Terrene Moon

by

Moxie T. Anderson

Gypsy Shadow Publishing

Terrene Moon
by Moxie T. Anderson

Gypsy Shadow Publishing, LLC.
Lockhart, TX
www.gypsyshadow.com

Library of Congress Control Number: 2022940013

eBook ISBN: 978-1-61950-373-2
Trade Paperback ISBN: 978-1-61950-675-6
Hardcover ISBN: 978-1-61950-676-3

Published in the United States of America

First eBook Edition: October 28, 2021
Print Editions: June 6, 2022

Dedication

For pulling me from the fire I had made
but could not quench
thank you, my darlings

And for my Kit, god among mortals

Chapter 1

As if embarrassed by the activities under its gaze, the full, golden Hunter's moon occasionally peeped in and out of the velvety blue clouds over the Crescent City. By the locals' standards, this was a perfectly reasonable October night sky, with a soft drizzle of rain lazily making its way down, misting the streets and leaving a fine witching hour sheen.

This wasn't the sort of rain to make the (mostly) sleeping inhabitants nervous, as so many rains are in New Orleans; hurricane season was nearing an end. Nor was this the humid light rains of a Louisiana summer that encouraged all manner of fetid smells to heat up from the asphalt—the unruly stomach content of an unruly reveler who'd had too many hurricanes at Pat O'Brien's, for example.

It was a perfectly dull, reasonable, and quiet evening in the Quarter, save for a hushed flurry of activity on St. Peter Street. From the windows of the apartment he shared with his mother, Winston Saunders focused his binoculars eighteen degrees to focus on the movement across the row.

"Who on earth moves in at 3:37 a.m. on a Sunday morning?" Winston grumbled, shaking his head with disgust. He zoomed in another precise three degrees to better observe the goings-on below.

The moving party was silent and stealthy, lugging heavy wood furniture up and down the inside stairs of the building as the men worked like a colony of ants, each seeming to sense the needs of the other wordlessly as they glided up and down, down and up the stairs for the better part of an hour. Slicked with rain, their olive faces against their dark clothes made them appear for all the world like lights appearing and disappearing under the dim moonlight. At the edges of their industry, a grim-looking man of about sixty watched intently and marked off contents on a clipboard.

Winston secretly admired the precision of their actions. He was himself an acolyte of order and precision, which accounted for his constant disgust with the city life surrounding him. To the man with the binoculars, humans were inherently chaotic, and the denizens and tourists of New Orleans multiplied that unnerving quality exponentially. Tomorrow, he decided, he would press his mother again to sell the apartment and move somewhere cleaner and more reasonable. Rhode Island, perhaps. Winston had never been to Rhode Island, but its size alone made it seem as if it would be more reasonable than New Orleans.

A flash of light from across the street stirred Winston from his thoughts of an Elysium Fields beyond the city. Refocusing his binoculars, he searched for the source of the light, hastily moving from window to window before eventually settling on the flicker.

From the second floor, a woman appeared in the window frame, silhouetted by the light behind her. Winston increased the magnification by another ten degrees to find the woman peering back at him with binoculars of her own. He could make out her teeth, grinning broadly as she raised her middle finger at him.

"Bitch," he hissed. He fumbled with the musty curtains in his mother's apartment, shutting them to *her*, to the constant nightmare that was the city. The discovery of his own spying unnerved him, and in his annoyance, he paced to the freezer and plucked out a dead mouse and headed back his room to feed Sophie. Although this early feeding would upset Winston's schedule by an hour or more in the next ten days, Sophie would adapt easily. Snakes, in that respect, were a relief to Winston—nothing of the reckless horror of humanity.

    Before the obnoxious pounding on her door, Charlotte LeNoir was blissfully dreaming of a lush space in the middle of Louisiana rice fields. The dream didn't involve any activity, just a feeling of hushed peace. It's awful enough to be torn from sleep; to be torn from a few moments of peace and calm in a hustler's city, living a hustler's life, is downright cruel.

    "Noooooooo," Charlotte groaned. "It's my ONE day off. GO AWAY!"

    "Bitch, don't make me bust this door down," came a deep growl from the other side of the door. "You *know* I will."

    Encouraged by the ruckus, Ghost, Charlotte's white shorthair, jumped on the bed and started yowling for breakfast.

    "Ugh, come on," Charlotte whined fruitlessly. "My one day off..."

    The knocking continued until Charlotte yanked open her front door to see her downstairs neighbor Tatiana with two loaded Bloody Marys in her hands. Normally in full drag, Tatiana was in her subtle Sunday wear of a headwrap and flowy pink muumuu.

    "Girl, I thought I was gonna have to bust in. Come stoop set with me." Tatiana thrust a Bloody Mary in her hand. "I know you had to work late, so I got you covered with a Bloody Mary. See? Bacon in it and everything, just like momma used to make for breakfast."

Despite her annoyance, Charlotte couldn't help but laugh. "All right. Let me feed Ghost and I'll join you. This best be important, Tati."

"That's right. Go on and feed her. Ain't nobody wanna fool with no angry pussy." And with that, Tatianna glided back down the stairs to wait for her friend. After Charlotte fed Ghost, she ambled down to the stoop, where Tatiana had two folding chairs waiting. The drag queen waved her well-manicured tips excitedly. "Come on, come on, baby. Look, look, look."

Charlotte's eyes followed Tatiana's hands across the street to find a group of burly construction workers negotiating the best method for fixing a pothole. Charlotte stared at Tatiana in dumbstruck anger. "You woke me up for this?"

"Sit down and drink your hair of the dog, bitch. And you're welcome."

And so it came to be that Charlotte (stage name: Snow White) started her one day off in three weeks with Tatiana Maneater (stage name, no need for anything else) hungover and watching construction workers.

"What time you get in, baby?"

"I finished at two but stayed up drinking and watching the rain. I *thought* I'd get to sleep in," Charlotte complained.

"Well, you know what white folks say: early bird gets the—oh YES, honey! Make sure you go on, get down there and check that hole, baby! We need to do something about these holes. You boys are heroes." The workers, surprised by the audience watching them fill the pothole, stared back at the pair. Tatiana waved to them vigorously. "I like that big boy with the beard. Ain't never had a big burly boy like that." Tatiana blew him a kiss, and Charlotte was surprised to see the man laugh and bend over jokingly and slap his own ass. "You ever have a big beefy man like that, Snow?"

Still resentful of the early hour, Charlotte ignored the question and responded with one of her own. "We have a new neighbor. You hear them move in?"

Tatiana sat back down, sucked on the straw in her drink, and kept her eyes on the bearded man. "Do what now?"

"Someone moved in above you last night. You didn't hear them?"

"No, baby. You know Saturday nights are reserved for Mr. D." Mr. D, a local politician with money and roots deep in Louisiana politics, was Tatiana's sugar daddy. "Please tell me they ain't no kids. Lord, I do NOT need little pussy goblins running all over them wood floors over my head."

"I don't think they got kids," Charlotte said. "No signs, anyway. Looked like an older white man."

"Gay or straight?"

"Well how am I supposed to tell that at 3 a.m. when I'm drinking and up in my place, Tati?"

Tatiana rolled her eyes. "Bitch, *I* would know. Was he at least good-looking? I need another daddy."

"I don't know. It was dark. Maybe ask the Creeper." Charlotte gestured toward Winston's window in the balcony across the street. "He was up with his binoculars."

Tatiana laughed a deep, throaty laugh. "That boy needs to get fucked. Bad." She scowled and looked across the way. "But not by me. You *know* he's a freak. You just *know* it Restraints, Prince Albert, all that Jeffrey Dahmer shit. Anyway, what you doing today on your day off?"

Charlotte sipped her Bloody Mary, hoping it would dull the throbbing of her temples. "I gotta make some more Sucka Punch for the girls, cultivate some herb, clean my place."

"Ooh, I need to get me some of that Sucka Punch. That shit is keeping Mr. D coming back and being generous. How much?"

"$20, with the neighbor discount." Charlotte yawned and stretched. "I better get going. Good luck with your bear over there."

Tatiana gazed at the construction worker lustily. "Come to think of it, baby, I'm a need a double on that love potion. I'm gonna get me a big boy."

Laughing, Charlotte stood and headed for her apartment to begin the long process of creating Sucka Punch for her coven, many of whom worked at Jack's Cabaret as exotic dancers and waitresses with her. Not that it was difficult to get the clients there to open their wallets, but the powder was a powerful aphrodisiac with the added benefit of encouraging men to be more generous with their money.

The original recipe, a family secret, was itself a simpler love potion that didn't incite the strong feelings of Charlotte's powerful concoction. Her great-great grandmother, Sally, a house slave on a plantation near what is now Houma, futilely created the mixture in the hopes that owner Richard Thibodaux would rekindle his love for his wife so he wouldn't rape Sally.

A raging racist to his core, Richard was unaffected by the love potion as he did not see blacks as worthy of love. After giving birth to two of his bastard children and faced with the brutal complicity and beatings from a furious Anne Thibodaux, Sally shifted her approach to her problem and abandoned the love potion, opting to dry and grind oleander over the course of a spring.

And as her misery with the Thibodauxs had brought her nothing but the ability to adapt, persist, and wait, Sally planned her escape. After the birth of her second child, Sally was no longer welcome in the house at night or without the bitter supervision of Anne. As the sugar cane harvest approached in October, she added the crushed oleander to the bottom of sugar jar. Once the newly refined sugar topped off the sugar jar, Sally would take her babies and flee on All Saints' night.

And Charlotte, great-great-great-great-great granddaughter, product of slavery, had the selfsame witches' blood coursing through her veins.

Exhausted by the end of her "day off," Charlotte stepped out onto her balcony. The soft light from the interior of her apartment glowed behind her as she sat down and lighted a blunt of the hydroponic OG Kush she was keeping alive and selling in her father Andre's absence. A warm wave of calmness washed over her, and sensing a rare peaceful moment, Ghost crept out onto the porch and hopped into her lap.

The night was still by New Orleans standards. Charlotte could hear a sax three blocks over, but the sad tune the musician was playing wasn't at all disruptive. The rise and fall of chattering voices occasionally wafted up from the streets to her perch, none of them angry or loud. Ghost purred in her lap, and for a brief moment, Charlotte felt completely at ease.

Nothing gold can stay, as the poet writes, and Charlotte's phone buzzed next to her, interrupting her respite. Exhaling a cirrus cloud of white smoke, she checked the number before answering.

"Hey, Papa."

"Hey, baby girl! What's good down South?"

A respected local jazz trumpeter, Andre was happily touring the West Coast with his band.

"Same shit, different day. You know how it is."

"You sound tired."

"Yeah, long day. I ran some deliveries for you, stopped by the store to drop off some mixes..."

"Twenties ain't no joke, especially in Nola. Try to go to bed early. You work tonight?"

"Nah. I'm gonna finish this blunt and take a bath."

"Everything okay with the setup? Producing well?"

"Of course. You taught me well. This OG is selling good, as always. I'll put your money in tomorrow before I go to work."

"*Our* money, baby girl. There's nothin' of mine that ain't yours."

Charlotte could hear the clinking of glasses in the background, the mike checks beginning—sounds of her life as a musician's child before she could capture a memory and enshrine it.

"Thanks, Papa. Love you."

"Love you, too. I'll check up on you in a few days. Try not to work too hard."

"It's all I know," Charlotte laughed. "It's what we do in this family."

Andre chuckled. "True. You come by it honest. I better go."

"Bye. Love you."

As Charlotte set her phone back down on the table next to her chair, Ghost prickled in her lap, growling. He arched his spine and hissed angrily before darting back into the open door to the apartment. Charlotte sensed something—some*one*—on the adjacent balcony, the one belonging to her new neighbor.

"It is *rude* to listen in on people's private business," she said to the darkness.

A figure to her right laughed from the shadows. "Apologies. I did not know if it was worse to interrupt your call or not. I am still trying to get accustomed to the city and its rules."

The voice was deep, the accent thick, pouring over Charlotte like a dark molasses. The interloper's voice, coupled with the effects of the Kush, disoriented her. She approached the gate separating their properties, gasping when she saw the white flash of his smile in the moonlight; she hadn't meant to approach him at all. Her erratic behavior both surprised and annoyed her.

"Well, now you know," she snapped. Charlotte grabbed her phone and returned to her apartment, turning the locks to the balcony behind her. Ghost blinked at her sleepily as she headed to her bedroom. "You're right. Let's skip the bath and go to bed."

And so they did.

Chapter 2

Winston stormed out of the apartment he shared with his mother, furious that the discussion they had about selling the place dragged out into an argument that was likely to make him seven minutes late for work.

Slamming the door behind him, Winston felt his mood sour further when the black drag queen across the street sang out, "Yoo-hoo!" and waved gaily to him. "Aberration," he hissed between gritted teeth. For Winston, the city was an all-too-welcoming host to anomalies in humanity. He felt rage swell up in his stomach, a hot bile scratching its way up to his throat. He *had* to escape. Every further minute he spent in the city was infecting him.

Winston spent his rapid walk to the post office in the Warehouse district in a sullen state, almost daring someone to speak to him or ask for money. His scowl and pace set the tone, however, so he arrived at his job unmolested.

Because he had been written up several times for his brusque manner with customers, Winston's managers found it best to have him sort mail in the rear of the office. Despite his tardiness, his arrival at his job set him at ease. He knew he would spend the next eight to nine hours sorting through mail, filling postal boxes, and generally being ignored. This suited him just fine; the less interaction he had with people, the more productive and relieved he was.

After clocking in exactly seven minutes late, Winston mumbled an apology to Tom, his manager, and scurried to his post. He began by pulling the cart from the letter slots, carefully stacking the letters to be sorted. The numbers, the crisp envelopes, the flyers—all of these familiar and predictable items soothed him, and he began to work rapidly, fluidly, instinctively.

Two hours passed as rapidly as a lover's farewell, with Winston performing his tasks with the nimble precision of a clockmaker. He would have remained at this post, almost content, had he not been interrupted by Tom calling his name.

"Yes?"

"We're picking up out there—first of the month. I need you to come help. Winston?"

Winston gritted his teeth. "I heard you."

Despite his annoyance at the thought of working the front, Winston passed the next hour uneventfully. An elderly woman did admonish him, "Smile, young man—it can't be that bad," but he looked at her flatly while returning her change and said nothing. Unfortunately, the stream of customers was steady throughout the morning, and it didn't appear to Winston that he would be returning to his quiet spot in the back before noon.

If only the morning had remained uneventful! It worsened for Winston at 11:48, less than an hour before his lunch break. The stream of customers remained steady, each customer demanding between four to seven minutes of his time. Winston handled the flow as well as he could—efficiently, with no extra time or effort spent on niceties.

"I need to send this letter as fast as possible."

Winston shook himself from his dreams of solitude to face a small, disheveled man with an unkempt beard across his counter.

"I'm sorry?"

"This." The man shook the letter mere inches from Winston's face. "I need to send this as fast as possible, and I want to make sure it gets to the address."

"So you want certified mail?"

"I don't know. What is that?"

"It means it will have to be signed for, and you'll receive notification."

The man raised his bushy eyebrows with understanding. "Yes, yes. That sounds good. How much will that set me back?"

"I will need to weigh it. What is the zip code, sir?"

"20500. Pennsylvania Avenue."

And with that, Winston knew this encounter would be unusual even by local standards.

"Okay. You will need to fill out form 3800, certified mail. It's in the divider on the counter behind you. There are pens there for your convenience."

The man looked over his shoulder and at the line behind him. "But I'll lose my place in line."

"Sir, you can return to my counter as soon as you finish. No need to wait again." Winston pressed his thin lips together and motioned with an extended arm.

Reluctantly, the man headed toward the counter and rifled through the forms. Winston signaled for the next customer, a young mother with children in tow. He managed that interaction seamlessly, mostly due to the antics of the bored children. As he handed the receipt to the woman, the elderly man had returned with his letter and form, thrusting it on the desk triumphantly.

"There. Now how much?"

Winston sighed. The man had mistakenly grabbed form 2976-E, customs.

"I'm sorry, sir. This is the customs form. You will want the form with the green strip."

A flush of red began to cover the man's face, highlighting the white of his beard and eyebrows. "Green. *Green.* Why didn't you say that the first time?"

"Apologies, sir. The boxes are labeled by form number. You will want—"

"Green. I got it." The man grabbed his letter and turned back to the counter with pens and forms.

"Yeah, yeah. Green, but 3800," Winston said. The man waved him off.

Winston handled another customer calmly, curtly—a package weighing 2.4 pounds (38.4 ounces) headed to Wisconsin—before the bearded man interrupted the end of the transaction.

"Here! Green. Can we finish this now?" Irritation was etched into every line on the man's grizzled face. Winston braced himself for the ensuing anger: the man had grabbed and filled form 3811, the domestic return receipt form.

"I'm very sorry, sir," Winston started, "but—"

"You gotta be *shitting* me," the man screeched. "How many goddamned green forms are there?"

"Sir, it's form 3800. I tried to tell you. We don't code them by color."

"You *said* green!"

"You didn't let me finish," Winston responded neutrally. "It is white with a green strip."

"*White with a green strip,*" the man mocked in a singsong voice. "Why the hell don't you idiots keep the forms up here? What happened to customer service?"

Winston gritted his teeth, imagining what he might do to this repugnant dwarf of a man under the right conditions. "I'm sorry, sir. It is form 3800, white with a green strip. Please check the labels."

The man scowled at Winston and spat on the tile floor before turning again to the counter with the forms. Winston motioned for the next customer, a woman who needed a package from her box (18317, second row, third column, middle set) in the office.

As he walked to the back to gather her package, Winston sucked air between his teeth. He could feel his back and neck tense. He knew the next interaction with the customer would include cursing, threats, perhaps even more spitting.

Not today, thought Winston. *Not today.*

He took his time gathering the package, hoping the irritable man would go to another counter. By the time he returned, though, the man was there, waving form 3800 at him. Winston handed off the package to the woman and pointed to have her sign before turning his attention to the irritable man.

"Ha! I have it now!" the man said triumphantly. "Now hurry up. I've spent too much time here already."

At that moment, Winston suddenly recalled an image he'd had deep in his subconscious from childhood. His mother was overprotective, never allowing him to explore the streets of New Orleans alone. He'd had no playmates as a child, only his own imagination and toys. Looking at the short, bearded man in front of him, Winston pictured one of his fairy tale books and an image of Rumpelstiltskin the dwarf having a tantrum at being bested. Unable to control the memory and the amusing likeness to the man before him, Winton began laughing.

Black rage crossed the face of the man across the counter. He sputtered and slammed his fist on the counter—all actions that only moved Winston to laughing tears. LaTonya, the clerk at the desk next to Winston, watched the interaction with wide eyes.

"I WANT THE MANAGER," the dwarf-man screeched. His actions and voice reduced Winston to a doubled-over fit of laughter. Hurrying to the counter for damage control, Tom hissed at Winston, "You're done. Get to the back."

Winston couldn't contain himself and spent an hour wiping away laughing tears of amusement at the stupidity of humanity as he tried to organize the letters and packages in his hands. Despite his usual precision, Winston and his brief interaction with the public did affect his usually fastidious work, with one package of 2.2 pounds (35.2 ounces) and two letters (98103, 03032) misfiled and sent to incorrect destinations.

Chapter 3

Dragging a plastic child's wagon filled with her potions and mixes behind her, Charlotte took a left turn from St. Peter's to Dauphine. Three blocks down and another left: Moonchild Metaphysical & Vodou, the LeNoir family business and a New Orleans fixture since 1889. There was no sign for the shop until the early 2000s, but the purpose of the store had not changed in well over a century.

Auntie Cassie had argued the name was too bold, even for the Crescent City, but her daughters convinced her the age of persecution for witches was long past. "Huh," Cassie snapped back. "If you're a white witch, maybe."

As matriarch, Mama Sally had the final say. "C'est bon. We'll be hiding out in the open for once." Her word was solemn, the final sounding of the judge's gavel; Moonchild Metaphysical & Vodou became the formal, taxable name of the shop.

For Charlotte, Moonchild was home. She had barely known a day in her life that she hadn't spent at the shop. With so many women in the family coven, Charlotte knew her feet barely touched the ground when she was a child, and she rarely cried.

To be sure, there was some familial guilt involved in her upbringing and her aunts' constant devotion. Taties Sylvie and Sybil made the fatal error of using magic to help Charlotte's mother Melissa conceive and carry a pregnancy to term after two previous miscarriages. Vodou priestesses themselves, Sylvie and Sybil should have known what their interference would cost: a life for a life. So it was that Charlotte came to be, screaming with fury, even as her mother slipped silently away.

Enraged by the family interference, Charlotte's father would have refused to enter the family store himself after his young wife's death, but as a young, struggling, and inexperienced father himself, he needed the help only an older generation of women could afford him. And over time and with many arguments and apologies, Andre forgave the twins for Melissa's death. For twenty-three years now, Sylvie and Sybil struggled only with forgiving themselves. And as a consequence, both women avoided the potions and herbs elements in the business, Sylvie focusing on ritual and vodou tours with their mother Cassie and Sybil perfecting her clairvoyance under Mama Sally's tutelage.

The loss of both her mother and the store's compounding skills had a strange effect on Charlotte, and similarly, the void in potion mixing left at the shop. Though her father had no interest in magic—despite having innate unusual luck and ability to influence people in most cases—he did possess a green thumb. He could get any plant to thrive, even when it was withering its last moments away.

As soon as she could toddle her way around, Charlotte followed in her father's footsteps. She loved the feel and damp smell of soil. She would squat down next to him as he potted, planted, replanted and listen to his instructions and descriptions of the plants and how to care for them. At age eight, she pulled a *Medicinal Herbs and Their Uses, Vol. I* from a shelf at the store and read the tome. Everything she absorbed from the book stayed in her young, green mind. Seeing her interest, Mama Sally brought her more books on natural healings and spells, even going as far as digging musty, yellowed family recipes from the shop attic for the girl to read and file into her mind.

By age fifteen, Charlotte perfected her first virility potion, Hot Spot, from barrenwort and ginseng, and it proved so popular that the first batch sold out in three days. The aunties were thrilled and pushed her to keep experimenting, and within five years, the *real* shop was stocked almost entirely with Charlotte's products. The front of the shop, with potions for tourists and newcomers, was stocked with the popular brands most customers of the arcane would be familiar with. Those products were ineffective and therefore cheap.

But Charlotte's concoctions—those were authentic and powerful. They could only be administered with extreme care with stern warnings to their users. As an added precaution, they could only be sold to longtime, trustworthy customers. The LeNoir family respected the potency of Charlotte's work, and by extension, so did the select customers respected enough to gain access to them.

It was 11:04 as Charlotte pulled her wagon over the stoop to the store, which opened at 11. Sylvie was at the counter and waved frantically. "Just in time, girl! The Patois are here!"

As she headed toward the counter, Charlotte smiled at hearing the voices in the shop.

"Charlotte, baby!" Mrs. Patois, a tiny woman of approximately 73, glided over to her and kissed her on the cheek. "We are so happy to catch you." Her blue eyes sparkled with genuine delight. "Maurice—look who it is!"

With a light-footed hop deft for his age, Mr. Maurice Patois hopped over to Charlotte and grabbed her hands and shook them vigorously. "Charlotte, my dear," he drawled in a thick Mississippi accent, "We are so fortunate you showed up. Miss Sylvie here says you made a new batch yesterday."

"I did," said Charlotte. "Let me take a look at y'all." Maurice and Joan Patois, high school sweethearts and New Orleans fixtures, always wore expertly tailored, matching outfits in bright colors. Today: sunshine yellow gingham. "You look like a field of daffodils. I love it."

"They here for the usual," Sylvie interjected. "I told them you'd have it."

"Sure do," Charlotte said. She tugged the wagon to the side of the register. "How many y'all need? A month? Two?"

The couple looked at one another, and Mrs. Joan covered her mouth with her hands and giggled. "We'll take two," Maurice said, pulling his wallet out of his dandy-yellow pants pocket.

Charlotte lifted two vials of a perfected version of Hot Spot from a box in her wagon. After eight years of toying with the brew, she had a virility recipe that was safe and effective, even for an elderly couple like the Patois. Charlotte wanted to patent the formula for wider distribution but her attempts at convincing her aunties had not been successful. *We don't need the Feds looking at what we make,* Aunt Cassie said, and the rest of the aunties agreed. Being audacious enough to open a black-owned magick store in New Orleans was one thing; inviting the government in to inspect their potions was a perilous idea.

Sylvie handled the transaction—$800—as the white-haired couple eyed each other like young lovers.

"You know I'll bring this to you," Charlotte told them.

"Oh, you're such a sweet girl," Mrs. Patois said. "We need the excuse to get out and dress up. And we love coming here."

"All right," Charlotte said. "Just let me know if you ever need, though."

Mrs. Patois kissed both of her cheeks and winked at her husband. "You know we will."

"Thank you, ladies," said Mr. Patois. He put his lemon-colored fedora back on his head and took his wife's arm. "We'll see you in two months."

As they left the shop, Sylvie and her great-niece watched them quietly. "I wish all our customers were like them," Sylvie sighed.

"Like who?" From the door leading to the back of the store, Sylvie's twin sister Sybil walked into the front of the store. "Hey, baby," she acknowledged Charlotte.

"The Patois," Sylvie said. "Big money and no drama."

"Oh lord," Sybil rolled her eyes. "They here for the sex oil?"

"Hey," reprimanded Charlotte, "Let them enjoy it. They're happy."

"You right, you right," Sylvie deferred, glancing at her sister sideways. "Ain't no harm. Let me help put them up." She motioned to packets and vials in the overburdened wagon Charlotte had with her.

Sybil snorted aloud, provoking her twin's ire.

"What?" Sylvie snapped.

"You think you strong enough to pull that thing?"

"I think we the same age, you old biddy," Sylvie countered. "You think you strong enough?"

Feeling an argument brewing, Charlotte interjected. "Is Mama in the back or upstairs?" The twins continued to glare at one another wordlessly. Charlotte sighed, annoyed. How her aunts had managed to maintain a rivalry for over one hundred years of their shared lives continued to astonish her.

"All right, then," she said, the twins ignoring her. As Charlotte walked to the kitchen in the back of the shop, the sound of her aunts' squabbling followed her down the hallway.

"Ma chere," a warbly voice called to her from the back and laughed happily. "Charlotte."

As Charlotte stepped into the kitchen in the back, she was met with a mimicking cry that mocked the sweet words calling to her. "PUTAIN!" a voice squawked. The French word for whore.

"Arrete!" said the first voice. "Hey, baby. Come give Mama a kiss."

At a green Formica table in the center of the kitchen sat Mama Sally, matriarch, head of the Moonchild coven, clad in her uniform of purple, down to her sneakers. At 173 years of age, Sally was plagued with cataracts that made her eyes look like opals, and she needed a cane to move around, but her mind and ability to see the three realms of time were as clear as a clockmaker's watch face.

Charlotte kissed her great-great-great-great grandmother on both of her cheeks and then her hand, the latter a sign of respect and submission to a greater power. "Mornin', Mama."

"HEY TRAMP!" a voice screeched.

"Tais-toi!" Mama Sally yelled back fruitlessly at Mischief, the African grey parrot out of reach at the top of the cabinets. The parrot had been a prize in a back-room poker game in the '80s, and Sally had regretted her win ever since as the bird's former owner, a sailor, had only taught the bird to curse in multiple languages.

"Okay, Okay, Okay, puta," the bird consoled itself. "Okay. Okay."

Charlotte slipped into a chair next to her great grandmother. "How you feelin' today?"

"I can't complain," Sally answered. "They behavin' up front?"

Charlotte laughed. "You know how the twins are."

"Mmm-hmmm. That's how come they still spinsters—they'd rather fight with each other than love a man."

"Men are overrated anyway, Mama," Charlotte said.

"I guess you right about that. Gimme your hands, baby."

Charlotte placed her hands into the papery-thin, coffee-colored veiny hands of her great grandmother and inhaled the sweet scent of frankincense Sally constantly burned in her kitchen-office where she held consultations.

As if stung by a yellowjacket, Sally jerked and pulled her hands back from her granddaughter's. She drew in a quick gasp of air, and a small cry escaped her lips.

"What? What is it? Are you okay, Mama?"

"Something new... something evil." Sally reached out for Charlotte's hands again. This time, she held onto them firmly, so much so that the pressure began to hurt Charlotte's fingers.

"What do you see, Mama?"

Sally's pale eyes searched but found only darkness. After a moment, she dropped her granddaughter's hands again, and Charlotte felt the blood slowly return to her fingertips. "It's gone. Are you safe at the club?"

"Yeah. Tatiana walks me home, or I get a cab. Don't worry."

Sally sat quietly.

"MERDE!" Mischief squawked, breaking the silence.

Despite themselves, both women laughed at the parrot's well-placed curse.

"Oui, c'est shit," Sally chuckled. "Damn bird."

"I better go help the twins. I brought some stock, and I know they're gonna wear themselves out fighting about how to organize it."

"Bon, but I want you take some mandrake. Not the cheap stuff up front. Here—" Sally turned in her chair and pulled open a kitchen drawer behind her. After rummaging briefly, she drew out a large root that looked like a miniature chubby infant. "You keep this on you at all times. You promise me."

"You know I will," Charlotte said. "Love you, Mama." Charlotte kissed grandmother's cheeks again.

"Love you, too, baby girl."

As Charlotte headed back to the sounds of the twins bickering at the front of the shop, her great-great-great-great grandmother sat silently, wrestling with her vexed thoughts of what might be watching her granddaughter.

When Charlotte left Jack's Cabaret at 12:35 a.m., the manager, Bobbie, told her to go as the club was fairly empty and the competition among the dancers for the available clients would likely escalate into bickering. As she'd spent the better half of the day at the shop listening to her aunts argue, Charlotte was content to be cut early.

As she stepped out into the cobblestone street right off Bourbon, Tatiana was waiting for her.

"Hey, baby," Tatiana said lowly.

"Hey," Charlotte responded. "You okay?"

Tatiana had just finished her own shift at the Honey Pot off Bourbon, where she was a drag performer. Usually upbeat, she was unusually somber.

"No..." Charlotte searched her friend's face under in the neon lights of storefronts they were passing and noticed that Tatiana's habitually impeccable makeup was smeared into a pallet of indigos around her eyes. She grabbed Tatiana's hand and stopped her.

"What's going on?"

Fanning her face with her hands Tatiana choked back tears. "You remember Miss Diamond? The tiny Latino bitch?"

Charlotte looked at her friend quizzically.

"You met her at my place last summer. Sweet little Puerto Rican thing. She bought a half off you and talked your poor sweet head off about *The Real Housewives of Miami*. Remember?"

"I do!" Charlotte said. "She told me her real name, though. Ricky?"

"That's her, yeah. Well, she didn't show up to work this weekend, and that bitch *loved* the stage. I don't remember her ever missing a night of work ever, not even when she had food poisoning and had to run offstage between sets to go shit." Tatianna sobbed. "The police found the beautiful bitch this morning, dead past the market."

Charlotte squeezed her friend's hand and stopped them both in the street. "Oh, Tati. I'm so sorry. What happened?"

"I don't know, but they investigating it as a homicide! The cops came tonight and scared off the customers, asking us who was she with Sunday night, did she leave with anybody..."

"Shit. I'm so sorry." Charlotte hugged her friend. "Come up and smoke with me. We'll talk."

Tatiana's eyes gleamed with tears in the streetlights, and the pair made their way back to their building on St. Peter's Street arm in arm, wordlessly in the way people often do when facing the senseless horrors of this world.

When they reached Charlotte's apartment, Charlotte popped some popcorn and rolled a joint. They headed to the balcony and sat side by side, passing the joint back and forth.

"Thank you, baby," Tatiana said as she exhaled. "I just can't believe it. She was so young, maybe 25? It's not right."

A shadow to their left and a tapping on the gate between the pair startled them abruptly. "Good evening, ladies. I am so sorry to interrupt, but I wanted to make my presence known this time," the voice from the darkness purred.

Startled, Tatiana jumped from her seat. "Mother-fucker, who the *fuck* are you?"

"I'm your new neighbor. It appears this is yet another bad time for introductions."

Seething for reasons she herself could not pinpoint, Charlotte stood up and took Tatiana's hand. "Yeah, you got bad timing, mister. Come on, Tati. Let's go in."

"No need," the stranger interjected. "I am heading out. Enjoy your evening." With that, he turned back into his place and closed the door firmly.

As Charlotte prepped to go onstage at Jack's, Bobbie came into the dressing room.

"Hey, Snow," she said. "We got a big crowd."

"I saw," Charlotte smiled. "We're ready."

"Awesome. I know you are. Love you, girl." Bobbie blew her a kiss and returned to watch over her father Jack's strip club. At 36, Bobbie Westhall initially had no interest in managing a cabaret in the Quarter, but her father's early onset Alzheimer's gave her little choice. The club was the only source of reliable income preventing Jack Westhall from entering a state-run facility.

Although Charlotte admired her new manager and coven member, her primary concern was the hustle. Played right, a full crowd meant the girls could all cover their rents for the next two months. As she finished preparing, she kept her makeup light, save for the blood-red lipstick highlighting her full lips. With her jet-black hair and fair skin, she looked like the embodiment of her stage name, Snow White. Knowing that the men in the audience fed on the pretense of naivete in the girls, she also opted for a pale blue baby doll dress with thigh-high white stockings and black Mary Janes.

Just as Charlotte stood to ready herself to perform, a light tapping sounded on the door. She tugged it open to find Johnny C, the club DJ, at the door.

"Oh cool—just came to see if you were ready."

"You know it," Charlotte tapped her fist to his. "Let's get it."

As she headed to the stage, Charlotte checked her dress pockets to make sure she had everything she needed. *Now coming to the stage,* Johnny called in the foreground, *Your favorite naughty princessssssss... Snoooooooowwwwww Whiiiiiiiiiiite!*

The bass thumped along to a Brazilian chanteuse's cover of "I Put a Spell on You" as Charlotte glided across the stage. As she moved to the music, arching her back against the pole and stepping around it gracefully, she inspected the crowd, assessing the easiest marks.

Though they had watched her hundreds of times before, other dancers were as temporarily stunned by Charlotte's beauty as the men in the audience were. Even without the use of magic, Charlotte was captivating, her beauty "beyond compare," the type of exquisite looks that compelled fairytale stepmothers to commit murder.

"She is so goddamn hot," Pixie Dream (real name: Vanessa Johnson), a tiny blonde dancer said aloud to no one, but the man on whose lap she was sitting squeezed her hip in agreement as he stared ahead.

Eyes locked on Charlotte, the cocktail waitresses forgot to serve the drinks on their trays, but none of the customers complained about the service as Charlotte slunk around the stage before them. All of the men in the club were mesmerized by the beauty in front of them. They were Herods to her Salome, ready and willing to abandon reason and sacrifice one another for her.

Evidence that clothing doesn't necessarily make the man, a silver-haired man in faded jeans and a Florida t-shirt pulled Amy, a cocktail waitress, to him and handed her a crisp $100 bill. "Get her to come to me," he urged, his greedy eyes never veering from the stage "and I got another hundred for you and ten times that for her."

Charlotte looked over the heads of the crowd to find Bobbie standing in a corner by the bar. The two met eyes briefly, and Bobbie nodded in assent. With that, Charlotte slipped to the stage floor, crawled forward, and reached into her dress pocket to grab a handful of Sucka Punch mixed with pink glitter.

> "You know I love you
> I love you
> I love you
> I love you anyhow
> And I don't care
> If you don't want me
> I'm yours right now..."

As she inched toward the stage front, Charlotte blew a red-lighting kiss to the audience, eliciting raucous cheers and whistles from the men watching. Reaching the edge, she winked and blew the glittery potion into the crowd.

Each knowing her role, the dancers followed suit, covering the club and its customers with glitter and potion. Thrilled with the party-like atmosphere, the oblivious crowd roared. Within seconds, the potion took effect, and the men opened their wallets and began spending freely. When they ran out of cash, they headed to the in-house ATM and ignored the exorbitant fees. With the effects of Sucka Punch seeping into their nostrils and minds, the men were captivated by all the women in Jack's Cabaret.

And the women, led by Charlotte, were more than happy to relieve them of their cash.

After pulling in almost $5,000 from three tables, Charlotte wandered to the bar for water as an excuse to escape the inane conversations. Behind the bar, Bobbie watched the exuberant crowd continue to enjoy the evening and the dancers. Their enjoyment translated to generosity with tips for the cocktail waitresses and bartenders as well.

"Whatcha need, baby?" Bobbie asked.

"Water. I'm gonna head out in a minute."

"Really? There's much more money to be had."

"I got what I need," Charlotte answered sleepily. "Balance in all things."

"You leaving already?" Pixie Dream hugged Charlotte's neck. "Don't go!"

Charlotte patted Pixie's arms and hugged her back. "I'm worn out, Pixie. I gotta open the store tomorrow, too."

"Awwww. Can I get some advice before you go? Five minutes, I promise."

"I gotta change," Charlotte said. "Let's walk and talk."

The pair headed to the locker room, Pixie holding on to Charlotte's hand like a child would. When they closed the door to the dressing room, the music from the club dissipated.

"What's up, Mama?" Charlotte asked.

"It's about Derek," Pixie started. "I think he's stepping out on me."

Charlotte rolled her eyes. Derek, Pixie's boyfriend, regularly hit on the girls at the club—so much so that Bobbie banned him from coming because she knew a confrontation was imminent. "You *think?*"

Pixie's round hazel eyes glimmered with tears. "I wouldn't care," Pixie said. "But my babies. They need their dad around."

Gritting her teeth, Charlotte searched Pixie's face. "What are you looking to do, Pixie? You can't keep a man who don't want to be with you."

"That's not true," Pixie sulked. "You know it's not true."

"It is in the long run, unless you want a zombie."

"I'm serious," Pixie's voice cracked. "I don't need forever. I just need him to remember why we fell in love and had these boys together. Please, Snow."

Charlotte sighed. "And?"

Pixie hurried to her locker and pulled a crumpled piece of paper from her purse. "And I know some of what I need to make a binding spell. I've tried altering Sucka Punch, but I can't—"

"Wait, wait, wait—you thought you could change the potion I made?" Charlotte laughed, but her laughter was tinged with bitterness.

"I know, I'm sorry! I was desperate. Snow, please. *Please.*"

Charlotte looked at the tiny blonde before her. Pixie was a great mother—no one in the coven would dispute that. Her fear and desperation with her boys' father were understandable: New Orleans wasn't a city that treated single mothers well.

"Please. Please, please, please."

Weary, Charlotte sighed and relented. "You're gonna need Mad Dog Skullcap. Fresh, nothing dried. Don't let it wilt. You're lucky we haven't had a cold snap yet."

"Skullcap. Okay, got it. Anything else? Do I hafta harvest under a certain lunar phase?"

"No, but try to find it in holy ground after midnight—churchyard if you can, better from the graves of lovers."

"Ooooh, Snow, thank you!" Pixie leaned up to kiss her friend on the cheek and hugged her neck tightly. "I owe you. I fucking owe you!"

"You will if he sticks around, I guess," Charlotte sighed. "I'm gonna take one of those cute babies of yours for my own."

"Pffft... some days, I swear, you could have them both," Pixie beamed. "Thank you! I better get back out and make that cash."

As Pixie spun around and headed to the front, Charlotte collected her belongings and shook her head. She knew what Pixie wanted was a short-term solution to an age-old problem: how to keep someone enamored. And in this city, Charlotte knew, hope was often what carried a woman through the night.

Charlotte rode home in an Uber, exhausted and yawning through the polite conversation the driver was trying to hold. Grateful that the ride would take only about eight minutes on the series of one-way streets, she tried to collect her thoughts about what she would need to do in the morning. Bank. Harvest. Feed Ghost. Pack herbs to make gris-gris sachets if the store traffic proved to be slow. Marinate a roast for Mama Sally, Cassie, and the twins in a crock pot while they limited their Saturday hours today to tours only at her insistence.

Mama Sally was to watch TV and sleep, let her mind and body rest.

As the driver pulled up to the building on St. Peter, Charlotte checked her phone. 2:17 a.m. She would get plenty of sleep before opening the store at 11. Feeling generous, she tipped the driver well and pulled her bag wearily from the back seat.

She hadn't even closed the door before hearing "Heyyyyyyyyyy, girl!" from Tatiana's stoop. Seated there with her frantically waving neighbor was a thin, swarthy man who Charlotte could only assume was Tatiana's latest conquest. Watching Charlotte exit the car, the man stood like a sentinel and watched her approach.

"Come sit with us," Tatiana instructed. "This is—"

"Vasile," the man interjected. Charlotte recognized his voice as that of her new neighbor immediately. The accent was unmistakable.

"He brought *champagne,* Charlotte," Tatianna exclaimed. "And not the cheap shit."

The man extended his hand. Unwillingly, Charlotte took it but released his grip as quickly as she could. His hands were blue-cold.

"An apology, the champagne," Vasile explained as his dark eyes bored into Charlotte's. "I fear I've made a terrible first impression."

"You think?" Charlotte laughed sardonically.

A heavy pall of awkwardness hung in the air. Tatiana laughed uncomfortably and poured an empty champagne glass next to her.

"Baby, be nice. I know you tired, but have a seat and let's talk. It's really good champagne." She took a long sip. "*Really* good." She poured a glass and thrust it up at her friend.

Charlotte sighed, her whole body too exhausted to argue. "All right. I'll have one glass. *One*, Tati."

"Excellent. To new friends," Vasile clapped his hands together. He motioned to the chair next to him and lifted a glass and poured Charlotte a glittery glass of liquid gold.

"Thanks," Charlotte said, easing into her seat.

"How was work?" Tatiana smiled, trying to ease the discomfort in the company.

"Good. I'm just tired. I gotta work tomorrow."

"What line of work are you in?" Valise asked politely.

Tatiana's eyes widened, considering the gaff she'd just made. "Oh, Charlotte is a dancer."

"Ah, how wonderful," the man said. "Ballet?"

Mid-sip of her champagne, Charlotte laughed and spat some of it on the ground. "No. *No.* I'm an exotic dancer. A stripper."

Vasile furrowed his brows. "Ah, burlesque?" he asked hopefully.

"Something like that," Charlotte acknowledged, glaring at Tatiana.

"Wonderful," their new neighbor said, clapping his hands on his knees. "Perhaps I can come watch you perform some time."

"'Scuse me—can I get a refill?" Tatiana interjected.

"Of course, of course," Vasile said.

"Mmmm, ain't nothing makes a beautiful man look even better than when he's pouring me a drink," Tatiana laughed. "Ain't that right, Snow?"

"I prefer he give me his wallet," Charlotte said pointedly. "Where's your glass?" she asked Vasile.

"I have to work tonight, so none for me, I'm afraid. I hope you ladies will enjoy."

"What do you do?" Charlotte asked.

"I'm a graphic designer, but the work I do is generally for companies overseas," he answered. "My schedule is... unusual."

"He's *Arabic*," Tatiana interrupted. "I ain't ever been with an Arab." She winked at Vasile.

The man emitted a deep-throated laugh. "Arabic, yes, something like that."

Charlotte ignored him and caught Tatiana's gaze. "So how did all this happen, Tati?" she asked, motioned to the table with the glasses and champagne.

"What, him?" Tatiana asked. "I felt bad we was rude to him, so I made him a pecan pie to welcome him to the neighborhood."

Incredulous, Charlotte glared at Tatiana and then met the stranger's gaze. "You made him *a pie.*"

"Bitch, that's what neighbors do."

Keen to the tension, Vasile shifted uncomfortably. "It was much appreciated. I should get back to work. Ladies, enjoy your evening and the champagne."

"Thank you, baby," Tatiana said, standing up. She kissed their new neighbor on both cheeks. "It was nice meeting you."

"Indeed," Vasile said. "The pleasure is all mine." He made a half-wave at Charlotte and then slipped into the darkness, back to his apartment.

Charlotte laughed. "I'm too tired for this shit tonight. A pie? *A pie?*"

"I ain't sorry!" Tatiana laughed. "He is CUTE."

Charlotte stood and drained her glass. "His champagne is good. Night, Tati."

"Mmmm-hmmm."

Sleep pressed heavily on Charlotte, like a stone, and she woke to the sound of Ghost's mewling at 10:08 a.m. "Come here," she urged, and the white cat leaped on the bed and rubbed his head against hers, purring loudly. It was the first sound night of sleep she'd had in a week.

With great reluctance, she pulled herself from her bed and headed to the kitchen to feed Ghost and make herself a cup of coffee. She looked forward to the day ahead, her aunts busy with tours and tarot readings, Mama Sally resting as she should be while Charlotte handled the traffic in the store with Bridgette (stage name, Lacy Monroe).

The promise of Sunday brunch with her family on a balcony was just 24 hours away. Despite the few disagreements she had with her aunts about the future of the shop, Charlotte knew she was lucky to have them and looked forward to a lazy afternoon with them before she headed off to work again.

And she still felt the power of the money she had pulled in from the club the previous night. If sales at the store were slow today, she knew she could secretly help her aunties and Mama Sally by filling the till with her earnings from Jack's. Her joy was the same kind she felt when she perfected a potion Mama Sally approved of, or a flower she plucked for the twins that delighted them so when she was a child. Their love for her was fierce, giving, protective; her devotion to them was just as strong.

When she reached Moonchild at 10:47, Charlotte's mood was slightly dampened by being greeted with the usual squabbling between Cassie and her daughters.

"Nooooo," Cassie growled. "I ain't taking a 'day off.' I know this city better than you two ever will. I'll do the tour and you—" she waved a hand in Sylvie's face— "You can help sell the customers goods on the way."

Visibly hurt, Sylvie looked to her sister. The twins fought like cats, but they defended each other ardently when attacked by someone else.

"Mama," Sybil chided. "We got this. I can go with her. We been here almost as long as you, and you taught us."

"Whose gonna read here at the store?" Cassie scoffed. "*Enough.*"

Sylvie and Sybil glanced at each other. Even at 136 years of age, they still felt the hurt and shame of humiliation at their mom's condescension.

"Hey," Charlotte interrupted. She tossed her bag behind the counter. "We got this. Sybil, somebody has to read if Mama's gonna sleep." Charlotte knew she was risking the twins' wrath, but there was no tangling with Cassie. Tall, broad, and pushy to the point of aggressiveness, Cassie saw her path as protecting the younger women in their coven, and there was no getting past it. Sylvie rolled her eyes, huffed, and stormed to the back of the store. Sybil met Charlotte's gaze and shook her head in disgust. Cassie ignored all three of them and read over her tourism schedule.

I can't win here, Charlotte thought.

As she cleaned the counters and set up the till, Charlotte pushed aside the family drama. They would have a fine day together tomorrow despite Cassie's undermining of her girls. Removed from Cassie by three generations, Charlotte intuited that her great-great-great aunt's anger wasn't directed at her daughters or her niece; she was still fighting a system she hadn't seen change much in her hundred-plus years in the city. Where Cassie's daughters were still battling her to make their own way at the store, Charlotte accepted it and tried to work around it where possible.

A gentle twinkling of the chimes at the door tugged Charlotte from her thoughts.

"Helllllllloooo," sang a loud, melodic voice that could only spring from Misty De la Rue. "Are we ready to have FUN?"

With a group of approximately ten tourists in tow and clad head-to-toe in an obscenely tacky magnolia blossom pantsuit, Misty held the door for her group and waved them all into the shop. "Heyyyyy, Charlotte! Y'all," she whispered excitedly to the tour group, "This is Charlotte, the great-great granddaughter of Miss Sally the vodou priestess!"

The heads of all twelve members of the tour group turned at once to gawk at Charlotte. Knowing the game, she nodded her head and lowered her eyes and waved her hand dramatically to admit them to the shop. "Welcome to Moonchild Vodou," she said breathily. "Prepare to have your lives changed for the better."

The faces of the female tourists—most in their fifties and sixties—relaxed at seeing a young, beautiful woman welcoming them. They took in as much as they could as they slowly wandered the store: *gris-gris* packets in multiple colors, mojo packets in the same jewel tones, dried chicken feet, vodou dolls in bright palettes, eggshell powder in jars, gold/silver/pewter metal sigils, skeleton keys in all colors of metals, enamel evil eyes in blues and whites, herbal potions not powerful enough to command Charlotte's prices, spirit offerings in dark monochromes, talismans from several cultures, tarot cards from Ryder-Waite to modern art, psychic readings, goddess statues, metaphysical books, prayer candles from Mexico to Hungary, incense from Arabia, crystals from mines across the world, brilliant scrying mirrors, ornate sacrificial knives, and a heavy wooden altar littered with candles and photos and tokens left (for a price) by prior tourists.

"Look around, and we will come right back here when the tour is finished," Misty urged. "You won't find this quality or knowledge in any other vodou or magic shop in the city!" She winked at Cassie, who ignored her to count heads.

Embarrassed by her aunt's cold people skills, Charlotte walked over to Misty and took her hand. "Thanks, Miss Misty," she said. "We definitely try our best."

"Baby, don't call me miss, please! You're all grown up now."

"Habit, you know this," Charlotte laughed.

"We ready?" Cassie interrupted, her clipboard clenched in her hands. "We have a 2:30 after this group. Sylvie, *allons.*" Her lips pursed tensely, Sylvie slung a bag of votives and incense over her shoulder, glared at her mother, and darted outside without a word, the door chimes ringing angrily as she shut the door firmly behind herself.

"Okay, are y'all ready, Steel Magnolias?" Misty clapped. "Let's get the real scoop on the magic and mystery of this fabulous city!" Like a small group of wrens, the women hopped and tittered excitedly and lined up to head out. Cassie heading up the rear, her mind filled with time frames, head counts, and price per tourist.

The atmosphere of the store changed almost immediately as the party left. Sybil continued to sulk, but she set herself up in her corner, surrounded by lush red velvet curtains she could draw around herself and any customer wanting a tarot or palm reading.

Brigette exchanged concerned glances with Charlotte, and the latter rolled her eyes. "Too many witches at the cauldron," she laughed wearily.

Winston had been dreaming of walking up a long flight of stairs and tripping repeatedly as he ascended. Right before waking up, he had nearly reached the top of the long staircase but tripped and tumbled backward head over heels. The dream sensation of his body slamming against the floor at the bottom of the staircase jarred him from his sleep with a sharp twitch.

He exhaled both with relief at being alive, but also with the annoyance of being shaken from slumber in such a frustrating manner. Sunday, six thirty-two a.m., and on his day off. *Why?* he groaned.

Knowing he would not be able to go back to sleep, he pulled himself from bed and shuffled into the kitchen. Coffee, black. Two eggs, hardboiled for exactly 3 minutes and 33 seconds, then split over toast. Shower, exactly four minutes from beginning to end. It wasn't his most efficient habit, but Winston could relax under the steam in the shower and forget, though briefly, the world beyond the bathroom door.

Two minutes twenty-eight for slicking his wet, dirty blond hair back, applying deodorant, and brushing his teeth. He caught his reflection briefly in the mirror, but there was nothing new or remarkable about his appearance. At any moment, Winston had the good fortune to look absolutely plain, and it pleased him. His features were ordinary to the point that no one had ever mocked his features for being out of place or too large or too crooked.

His eyes, the purported windows to the soul, were also a plain shade of brown. They would not ever captivate anyone; no one would write a paean to them. Winston had recognized his complete ordinariness when he was 15, and he had long ago accepted it.

Considering the time, Winston decided to head for the Immaculate Conception Jesuit Church for 8 a.m. mass. He checked in on Sophie, who was still curled up in a series of sleepy coils, picked up his mother's Social Security check to deposit on his way home, and headed out into the city.

Winston was pleased his ten-block trek to the church was as unremarkable as his visage. Worn out from its merriments of the night before, the city slept in late. He reached the 1930s red brick edifice with six minutes to spare before mass and slipped into the right corner, back pew, making sure to sit near the end of the bench so no one would try to sit next to him.

Winston was not Catholic, nor remotely religious. He had attended Catholic mass only as an adult, out of curiosity, by wandering into St. Louis Cathedral one day. He was fascinated by the language and the ritual, the aerobic routines of the parishioners standing and sitting and responding in unison.

Although he was an interloper in the community, he learned the sequences of the service within a few months' time. Once comfortable with one church, he farmed around to see if the others in the area were similarly organized. The Spanish mass at Our Lady of Guadalupe & Shrine of St. Jude's confused him, as did the Latin mass at St. Patrick's, but he found he understood the routine well enough, even if he could not the language.

There was something soothing about this ability to transcend the limitations of language, so Winston learned the church schedules and tried to alternate locations just to make sure he could keep with the patterns of the mass.

He could not take communion, though he was tempted to see what was happening at the altar.

The gospel reading on this October morning at Immaculate Conception was the parable of the mustard seed, and try as he might, Winston could not stay focused on Father Byrne's homily. He found himself daydreaming of the church, the entire city burning to the ground, reduced to embers, then ash, with the potential for new growth to overtake it all—the wrought iron, the brick, the bones of the dead.

He was relieved to find no one sat near him for the sign of peace, a part of the mass that demanded human contact. His first experience with the act initially saw him scurrying from St. Louis Cathedral in horror in his early days of exploration. Now he knew when the moment approached and would slink out of the pew, out of the church, if anyone was near enough to try to touch him.

As he watched the parishioners line up for communion, Winston found himself exhaling a sigh of relief at the order. Here, there was no pushing, shoving, haggling, heckling, or arguing—just humans lining up dumbly, like cattle, making as little noise as possible while they approached the priest. He watched them advance, then turn, return to their pews, and kneel to pray. The organist played "O Lord, I Am not Worthy," with a light hand, and Winston waited for the last congregant to take communion before slipping out the back doors. He always left before the reading of the church bulletin—it varied in length and was the only moment of disorder in what was a comfortably numbing, predictable affair of highest orderliness.

Winston walked to an ATM to try to deposit his mother's check, but an error message crossed the screen. This problem meant he would now have to walk out of his way to the next ATM that would accept the check. He scowled and picked up his pace. The plan was to deposit the check, stop and have a cup of coffee, black, hope that no one spoke to him, and then be on time when Jazzy Pets opened at 11 so he could purchase more feeder mice for Sophie. Inefficiency in the city, as always, interfered with his plans.

He found himself wondering about the reliability of ATMs in Rhode Island and made a mental note to look them up when he returned home.

The trek to another ATM set him back about ten minutes, but the transaction glided through seamlessly, which relieved Winston. He would have to head southwest toward the pet store, leaving him nearly twenty-five minutes to order coffee at JB's Java. Winston liked JB's as the baristas were not overly friendly, and the young man who worked Sundays hardly seemed to like customers at all. His interactions with customers were succinct, and Winston appreciated his disinterest and tipped him moderately for the service.

The air was cool this blue fall morning, and to avoid the bustle of the locals buying coffee inside, Winston took a seat outside. The smell of the dark roast wafted up into his nostrils, wiping out the general funk of the city. Winston closed his eyes. Perhaps the day would not be so terrible, especially if he could get back home before the Sunday crowds were up and about.

"Ay—ay man. Pssst."

Winston opened his eyes to find a gaunt man of indiscernible age seated next to him. The man had the leathery, tan skin of someone in the sun too many hours of the day. He was seated too close, close

enough for Winston to smell stale liquor on his breath
and sweat on his clothes.

"You got a cigarette?"

Leaning back to escape the radius of the man's
sour breath, Winston shook his head.

"Damn." The man's bloodshot eyes darted around
them. "*Damn.*"

Hoping the man would find another target, Winston lifted his coffee to his nose and inhaled.

"You wanna hear something, man?" The stranger
leaned into Winston's space again.

"No," Winston growled.

"No, man. This is important." His eyes darted back
and forth across the perimeter. "I figured it out last
night, man." He paused and looked Winston in the
eye. "*Illuminati,*" he whispered dramatically. "They're
here, man. I know exactly where, too. I found the clue
on the Joan of Arc statue."

Winston closed his eyes, a futile attempt to block
out the chaos unfolding in front of him. *Why? Why
can't I just get through the day—*

"For real, man, listen. Listen!" The stranger
clamped his leathery hand onto Winston's arm.

It was too much. "Look at me," Winston seethed.
"I mean it, you fuck. Look at me."

Surprised by the tone, the man's eyes widened as
he looked into Winston's deep brown eyes and saw the
monstrous buried in them.

"If you don't get your hand off of me and get the
fuck away from me, I'm gonna gut you and donate
your skin to the Illuminati. They'll tan your worthless
hide and then engrave it and write on it with your
blood to bring on the New World Order. *Do you understand me?*"

Rheumy eyes wide, the man pulled his gnarled
hand away from Winston and recoiled in horror.

"You—you're one of them!" The man pushed himself away from Winston so rapidly that he nearly fell

backwards and flailed his arms to steady himself. He leapt up and walked away backwards, keeping his eyes on Winston, and muttering about the Illuminati until he reached a corner and dashed around it, like a frightened cat.

Despite himself, Winston chuckled. Perhaps this small victory was a sign of hope that he shouldn't head home to his small apartment and his mother so soon. He sipped his coffee triumphantly and thought about the day ahead.

The cool twilight sky illuminated the upper half of the buildings and balconies on Charlotte's block in an ultraviolet purple. Illuminated by the waning moon, the night sky continued to glow a periwinkle blue while the lights on the bottom halves of the buildings switched on to their warm golden hues. The combined effect of the sunset colors resembled a pop art painting, filled with energy and promise.

Charlotte's apartment was crowded and humming with activity. The aunties had helped Sally make the creaky climb up the wooden stairs to the apartment, and having deposited her safely to a rocking chair on the balcony, they bustled to the kitchen to warm up a large cast iron pot of gumbo, a pan of jalapeno cornbread, and set a large pot of rice to boil.

For her part, Charlotte was in charge of mixing drinks to the small party that began to arrive as the last indigo vestiges of daylight retreated from the night.

First to arrive was Bobbie, and she came carrying her famous peach cobbler. Bridgette had followed her from the club, and both represented the younger witches from Jack's. Alyssa, a realtor to the wealthy who often helped procure clients for Mama Sally, showed up shortly after in a bright green caftan and a wide smile. Monique and Chantelle, two gifted vodou priestesses who worked reading cards in Jackson Square, showed up last and planted themselves at Mama Sally's feet on the porch.

"Y'all come get a plate," Cassie insisted. "Mama, here you go," she said as she surveyed the group and handed her mother a bowl loaded with fragrant, steaming gumbo.

"What can I get you to drink?" Charlotte asked her great grandmother. "You want a soda, or...?"

"Just water, baby," Sally chuckled. "I can't drink that other stuff. You know that."

"Okay. You know I gotta ask."

The women settled into their seats on the balcony, either in chairs or on the wood planked balcony itself. As the youngest LeNoir, Charlotte's role was to replenish glasses or plates, provide napkins, offer desserts. After the plates were cleared, she brought out a joint for herself and the younger girls—though sometimes the older witches surprised her and wanted to smoke with them.

Full of gumbo, cornbread, and cobbler, the ladies sat quietly for a few moments and passed the joint, waiting for Mama Sally to speak.

"Feels good out here," she said at last, breaking the contented silence. "I wish it would be like this for Samhain."

"Rain, then?" Chantelle asked for her position at Sally's feet.

"I think so, girl. Yes, rain and sadness. That's what the moon says."

Charlotte drew a deep drag from the joint before passing it to Bridgette and looked at the beautiful faces of the women on her balcony. Even with her need for planning, a concerned furrow on her brow, Cassie's eyes glimmered, and her sharp cheekbones cut across her face like the edge of a shard of glass. Monique and Chantelle glowed blue-black under the glowing moon, their faces filled with devotion to Sally, the current queen of New Orleans magic. Their stomachs warm and full, even the twins momentarily abandoned their rivalry and enjoyed the moment, Sylvie even opting for a drag of the blunt, which led to gentle teasing and laughter. Charlotte felt a warm rush of adoration run through her body for all of them.

"What do you need us to do, Mama?" Cassie asked. "Just let us know what you want, and we'll get it done."

Reaching for her daughter's hand, Sally smiled enigmatically. "I want you all to remember who you are. Who *we* are. Remember those who came before us and make the appropriate tributes. You know what to do."

The pearly whites of her cataracts reflected the moon's light, flashing with a strength and stubbornness the coven knew well.

Suddenly, Sally gasped. Monique leapt up from her seat and took Sally's hand.

"What? What is it?"

Sally closed her eyes and inhaled deeply.

"Blood. I smell death," she croaked.

Charlotte hurried to her side and took her other hand. "I'm here, Mama. What is it? What do you see?"

Sally motioned ahead, toward the wrought-iron bars of the balcony. Charlotte looked up and caught sight of the twins, their faces pinched with worry. The women rushed to the edge of the balcony, only to find the grim-looking older man Charlotte had seen moving in her neighbor's goods. His face was full of purpose, and he hastened to the stairwell, his left hand clutching a large blue cooler.

He disappeared under the balcony and into the dark corridor of the staircase, his steps rhythmic and heavy as he hurried up them.

Charlotte's eyes narrowed as she listened for Vasile's door opening, the shuffle of footsteps, the closing of the door. "What do you see, Mama?"

Sally closed her eyes and listened intently, but the threat was closed off to her, occluded by the night. Charlotte walked to the edge of the balcony again, hoping to hear something in the apartment next door. The women of the coven looked to one another uncomfortably, the silence hanging over them like a shroud.

Suddenly, Charlotte heard the rhythmic clicking of heels on the cobblestone walking toward the apartment. Cloaked in black, Tatiana appeared with an entourage of young, beautiful queens. She held a black parasol over her head and her makeup ran in inky rivulets down her cheeks. Only then did Charlotte remember that this evening was the wake for Miss Diamond.

With silent respect, the witches understood the sorrow of the party below them and whispered incantations of solace as the group passed below them and into the grief-stricken Tatiana's apartment. While most of the gathering's evenings ended with elation and women's voices cackling up into the night sky, this evening was sour, troubled, and as the women left in pairs, each one felt the heaviness of what had transpired.

Chapter 4

Although it was a Sunday night and business was steady due to a Saints home game, Pixie left Jack's at 11:05, her heart set on finding Mad Dog Skull Cap to repair her floundering relationship with her children's father. Pixie met Derek the first week she'd arrived in New Orleans, and they'd been more or less inseparable until recently. While the girls at the club told her to ignore him or leave him, she couldn't picture herself with anyone else.

Since her pleas for reconciliation with her partner had failed, Pixie set off on foot to catch the 11:20 from Rampart Street to City Park @Louis to walk the short distance to Holt Cemetery. Founded in 1897 as a potter's field for the indigent and named after a Confederate army surgeon Dr. Joseph Holt, and later obstetrician and smallpox and yellow fever expert in New Orleans, the graveyard was the final resting place for many deceased black New Orleans natives.

Pixie knew the cemetery because of the coven: Mama Sally's son Apollo, grandson Armand, and Cassie's daughter Honoré were buried within the wrought-iron gates, and the coven conducted most of their rituals there.

And although Pixie knew of many cemeteries closer to the Square—St. Roch's, Lafayette, St. Louis among them—Holt was the only graveyard where she had any hope of procuring the skull cap root during a waning moon. Unlike the many elaborate and above ground marble and concrete necropolises that made New Orleans unlike any other city in the world, Holt's was on a flat plain, and its plots much simpler. Rains regularly swept away topsoil and created wide puddles on graves. The dead here were not buried in expensive metal caskets and liners but wood, so that the bodies disintegrated rapidly and mingled with the soil, nourishing the grass, weeds, and beautiful oak tree in the center of the yard.

By 11:50, Pixie was hoisting herself over the locked gates at Holt, using her backpack to protect her hands as she climbed over the iron posts. She crept quietly against the back wall and felt relieved as she noticed one of the streetlights near the cemetery had burned out. This meant the closer she moved toward the tree at the center and toward the graves adjacent to it, the better concealed she was.

Holt had the unfortunate setting and history not only to be a pauper's cemetery, but also attracted graverobbers and practitioners of darker magic than Mama Sally's coven. Without caretakers on site, the cemetery was vulnerable to all manner of the city's denizens.

Pixie stumbled over a large, half-buried PVC pipe serving as a part of a rectangular plot for some beloved family member and crept closer to the tree, searching the ground for the telltale violet flowers. In October, finding the weed was unlikely, but not impossible; September had been as warm as August, and the first cold snap had not hit South Louisiana yet.

Pixie kept her eyes on the ground, watching her footing as she walked around plastic gravestones with hand-painted lettering, wooden markers with crude wood-burning, garden fencing, shoes and markers, shirts on T-bars, empty beer bottles resting near markers—signs of respect and grief for the dead. She circled near the back side of the oak tree, closer to where the LeNoir family members had some of the rare marble headstones in the yard.

Approaching the trio of headstones, Pixie knelt and paid her respects and asked for guidance from the dead. Above her, the Spanish moss swayed gently in the October sky, dancing slowly above the bones interred under the shadow of the oak. Beads and conch shells on cords clinked gently over Pixie's head, and she felt a sense of serenity.

Hearing a rustle over her shoulder, Pixie turned with a start, but was met only with the illuminated eyes of a rabbit grazing on clover... and skull cap!

"Yes!" Pixie squealed, and kissed her hand and held it to Apollo's headstone. "Thank you!" She jumped to her feet, and the frightened rabbit dashed off as she rushed to the plot with the Mad Dog plant. Pulling her backpack off her shoulder, she knelt down and unzipped the bag to pull out a scuffed steel spoon. As she dug carefully around the plant and its roots, her mind raced with images of a happier future for her family.

Fixed on her task, Pixie never saw her killer creep up behind her, but only felt a swift, sharp pain on her neck. Eyes wide, she watched as her blood fell into her cupped hands, staining the gentle blue of the treasured skull cap. As her life slipped from her body, she looked up to see the crescent moon, watching her hopes for love slip from between her fingers.

Alyssa pulled her Cadillac to the side entrance of Moonchild and honked twice. In the back seat of her immaculate ride: local socialite and co-chair of the Loyola University alumni fundraising board Tillie Bond-Kennedy (distant relation by marriage).

Wanting to convince Tillie to purchase a lakefront second home, Alyssa had wooed her with a champagne lunch and knew she would be enchanted by a reading from Mama Sally.

And Sally would give her an honest reading and benefit greatly from it: coven mutualism.

Sybil peeked through the back doorway and grimaced as rain slapped down against the cobblestone streets, jettisoning up into the air with vexed fury, a toddler railing against the rules of humanity. Sybil waved and held up a finger and mouthed *wait.*

Sally chuckled. "Rough day for reading. What's wrong with these folks?"

Sybil bustled about for an umbrella. "It's Alyssa, Mama."

"I know that, child," Mama laughed. "What these people want with Mama in this rain that can't wait?"

"Money can't wait, that's what," Sybil said, her words punctuated by the snap of her opening umbrella.

"BUTANNA!" Mischief screeched. "RAIN. OH BUTANNA!"

"Hush, you. We got company." Mama placed her hands on the table in front of her as Sybil stepped out into the rain to usher in the money. The car doors thudded open and closed, and heels clacked in the kitchen. She could sense quiet hesitation in the new energy crossing the threshold, unusual for a city like New Orleans.

"Hey, Mama," Alyssa said. "Y'all staying dry back here?"

"I am baby, I am. Come in. Sybil, get these ladies something warm. Tea, black." Mama's kitchen, Mama's rules; there was no coddling here, and her presence brooked no special requests from anyone, regardless of status or paycheck. "Sit down, sit down. What you need from Sally in this weather?"

Alyssa pulled back a chair for Tillie, and the pair sat down across from Sally. "Mama, this here's Mrs. Tillie Bond-Kennedy."

Sally extended her gnarled hands, and Alyssa nodded to Tillie.

Tillie placed her delicate hands into Sally's. "Thank you for seeing me, ma'am. I know this is last minute."

Sally gripped Tillie's hands and held them in silence. Alyssa nodded to her client, comforting her through the awkwardness.

"Sybil," Mama said at last.

"Got it, I got it," Sybil answered as she hurried over with two steaming cups of tea. She placed the teacups in front of the visitors and stepped back quietly.

"What you came to ask me isn't the question you need to be askin' me, baby," Mama said solemnly.

Confused, Tillie looked to Alyssa for help. "I'm sorry, Miss Sally," she drawled. "I'm not trying to waste your time—"

Sally smiled. "I know that, baby. Sometimes folks who come to me don't know they're lost."

Alyssa looked to Sybil; the latter could only shrug.

"You wanna know if you should buy that place on the lake, bring your grandbabies there," Sally said. "Yes, you do that. They gonna love it there, and you'll be happy."

Alyssa shot Sybil a relieved look.

Mama lifted her arm and reached it up into the air, shakily, to meet Tillie's face. Tillie looked first to Alyssa and then to Sybil, but both women knew Sally's truth could not be bound by either of them.

Tillie relaxed under Sally's hands and closed her eyes as the coven mistress ran her fingers over Tillie's face and down to her neck, pressing against the woman's carotid artery and jugular veins.

After a fly's lifetime, she pulled her hands away shakily.

"Listen to me close, baby," Sally warned. "You go see the doctor. Then you go see another. They gonna ignore you the first two times, like Peter denying

Jesus. The third gonna listen to you. If you don't do this, you won't see that lake house with those beautiful grandbabies."

Tillie's eyes widened, and she looked at the pale eyes that couldn't meet hers, though they could see all.

Sally reached for her hands again. Tillie slipped her hands into Sally's worn and calloused hands. "I—I don't know what to say," she said.

"Ain't nothing to say," Sally answered as she dropped Tillie's hands.

"I'm—I'm sorry," Tillie started. "What do I owe you?" Alyssa shifted uncomfortably.

Sally rocked in her seat. "You come back pay once you see what I see." The tea remained untouched as the women stepped back out into the merciless rain, and Sally sat unmoved by the truth revealed to her.

The pouring rain meant business was slow in the front of the shop. Sibyl left her place by her mother's side and pushed aside the beaded curtains separating the store. She scowled upon entering the room, and her twin noticed her mood immediately.

"What's up?" Sylvie asked.

"She just gave a free reading," Sybil said, nodding her head toward the back.

"Excuse me?" Cassie interrupted. "Has she lost her damn mind?"

Sybil shrugged. "No idea what she's thinking."

Cassie set down the paper towels and window cleaner she was using on the display case by the register. She strode to the back, pushing aside the beaded strings, which continued to ripple, reverberating from her frustration.

Sensing the tension, Charlotte, notebook in hand, approached her aunties tentatively. A rainy, indoor day at Moonchild had the potential for a dangerous storm conjured by a family of intense, stubborn witches.

"What's wrong?" she asked.

"Oh, Mama just did a reading for some Garden District mark Alyssa brought in and didn't even charge her for it."

"That don't sound like her," Charlotte mused aloud.

The twins looked at her simultaneously, confused by the obviousness of the comment.

Figuring it best to remain quiet, Charlotte moved away from her aunts to watch the rain briefly through a window. She tuned out the twins discussing, then debating, then arguing what had transpired in the back. The rain soothed her, and she could briefly ignore the stress of working with family.

The door chimes pulled her from her thoughts and quieted her aunts, who shot disgusted looks at one another before moving to their separate corners of the store—Sylvie at the register, Sybil at her reading table.

Giggling and soaked from the rain, two neo-hippie women stepped into the shop. One, tall and thin, wore yoga pants and a tie-dyed shirt and a long cardigan with a soaked pair of sneakers. The other, shorter and slightly rounder, wore intricate harem pants and a t-shirt reading "Ganja Run 2016" on it.

"Welcome, ladies," Charlotte said. "Looking for anything specific?"

"Oh, no," the taller of the pair said. "I just pass this place all the time and wanted to see what the inside is like."

"Well, have a look around. We do have essential oils and crystals if you're into the natural magic energy. Our tarot and palm reader Miss Sybil is in the corner if you need a reading."

"Great, thanks!" the taller woman said.

Charlotte returned to taking notes of items that were running low. She had already counted bottles and packets behind the counter. She knew Sylvie would keep an eye on the women in case they tried to pocket anything, but the pair looked moneyed, despite their casual appearance. She heard bits and pieces of their conversations as they wandered through the store. *Nag champa soap! Ali, they have an obsidian crystal...could use this vitality potion for Marc...* Their murmuring blended with the steady vibrations of the rain.

Storming through the beaded curtains, Cassie stepped up the register, her face twisted into a scowl. Whatever Mama Sally's reason for not charging a customer, the excuse did not appear to satisfy her daughter. Sylvie stepped out of her mother's way and moved to busy herself.

Charlotte avoided her great aunt's eyes as Cassie surveyed the shop, her eyes resting on the two women as she sized them up. Both women were happily moving around the shop, and both had several high-price items in their arms, including the overpriced crystal.

After shopping, the pair approached the counter. Cassie met them with a weak, forced smile. "That it for you ladies?"

"I think so," the shorter one said. "I just wanted to ask if this soap is vegan." She held up the wrapped bar of soap.

"What do you mean?" Cassie asked. "*Vegan?*"

"She wants to know if any animals were harmed in the soap processing," the taller woman explained. "Some soaps use animal fats."

Cassie looked at both women blankly, and the women stared back, waiting for her answer.

Sensing disaster, Charlotte approached them. "Ma'am, that soap is 100% cruelty free."

"So no animal byproducts."

"No ma'am."

Cassie made a mocking sound with the back of her throat. "You know where you are?"

Too late—having picked up wind in her argument with her mother, Hurricane Cassie was determined to make landfall and cause more destruction.

The smaller woman furrowed her brows. "I'm not sure I—"

"This is a vodou shop." Cassie reached into the case next to her and pulled out a brightly painted chicken foot. She placed it on the counter emphatically. "You comin' into to my house to complain about the cooking?"

The women looked at each other uncomfortably. Cassie continued to stare them down. Charlotte glared at her aunt, but Cassie would not be moved off course.

The taller woman set her purchases down on the counter. "I think we'd better go, Ali." Wordlessly, the smaller of the pair set down her items and looked at Charlotte with a pained expression. *Sorry,* she mouthed. They left the shop silently, humiliated.

Charlotte shook her head with disgust.

"What?" Cassie challenged. "You got something to say to me?"

You just lost us $500 easy, Charlotte thought, but she knew better than to give her anger a voice.

Cassie continued to look for a battle and began to rant. "I haven't spent over one hundred years of my life to educate myself on this art just to have some ignorant white women come in and try to tell me how to run this place and what I can sell."

It was a losing battle, like sandbags meeting a six-foot tide. Charlotte turned back to her work of cataloguing and hoped the women wouldn't leave them awful reviews online.

◖

The rain refused to abate when Charlotte left Moonchild on foot to start her shift at Jack's. While a downpour would probably deter clients from stepping out into the rain for a strip show in other cities, the revelers and visitors to New Orleans were unpredictable, so that a rainy Tuesday night could be packed or dead as the late-night, permanent inhabitants in St. Louis no. 1.

Despite having an umbrella, Charlotte stepped up the back steps to the club soaking wet, her long black hair plastered down the back of her blouse. She no sooner stepped into the dressing room when Mandy Love jumped up. "Girl, good thing you're back here. Twelve is up front."

"Shit—a bust?"

"Nah, not a bust. Bobbie said to let you know and to come up front when you get here."

Charlotte rolled her eyes and pulled a small vial of White Out from her locker. White Out was one of her most ingenious potions, and she didn't sell it. It had a rapidly acting effect if inhaled, making the user highly susceptible to persuasion and temporary forgetting. It had gotten Charlotte out of several dicey encounters with NOLA police. She loosened the cap and slipped it into her back pocket, ready to be put to work if needed.

As she headed toward the front, she saw two officers with Bobbie, who had pulled them into a champagne room in the back of the club, one usually reserved for private dances. Bobbie's face was clearly troubled.

"Hey," Charlotte said as she walked into the room. "What's up?"

"Oh, thank God you're here," Bobbie said. "They're here about Pixie—"

"Vanessa," one of the officers interjected. "Vanessa Johnson."

"We all just call her Pixie. What'd she do?" Charlotte said, slipping into a seat.

"She's missing," Bobbie interrupted.

"Ma'am," the officer said, placing his hand on her shoulder. "Thank you for talking to us. If it's all right, we'd like to talk to Charlotte here alone."

The women looked at each other, and Charlotte shrugged. "It's cool."

"If they hassle you, don't talk," Bobbie instructed. "We have a great lawyer and lots of powerful clients willing to pay to help us," she warned, as she narrowed her eyes at the men.

The second cop snorted. "Sure you do." His partner held out his hand to quiet him. "Thank you again for your help, ma'am."

He slid into a booth next to Charlotte as Bobbie left the room but stayed just within view, like a worried mother.

"Sorry to cut into your work hours," he began, taking out a notebook. "I'm Sergeant Wilson, and this is Sergeant Mansfield. We got a call from Ms. Johnson's partner Derek Jenkins. He says she hasn't returned home for three days now. Derek tells us she's close with a lot of the women here."

"Yeah, she is." Charlotte's defenses relaxed. "We all like her a lot." She frowned. "Where are her boys?"

"At home, with their father. He says she wouldn't leave them."

"She wouldn't," Charlotte agreed. "Not a chance."

"When's the last time you saw Vanessa?"

"We both worked Friday."

The policeman scribbled in his notebook. "And what frame of mind was she in that night?"

Charlotte thought about how bubbly Pixie had been. Full of hope. "She was really happy," she said. "She made good tips and was looking forward to being home with her man and babies."

"Any problems with customers? Your boss said you ladies on the floor have a better sense of the atmosphere with the customers because she's usually working in several areas."

"Yeah, she's right." Charlotte searched her memories. "I can't think of anything unusual. Before I left, she came to talk to me. She was getting ready to leave, too. We both banked, and she wanted to get home to her kids."

"What was your conversation about?"

"She wanted... advice. Relationship advice."

"Right, not unusual for a young woman. Your boss Bobbie said she had to ban Derek from this place?"

"He can't seem to keep his hands to himself when he's drunk. He's all right if he's not drinking, but..." Charlotte trailed off. She knew the statistics of domestic abuse and murder. Lots of girls had come to the club to work and had to leave because of black eyes at the hands of jealous partners.

"When you say he can't keep his hands to himself, do you think he could harm her?"

"I don't know," Charlotte answered honestly. "I've never seen any sign he hurt her, and she never says he did. His kind of abuse seems to me to be emotional, but we both know that shit goes hand in hand a lotta the time."

"True," the cop continued to write in his notebook. "We will definitely look at him closely. Vanessa have any history of drug or alcohol abuse that you know of?"

"You know, a lotta dancers have problems like that. I don't think Pixie does. She's a devoted Mama and just works and goes home to them. I've never seen her out partying."

"That seems to be the consensus among both her family and coworkers. I know this can be a touchy subject, but did she have any clients she would see privately, in her own time?"

"Nah. Bobbie or one of us would catch that. Bobbie doesn't hire prostitutes."

"I understand. So not a chance she would—"

"No," Charlotte said flatly. Her tone let the officer know that line of questioning was finished.

"Okay. Do you have any thought about where she might be? Your boss said her last shift was Friday night, and that she took off Saturday and Sunday to spend the weekend with her kids."

Charlotte thought back to her conversation with Pixie, her hopes for collecting the skullcap roots. There was no conceivable way to explain this to the man in front of her honestly. "No," she said at last. "I'm pretty sure she was heading home."

The officer stood. "Thank you for your time," he said, and pulled out a card. "Here's my number. If you can think of anything else—"

"Yeah, I'll call," Charlotte said.

The pair left the room, stopped to thank Bobbie, and headed out of the club. Once she was sure they were safely out of sight, Charlotte approached Bobbie.

"What are you thinkin' about this, Bobbie? You think Derek hurt her?"

"After ten years in this place, baby, nothing surprises me anymore."

When she left Jack's at 1 a.m., Charlotte's heart weighed on her. The rain, relentless, hadn't eased up in the few hours she had worked, and the police presence in the club scared off the few customers that might have braved the deluge to see semi-nude women dance.

As she waited under the eaves for an Uber, Charlotte scanned the rain-slicked streets around her. Rainy, desolate streets could sometimes make the nights in the city more dangerous as they presented an opportunity for crimes to go unnoticed. Charlotte had been robbed twice before, and although she didn't have much in the way of tips this evening, she was still wary of her surroundings.

Suddenly, her eyes landed on an unusual sight, even for the quarter: the small, older man from Vasile's apartment was scurrying through the rain, rat-like, with the blue cooler he'd had Sunday.

It wasn't the rain that sent a chill up Charlotte's spine. Though she didn't share the seeing skills of Mama Sally or Sybil, she felt something foul in the night air. As she watched the man turn a corner to head east, her Uber pulled up to honk at her. She approached the driver side, and a sleepy looking man rolled down his window and blinked into the raindrops hitting his window.

"Hey, man, sorry. I forgot something," Charlotte apologized.

"For you? I'll wait," the man smiled.

"Naw." She thrust a $10 into the window. "I gotta head back in for a while. Thanks, though."

"All right. You want my number for when you do leave? Better for me," he winked.

Charlotte repressed the urge to roll her eyes. "Thanks, no." She waved him off and pretended to head back to the threshold of the club. When his car was no longer in view, Charlotte half-jogged off in the last direction she had seen Vasile's man.

Running in the Quarter is a precarious enterprise on any given day; the cobblestone and curbs are uneven and tricky. Running through them in the rain, at night, more dangerous still. Charlotte had several advantages on her side: her subject had only two blocks' head start on her, and his steps were much more trepidatious than hers. Also, she had fallen and skinned her knees on these same city streets from the moment she began to walk, so each dip or flaw was imprinted in her memory.

Had the strange man looked back, he likely wouldn't have been intimidated by the slight build of the woman following him in the darkness. By sheer luck, Charlotte had worn a black hoodie and jeans with a worn-out pair of black Chucks, so she was even harder to spot in the inky darkness and rain. She slipped in and out of hidden corners of the city like a cat, sleek, stealthy, quiet as death.

The pair—only one of whom knew they were a pair—slunk through the city streets. Block after clock, Charlotte was only more determined to see this spying of hers to its end. After almost half an hour, she watched him cross a mostly empty Canal to Basin, then left on Cleveland.

After he slunk around the dim corner on Cleveland, Charlotte stepped around the corner, then jumped back suddenly. She had nearly stumbled right into his back as he pulled a white lab coat from his cooler. Luckily, the rain and his intentions preoccupied his mind and covered her own footsteps. She dipped her head around the corner to watch him slide into a door to Tulane Medical Center, leaving his umbrella leaning on the wall.

"Shit," she breathed, wondering if she'd just wasted half an hour following a lab aid or doctor to nothing. Charlotte bit her bottom lip and shuddered in the rain. *I'll give him fifteen minutes. If it's nothing, it's nothing, and you're an idiot who could be home in a warm bath.* She headed into the darkness down Cleveland, across from the hospital, and squatted into a doorway out of the rain to wait.

As the time slid closer to 2 a.m., she shivered in the doorway and watched the back of the hospital door the man had entered. The rain had revitalized her, and she felt even more certain something was wrong with the man. After waiting no more than nine minutes, Charlotte saw the door open, and the man stepped back into the rain. This time, his pace had quickened, and he looked over his shoulder quickly, as if worried he'd been detected. He abandoned his umbrella and crossed the street with a hastened trot.

I knew it, Charlotte thought triumphantly. She also knew where the man was likely to end up: back to the apartments on St. Peter's.

This time, she took short cuts back to her place, running through the rain to make sure she would reach her apartment before the stranger did. As she turned the corner to her block, she scanned the balcony but couldn't see if her new neighbor was out in the rain. Doubt crept into her mind again, but she slipped into a small crevice by Johnny's Bar and waited.

The rain slowed to a dull, steady hum, but that was little comfort from her spot in the darkness. Charlotte tried not the think about the rats that might currently be at her feet. Hopefully, they had more sense than she did and were indoors. She tried to calculate how long a man of about sixty might lag behind her, but she soon tired of the attempt, and shivered, hoping he would not be long.

After eight minutes of waiting, she heard a set of tired footfalls heading south toward her apartment. From her vantage place in the darkness, she watched the small man walk past her. When he finally slipped into the stairwell to Vasile's, she followed, her mind and heart racing.

As she reached the top of the landing, Charlotte jerked back in fear. There, at Vasile's doorway, the small man was triumphantly pulling the stolen fruits of his labor from his cooler to show to Vasile. Both men started at her presence, and Vasile pulled the man into his apartment quickly and shut the door.

Confused by what she had witnessed, Charlotte dashed into her apartment and double bolted the locks. She checked the doors to the patio as Ghost meowed his welcome and then checked the bolts on all the windows.

It took two joints and several texts (unanswered) to Tatiana before she finally drifted off into a fitful sleep.

Chapter 5

Charlotte jolted awake suddenly, scaring Ghost, who jumped off the bed and darted under her bedroom armoire. She had been dreaming of a shadow: it crept onto her balcony and peered at her as she slept. As the ominous figure jostled the locks, it grew larger, angrier, and shook the window frame. Charlotte's dream brain amplified the sound so that it clattered like a hurricane shaking glass.

After taking stock of her surroundings and listening to her elevated heartbeat thump in her eardrums, Charlotte groaned and swung her feet to the side of her bed to touch the cool wooden floor.

No sooner had she gathered her bearings, yawned, and stretched when a loud battering on her door had her heart skip a beat.

"... better open this door or I'ma bust it down!"

Charlotte breathed a sigh of relief. *Tatiana.* She unbolted the locks hastily and pulled Tatiana inside by her arm, looking over her friend's shoulder at Vasile's door.

"Okay, okay, girl, damn," Tatiana protested. "I'm here."

Charlotte slammed the locks shut and led her friend to the kitchen, as far away from the front door as possible. "You not playing, huh?" Tatiana said.

"Shhh," Charlotte hissed. "Lower your damn voice."

As if to protest, Tatiana raised her eyebrows and opened her mouth, but seeing the genuine distress on Charlotte's face had her clap her mouth shut. "Okayyyyy," she said in a stage whisper. "I got your texts, but they sounded like you was smokin' wet."

Charlotte shook her head. "I saw that little dude last night when I left the club," she nodded her head toward the direction of the front door. "His gnome or whatever he is."

"Okay, okay. What's a gnome?"

Charlotte groaned. "That little guy. The one with the glasses, pressed shirts? Come, Tati. It's the only visitor he's had over."

"Ohhhh, Mr. Andrei."

"What?"

"That's his name. The old guy. I met him when I gave him the pie to give Vasile."

Charlotte grabbed Tatiana's hands. "Enough with the fucking pie! Listen, I followed him to Tulane Medical."

"Okay, I got that part. And you followed him back here. But what was you doing following old people out in that rain last night? You sure you—"

Charlotte waved her off. "I just—I don't know. I had this feeling. Like, the kind you don't ignore."

Tatiana's eyes grew wide. "Ooooh, okay. I get that, with the vodou and whatnot."

"I guess," Charlotte sighed. "He had a cooler with him. I thought he'd gone into the apartment when I got up the stairs, but they were both at the doorway, and I saw what he had in the box."

At this point, Tatiana was completely engrossed, her eyes wide, waiting on every syllable coming out of her friend's mouth.

"And?!"

"And he had packets of blood, like they have in hospitals or when you go to donate blood. He was handing them to Vasile."

"And?!"

Charlotte dropped Tatiana's hands. "What do you mean *and?!*"

"I mean what about the blood?"

"You don't think that's weird? I just get this feeling..."

"Baby girl, my Gigi had anemia and sometimes needed blood."

"Your Gigi got someone coming to her house at 2 a.m. with blood?"

Tatiana thought earnestly.

"I didn't think so," Charlotte said.

"So you think they selling shit? Like the black market?"

"No. I mean, I don't know. I'm gonna go talk to Mama."

"That's a good idea, baby. I'll go with you. I need to check out what new shit y'all got, maybe a love potion. They got a cute little new barback at the Honey Pot."

Charlotte sighed and ran her hands over her hair. "Okay. Lemme grab my keys and my bag."

Before they left the apartment, Charlotte peeked out of her door to make sure the men were not in the hallway. Tatiana stepped out first, and no sooner had Charlotte turned her back to lock her door than Tati beat on their neighbor's door with an open palm.

"What the *fuck* are you doing?" Charlotte snapped.

"I got this," Tatiana said.

Incredulous, Charlotte leaned back against her own door, mouth hanging open, as Vasile's door creaked open. There, in the dark entryway, stood Mr. Andrei. He could not have been more than 5'3", and that was in dress shoes. His white hair was slicked back neatly against his scalp. His pale blue eyes peered into the dim light of the hallway over his glasses, and he forced a polite smile.

"Yes?" he asked, his accent as thick as Vasile's, though his voice was much gruffer.

"Heyyyyy," Tatiana drawled. "We just thought we'd come by to say hi. My friend here—" she pulled Charlotte forward by her hand, "came home late from work last night and was worried about y'all. Said she saw blood?"

Charlotte refused to meet the man's eyes, focusing on the stairwell in front of her and promising herself she would slip Tatiana something nasty later—maybe some Weeping Willow, make her dick soft—before she headed out with Mr. D on Sunday.

Mr. Andrei stepped out into the hallway and closed the door to the apartment quietly. Tatiana smiled at him brightly.

"Ah yes," he said. "My apologies for the late hour— Ms. Charlotte, is it?"

Tatiana tugged at her friend's hand. Charlotte begrudgingly met the man's gaze. She shrugged and refused to answer.

"Mr. Vasile is very private about his condition," the small man offered apologetically. "I'm not even sure he approves of my having this conversation with you."

"Hah! I knew it!" Tatiana said triumphantly. "I *told* you, Snow. He's *anemic.*"

Charlotte kept her eyes on the man before them. He remained expressionless, crisp and sharp as his pressed white shirt.

"If you'll excuse me," Mr. Andrei said. "I must go tend to him so he can work this evening. Good day to you both." With that, he closed the door quietly behind him, leaving the pair in stunned silence.

As they headed down the stairs and off to Moonchild, Tatiana started, "Girl, you really need to get some sleep."

"Don't," Charlotte seethed and fantasized anew about sabotaging her friend's weekend date.

"Bitch, slow down. I can't run in these heels on these streets."

Dressed in jean capris, a gingham blue shirt tied over her navel, and matching gingham wedges, Tatiana struggled to keep up with Charlotte as they walked through the uneven Quarter streets toward Moonchild.

Annoyed, Charlotte shot a glance at Tatiana over her shoulder and marched ahead silently.

"Owwwwww!" Tatiana screeched. Charlotte turned around to find the queen on her knees, gasping for breath and reaching for her ankle. "Girl, please! I think I broke something."

Charlotte narrowed her eyes and put her hands on her hips.

"I'm for real, baby. Now help a bitch out. No hos left behind, and all that shit."

Despite her anger, Charlotte inched forward and extended a hand to help Tatiana to her feet. The latter teetered on her heels and leaned onto her much shorter friend for support. "Thank you, baby. I ain't playin'. I think I mighta twisted something. Ow, ow- ow."

"Huh," Charlotte grunted.

"I know you mad at me, but—"

Charlotte stopped mid-step and tried to temper her words. "Tati—it's not even that I'm mad at you. I'm *telling* you something ain't right, and you bust over there like the Kool-Aid man. You need to think before you jump into shit. You know better than anyone that this city can eat people up for dumb shit like that."

The pair met eyes, and Tatiana's big brown eyes brimmed with tears. "Hey," she reached for Charlotte's hands. "Hey, you're right. I'm sorry. It's not an excuse, Snow. I'm just so angry about Ricky that I'm not seein' straight, just ready to fight."

Charlotte exhaled a deep sigh of relief. Finally, truth. "I get it. I do. But you gotta stay smart. I want you to stay away from that man—those men. We'll see what Mama thinks, but I know something ain't right there. This city can be beautiful, and can be rotten. People like you and me know the game better than anyone."

"You right, you right," Tatiana sniffed, and she pulled Charlotte close. The pair hugged tightly.

"Now, you really hurt, or—"

Tatiana scowled. "You runnin' though these god-damn streets in tennis shoes while I'm in these fine-ass shoes from Neiman. You *think* I'm faking this shit? For real?"

Tatiana's indignation set Charlotte to giggling, and Tatiana soon joined in, wrapped her arms around her friend, and the pair hobbled to Moonchild together. By the time they entered the storefront under the tiny door chimes, the neighbors were giggling like school-girls, arm in arm.

"Hey, Heyyyyy, witches!" Tatiana called as she stepped into the store.

Stocking items into the glass counter, Cassie shook her head. The twins rushed to their niece and Tatiana, who they considered both a local and wic-can/vodou cross-gender treasure.

"Blessings, blessings," Sylvie said as she kissed Tatiana's cheeks. "It's been way too long since you been here."

"Yes, blessings," Sybil said, pushing her sister out of the way. "You honor us, queen."

"Oooooh, lawd, no," Tatiana demurred. "Royalty ain't supposed to kneel before the common people." She hugged the twins heartily. "I'm sorry I ain't been in for a minute."

"You working today or what?" Cassie interrupted flatly.

"Nah, Auntie," Charlotte said. "I'll be here tomorrow. We came to see Mama. She busy?"

Cassie shrugged and continued her stocking. Sybil and Sylvie exchanged eyerolls. "She's here," Sylvie offered. "She don't have a client until 2. Go on back."

"Thanks," Charlotte said as she took Tatiana's hand and led her to the kitchen. Before they reached Sally, Charlotte could hear Mischief screeching ASOKO! in Japanese.

"Can you eat them birds?" Tatiana whispered. "How she put up with that shit?"

"Well, well, lookit who we have here," Mama Sally said, her voice full of joy. "Come, come, sit, sit. I knew you would come to see me today."

Charlotte knelt before her great grandmother and kissed her hand. "I have Tatiana with me, Mama."

Sally laughed. "I know, baby. Welcome, welcome, Tatiana, bride of Erzulie!"

"Okay, okay then," Tatiana laughed, extending a hand. "You lookin' good, Mama."

"BULLSHIT!" Mischief screeched.

"I ain't one to commit animal cruelty, Mama," Tatiana joked, "But some flour and Tony's..."

"Heh. That bird gonna outlive Mama," Sally shrugged. "But let's talk about why you're here, baby." She reached out to Charlotte, her gnarled hands shaking.

Charlotte took her great-great grandmother's hand. "I don't know if I'm wrong, Mama, but—I feel like something close is wrong. I know you see it."

Mama Sally searched the present and future in front of them. Her eyes, though occluded, darkened with what they saw. "You see and don't see," she said at last. "What's right in front of you, you can't see."

Tatiana's eyes grew wide, and she looked to Charlotte for answers.

"The blind see, and the seeing are blind," Sally continued.

Mischief cooed and preened his feathers on the kitchen counter behind Sally, though his actions did nothing to decrease the tension.

"What do we do?" Tatiana cried, breaking the silence. Charlotte pressed her friend's wrist with her hand.

"Blood is what it seeks. Teeth and claw. The old ways aren't always gone work. Try them anyway. Then you—" she seized Charlotte's hands, "You will know what to do. You always have."

"VA LA MERDE!" Mischief screamed. Despite themselves, all three women laughed.

"You right," Tatiana laughed. "You right."

"You," Sally croaked, as she reached for Tatiana's hands. "Something is after you, too. The hunter becomes the hunted."

"Oh, girrrrl, all these mens be after Miss Tatiana, Mama Sally. That ain't nothin' new. Oooh, Mama, your hands are dry. Lemme rub 'em. I got some lotion in my purse."

Dumbfounded into silence by all she had heard and witnessed, Charlotte watched quietly as Tatiana pulled coconut butter from her purse and massaged Mama Sally's hands.

Chapter 6

Although he normally wouldn't risk sitting on his balcony for fear of interacting with the people living nearby—Winston refused to think of them as neighbors—he needed an escape after another long shift at the post office. His feet hurt, so he had them hoisted onto the latticed ironwork on his balcony.

Winston inhaled deeply and dared to relax and enjoy the cool October evening. He kept the porch light off and sat in the darkness with Sophie slung around his shoulder. She had coiled herself loosely around his neck and occasionally flicked her tongue around his ear. His mother could no longer make it out onto the porch, so he knew he would not be interrupted by her demands.

The streets were unusually quiet, with none of the usual buskers squatting below, blaring trumpets or playing plastic bucket drums. Noise in the Crescent City is endless, and no manner of threats or bribes convinced locals to move along or shut up. Winston spent a good portion of his twenties using the system, trying to call the police on the buskers, the drag queen's parties, the open drug trade from the hooker—or whatever she was—across the street. All this got him was a warning from the police as if he—*he*, the only quiet person in this damned city—were the nuisance.

Movement directly across from his vantage spot caught his eye: a tall, thin figure stepped onto the balcony and surveyed the streets below. Like Winston, the man also rejected the light, choosing to stay in darkness. He walked to the edge of the balcony and rested long, greyish fingers on the edge of the railing. Winston couldn't make out much of the expression on the man's face as it was only dimly underlit from the lamps on the streets below, but he could see distinct features: a sharp nose and deep cheekbones.

Winston delighted in spying on people but hadn't dared to take out his binoculars since his last unfortunate interaction with the young woman across the way. He held his breath and the man glanced around the balconies, perhaps looking for someone to spy upon as well. As the stranger's gaze crossed over Winston's flat, Sophie tensed, constricting her coils around Winston's neck. Despite his best effort, Winston coughed and sputtered, pulling her loose by her tail.

Across the way, the man smiled widely, his teeth gleaming eerily from the blue lights of the street below. "Good evening," he said at last, and it sounded to Winston more of a challenge than a greeting.

"Sure," Winston said, standing up to head back in.

"What a beautiful animal you have there," the man offered. "So many people suffer from ophidiophobia, the fear of snakes. Shame, isn't it? They are such efficient hunters—very meticulous. Not one part of their prey wasted."

Despite himself, Winston felt mesmerized by the man's voice. He had never heard an accent quite like it, and no one ever had addressed him so comfortably—much less about Sophie. He stepped backward, dumfounded, unsure of what to do.

The man let out a throaty laugh. "I will leave you to enjoy this beautiful evening." And with that, he turned around and stepped back into his apartment.

Once he was alone, Winston gasped suddenly, unaware that he had been holding his breath. He felt a red-hot flame of anger well up in his chest. Where Winston was usually in full control of his emotions and could avoid interactions with others when he felt less than they, the stranger unsettled him, and this angered him.

Although the night was cool and crisp and beautiful, Winston stormed back into his apartment and headed to his room to look up articles about Rhode Island life.

"Hey," Charlotte said to Sybil as the pair ran the storefront. "Bobbie wants me to come in. She just sent a text that said bring Cassie with me."

"What? It's the middle of the day."

"I know. Tantie Cassie!"

"What?" came a voice from the back.

"Come here!"

Cassie walked to the front slowly, a bowl of shrimp and grits in her hands. "I swear, never a quiet minute in this place, even to eat. What you need?"

"Bobbie wants you and me to head to Jack's."

"What, now?"

"Yeah." Charlotte frowned at the text on her phone.

"Why?"

"She didn't say, just said it's important."

Cassie scooped a large bite of her food into her mouth and set the bowl down on the counter. "All right. Let's go. Sylvie, you gonna be okay running shit here if Sybil has to read? I think Mama has a 5:30, so we should be back."

"We got it. Y'all go ahead," Sylvie responded.

As Cassie and Charlotte headed to Jack's, Charlotte took her great auntie's arm and walked a slower pace than she would have liked, wracking her brain about the meaning behind this impromptu meeting. Samhain was approaching, and most of the girls at Jack's were in the coven, but still—Bobbie's request was unusual.

"Can you get any idea of what this is about?" Charlotte asked, breaking the silence.

"Huh," Cassie grunted sardonically. "I don't have the sight. You know that. You?"

"No," Charlotte said. "No clue. She just says it's urgent and get here quick."

Though she knew deep down that Cassie loved her, Charlotte wished she could reach her aunt. The twins said that when their brother Honoré died of the ague at age 3, Cassie grieved for years and never seemed to be happy again. Like Sally before her, Cassie raised her children alone, their father having died after a barroom brawl moved from fists to knives. "Too much pain all at once," Sybil said, and Charlotte believed her. Cassie shut down even with her girls, who learned to seek out comfort and love from Mama Sally.

It was 1:15 when they reached Jack's, Charlotte helping Cassie negotiate the stairs. Despite her age, Cassie, like Sally, was still nimble, a testament to the use of magick and to Charlotte's elixirs. As they walked through the back entrance of the club, the dancers parted ways quickly at the sight of Cassie and followed Charlotte and her great aunt toward Bobbie's office.

"Charlotte's here," said Mandy Love, an athletic and popular dancer with auburn hair who had a way of making the customers at ease.

"Thank heavens," Bobbie said from in her office. She stepped into the doorway and took Charlotte's hands and then Cassie's. "Let's head to the dressing room."

When they reached the back, one of the girls led Cassie to a plush chair. It was then Charlotte noticed Bobbie's eyes were red, her cheeks stained with tears.

"Thanks for coming so quickly. I'm gonna let Mandy explain why you're all here." With that, Bobbie sat down and reached for a tissue. Mandy looked uncomfortable, the way one does when delivering awful news.

"I don't know how to say this," she started. "But I learned from the cop I see sometimes that the police found a body last night and are going to announce to the press today that they found Pixie."

A graveside pall settled over the women. "Oh my god. What happened?" asked Sapphire (real name, Deanna). A cry of pain from another dancer escaped into the room.

"He wouldn't tell me too much, just that they'll probably come talk to us again. She was at the cemetery."

Charlotte sucked in a breath of air through her teeth, causing Cassie to look sideways at her.

"*Our* cemetery?" Cassie asked.

"Yeah, Holt," Mandy said. "It looks bad, y'all. He said he was there to help cordon off the place. 'Ritualistic' is the word he heard the detectives use."

"Who would wanna hurt her?" Bridgette asked. "She was the sweetest thing."

The girls and Bobbie looked to Cassie for comfort and answers.

"I'll bring this to Mama Sally," Cassie promised. "I don't see things like Sybil and her do. You do what you gotta to get more outta this cop, you understand?"

Mandy nodded solemnly.

"I'll try to get information from the boyfriend on her family and arrangements. I just can't believe this." Bobbie wept.

Charlotte felt a chill crawl under her skin and down into her chest. She knew why Pixie had gone to Holt but never imagined she would go alone. She fought against the tears welling up in her eyes and looked at the floor as the women talked about helping Pixie's boys. *This is my fault,* she thought. *I never should have told her what to look for.*

Chapter 7

Charlotte walked Cassie back to Moonchild around three and then headed back to Jack's to grieve and work with the rest of the coven. It was, thankfully, a weekday, and slow at that, so the girls did what they could to get through the night. Tips were slim, a sign of their own diminished energy and interest in making money. Pixie was well-loved, and the news of her murder affected all.

Although she would usually text Tatiana so they could walk home together, Charlotte didn't want to share her grief—especially since so much of it was still something she couldn't voice. She stopped to pick up a bottle of whiskey so she could be alone with her sorrow. Tomorrow, she would regroup and seek Mama's help. Tonight, she would mourn and drink herself to sleep.

Ghost ran to the door and rubbed against her legs affectionately as soon as she entered the door. He followed Charlotte to the kitchen on silent paws and watched as she took a glass from the cabinet, poured a drink, and took the bottle outside on the balcony with her. As she sat down, Ghost jumped onto her lap and purred loudly, rubbing his head against her hands. Coupled with her guilt, Ghost's innocent affection made Charlotte gasp in pain, releasing the agony of holding in her emotions.

She sat quietly in the darkness, grateful for the quiet humming of the city life around her. She could hear the thumping of club music north, toward Bourbon, the buskers drumming to the south, in the square, the clip-clop of horse hooves from the carriage rides that could still be purchased at this late hour. These were the sounds she'd grown up with, and they comforted her in their familiarity.

And she wept because the beauty of the city was rivaled only by the ferocity and indifference with which it could destroy a life like Pixie's, leaving her dreams unfulfilled and her boys without their mother.

Charlotte filled her glass again as Ghost purred contentedly in her lap as she stroked his back. *I should have known,* she thought. *I shoulda told Pixie not to go alone.*

A click on the balcony to her left made Ghost lift himself in her lap, and he arched his white back, hissed, and scrambled back into the apartment.

"GODAMMIT!" Charlotte yelled and stood up. Not only had Ghost torn up her thigh with his back legs as he scrambled to escape, but once again, her neighbor was invading her space when she needed to be alone.

Vasile raised his hands. "I did not mean to scare it."

"Him. *Him.* And he doesn't like you a bit. Wonder why," she said, draining her glass.

"He doesn't know me?" Vasile offered.

Charlotte poured herself another draught and headed toward the locked gate separating Vasile's balcony from her. "Or maybe he does," she scoffed.

Uncomfortable, Vasile looked off his balcony, down the block. "I find myself apologizing again. I feel I have offended you often, and that is not my intention."

Charlotte looked through the gate and met her neighbor's eyes. They were black and shiny, but even in the darkness, she could see pain. "Shit," she said. "Look, it's been an awful day. I don't think it's a good time to be talking to me." She fumbled with the whiskey bottle and poured herself another glass.

"I'm sorry," Vasile offered. "I can see you are suffering."

"Yeah," Charlotte acceded. "This place—" she gestured over the balcony, "It's the most beautiful, cruel place in the world. It's the worst lover you can imagine, one you want so bad that beats you daily. But you're new here, so you don't get it."

Vasile circled his pale fingers around the black wrought iron separating them. "You're right, of course I don't know this city, but I do know misery, and all too well." His tone was so crestfallen that Charlotte had no response that seemed appropriate. The warm whiskey was settling into her veins and her mind.

"Men are a fucking misery," she snapped, and filled her glass, slumping into her chair.

"I see," Vasile said. "I am sorry you are hurting. Good night, Charlotte."

His shoulders slumped, Vasile walked back into his apartment and locked the patio doors.

Charlotte chuckled. "Like this man is scared of *me.*" She drained her glass and made kissing noises, trying to coax Ghost to join her in her sadness, but she was completely, utterly alone.

Chapter 8

The following night, the collective mood of the dancers, bartenders, bouncers, and proprietor at Jack's was not much better than the night before. The girls tried to keep the mood light for the customers, but during breaks, they often stepped behind the bar to get a drink or headed to the back to cry.

Charlotte abstained from both tears and alcohol, focusing instead on her anger and acting more disdainful and aggressive with the men in the club than she normally would have. Every man in the club was, in her eyes, a potential suspect, and she resented them all. Leaving work at midnight was a relief, as was Tatiana's presence at the back door.

"Heyyyyy, little Mama," she said, handing a warm bag with a poboy to Charlotte. "Brought you a poboy from NOLA's. Loaded, with pepper jack."

"Thanks, Tati," Charlotte sighed, hugging her friend. "It smells so good."

"Gotta oyster for me. Let's go hang out and chat. Your Tantie Cassie wanted me to make sure you get home safe."

"What?" Charlotte hesitated before biting into her poboy. "She called you?"

"No, texted. She asked me to pass by. Mama said make sure you got the mandrake doll on you."

"Yeah, I do," Charlotte said. "Cassie really texted you? I didn't even know she knew how to text."

"Well, she don't really, but I got the message," Tatiana laughed. "I had a good time talking to them. Sybil and Sylvie crack my shit *up.*"

"Uh huh. They ain't as funny when you gotta work with them arguing all the time."

"No doubt. Family is messy, and y'all all got strong personalities."

"What did Mama have to say?"

"Well, she gave me some ideas and plants on your thinking on our new guy." Tatiana hoisted a large plastic bag with potted plants in them, one stalk of a plant peeking from the top of the bag.

"Okay, what is that?"

"Garlic and onions. She said see if he reacts to them. We gone put them by the gate on your balcony." Tatiana's eyes glowed conspiratorially in the dim streetlights. "Find out he if really is anemic, or—" she looked over her shoulder and whispered, "*or if he's a revenant.*"

Charlotte struggled to suppress a laugh at her friend's earnestness. "A what?"

"A vampire," Tatiana explained. "It's what Mama Sally calls 'em. I didn't know, either."

"Oh lord," Charlotte said. "Really?"

"Hey, if you woulda told me six years ago I was living next to a real-life witch, I wouldn't have bought it, either. Ain't nothin' surprise me now. She also gave me some rosaries, said to hang them around all entries and windows until we know for sure."

Charlotte stopped and tugged Tatiana's arm, "She's serious?"

"She sure didn't act like it was a joke, baby. She said she already told you something ain't right, and you heard what she said about me being hunted. Tatiana Manhunter ain't about being on the dinner menu for no revenant."

As they neared their apartment, Charlotte and Tatiana both scanned Vasile's balcony, but it was empty. Surprisingly, Tatiana was quieter than usual, and Charlotte could sense her tension. They walked up the stairs gingerly, though the wood still creaked and groaned below their feet. Not until they both entered Charlotte's apartment and locked the double bolts behind them did the pair relax.

Ghost was waiting by the door and mewled a hello, proceeding to rub the sides of his body against Charlotte and then Tatiana. "Let me feed him. You want a soda or water? I'm out of booze."

"Thanks, baby. I'll take some water. Lemme go put these plants out on your veranda."

"Veranda, revenant—you're fancy today, Tati."

Tatiana flipped her wig playfully as she headed to the balcony. When she came back in, she locked the door and pulled a rosary out of the plastic bag to hang over the door. She did the same with the front door before sitting down to eat her oyster.

"This poboy is delicious," Charlotte said, walking back to the living room with water. "Thanks again. I owe you."

"Girl, please. You and your family feed me all the time. I hung up two of the rosaries, but you gonna need to do the ones over your windows. We gonna see what he thinks of that garlic, too."

Disinterested in his own food, Ghost hopped onto the sofa and begged for an oyster. "Can he have some of this? Do cats eat oysters in nature?" Tatiana asked.

"Tati, how would they get the shell open?" Charlotte laughed, and Tatiana joined in. "I'm so glad you're here. Work has been rough."

"I didn't wanna ask, but Cassie said one of y'all dancers died."

"Not just died. Murdered."

"Yeah, she said. I didn't wanna ask. Was she turnin' tricks?"

"No, not that any of us could tell. She just came to work, did her job, and headed home to her boys.

'Course she coulda run something outta her place, but Bobbie don't play with that shit at the club."

"I'm so sorry, baby girl. This is some crazy shit—like what happened with Ricky. They got all kinds freaks out there lookin' to hurt girls like us. You gotta promise me: no more sneakin' around late at night to follow men around this city. You text me or call me anytime, and I'll come walk you back home."

"I know, Tati. I appreciate that. Same goes for you."

This time, it was Tatiana's turn to laugh. "What you gonna do for me, Snow, all 5 feet nuthin' of you?" At 6'3", Tatiana was a tall queen with impressive biceps and plenty of experience protecting herself from a world that hated her kind.

"Okay, point taken, but still—we're all safer in pairs, Tati. And if something is after both of us, maybe it's better to meet that evil together."

"True, true. Ain't nobody invincible. This city just has a way of making you think you are, and then it cuts you deepest when you ain't lookin'."

The women ate in silence, sobered by the reality of Tatiana's assessment of the Crescent City and the fear that something was stalking them both.

Chapter 9

"Cops coming," Sybil said suddenly as she looked up and shuffled her tarot deck. Sylvie stopped cleaning the counter to assess their surroundings; the police had not harassed them for many years, not since white people began running Wiccan stores and rituals in the city. Though this incursion frustrated Cassie, Mama rightfully pointed out that the popularity of vodou and magick would only make their lives easier with respect to cops and city officials.

As usual, she was right, and rarely had the police darkened their stoop in the recent years—usually just coming to ask about grave robbing for ritualistic purposes, and even in this the LeNoirs weren't suspects, just storehouses of knowledge.

Within three minutes, the door chimes tinkled as two men in dress shirts and slacks entered.

"Ah, detectives," Sybil corrected herself without looking up from her cards.

"Good afternoon, ladies," the larger of the two, a black man with skin like cherrywood said. "I'm Detective Ardoin."

His partner gave a nod. "Detective Hills," he offered.

Sylvie placed elbows on the edge of the countertop and leaned into the conversation. "What you boys need?"

"We're looking for one of your employees. Charlotte LeNoir?"

"Our niece, you mean," Sybil snapped as she laid down a card. "We all family here."

"Your niece then," the Detective Hills said. "Is she around?"

"I'm right here," Charlotte interrupted, stepping in from the beaded curtains. "You can follow me."

"Please," Sylvie said, motioning to the doorway. "No offense, but y'all terrible for business. Charlotte, can you show them out back when they finish?"

"Yeah, I got it. My great grandmother said y'all might wanna talk to her, too," Charlotte said as she led the way. Detective Hills looked over his shoulder curiously at his partner.

"МУДАК!" Came a screech from Mischief. Charlotte smirked; maybe the parrot knew more than he let on.

Charlotte ushered the men into the kitchen and motioned to two folding chairs across from Mama Sally. She walked behind the table and rested her hand on her great-great grandmother's shoulder.

"Now what do we have here?" Sally asked. Although she knew very well what the two men across from her needed, she also knew enough not to show her own hand.

"Ma'am. I'm Detective Hills. This is Detective Ardoin. We came to talk to Charlotte here about a friend of hers."

"Huh. Charlotte, baby, you get their ID?"

Charlotte met eyes with the detectives. "I'm sure they'll let me see them, Mama."

The detectives exchanged glances again. "Ma'am," Detective Hills said, his voice raised a notch in frustration, "We just have a few questions for Charlotte. We can always continue this at the station if there's a problem."

Sally laughed and patted her granddaughter's hand. "Of course you can," she cooed. Something about the comforting tone of her voice and the warm, strange spice smells emanating from a pot on the stove lulled the detectives into silence.

"I don't think that will be necessary," Detective Ardoin interjected. He pulled out his identification and slid it across the table. Grateful for her grandmother's strength, Charlotte kept her eyes locked on Ardoin's, breaking contact only to look at his identification. She slid it back to him wordlessly.

"What can we do for you?" Mama Sally asked.

"I'm afraid I have bad news," Ardoin said. "We just stopped into Jack's Cabaret—I understand you work there?"

Charlotte nodded. "I do."

"A body was found at Holt cemetery two nights ago. She has been positively identified as Vanessa Johnson. I believe she went by Pixie at the club?"

"I just spoke with some officers a few days ago. What happened?"

"Ma'am, that's what we are trying to find out, so we're interviewing her friends and—" Ardoin struggled for the right word. "And her associates. How well did you know Vanessa?"

Although Charlotte already suffered through the awful revelation of Pixie's death, she felt hot tears run down her cheeks. "Pretty good," she said. "We're all close there at the club. Everyone liked Pixie—Vanessa."

"That's what we've come to understand, and I'm sorry for your loss. We will do everything possible to bring her killer or killers to justice. We're especially interested in talking to you since we understand you also work here at Moonchild. Can you talk to us a bit about the shop?"

"What you need to know?" Sally interrupted. "It's everything you see. Ain't no secrets."

Ardoin chuckled. "True, but Miss—?"

"Sally. Long time since I was a miss. Long time." Sally leaned back from the table, her hands on the top, her opaque eyes tracking nothing, and laughed. "We wanna help you boys, but you can see what we do. Vodou. Magick. Readings. Tours. How can we help catch this poor baby girl's killer?"

Ardoin shuffled in his seat and looked askance at his partner. "We can't get into the details of her death, Miss Sally, but... it appears ritualistic in nature. We're hoping you can give us some insight into what we found." He nodded toward Hills, who pulled a photograph from a file in hand, then slid a photo across the table.

Charlotte looked down at the photo, gasped, and covered her mouth. There, on an 8x10, was Pixie, her face a pale gray, her lips purple and swollen. She was nothing of her vivacious, former self, and the image made Charlotte sob. Sally reached for her hand so she, too, could see.

"Like I said, she was found at Holt cemetery," Ardoin said. "I believe y'all got people buried there."

"We do," Charlotte said solemnly. She pushed the photo back across the table to the detectives and looked the detective in the eyes. "You gotta promise me you're gonna catch whoever did this to her—" her voice cracked. "She's got babies who needed her."

"Ma'am, we will do everything we can," Ardoin said. "But we need help. Her body was laid out, like you see there. We need to know anything you can tell us about how that might relate to vodou, or..." he gesticulated around the kitchen, "...anything else you all know about."

"Sheiße," Mischief cooed, hopping from one foot to another. *Sheiße, sheiße.*

"Hush," Mama fussed at the parrot. "You hush." She extended a gnarled finger at the detective. "You ain't lookin' for someone like us. This ain't about vodou ritual, or Wiccan ritual, nor magick. Wastin' your time. But it *is* ritual for the killer, yes. It's someone who hides in the shadows."

Thinking Sally could not see his reaction, Detective Hills tapped his partner, rolled his eyes, and stood to leave.

"You doubt all you want, boy," Sally bit back, lingering on the boyyyy. "You outta your element here."

Speechless, Ardoin looked to Charlotte for help, but she was lost in her own pain. "Well, thank you ladies," he said helplessly. He reached in his pocket and slid a card across the table, but neither woman touched it. "Call me if you remember anything. We really need all the help we can get here. For your friend."

With that, Charlotte directed the men to the back stoop, and closed the back door firmly the minute they were gone. "Mama," she started.

"I know what you want to hear," Sally interrupted. "Sit down. Let's talk."

The night was cool and breezy, and Winston longed to sit on the balcony. However, he noted with annoyance that the tall stranger was already out there with the older man who had helped him move in. Winston tried to guess at the nature of their relationship as he listened to their conversation from his place by the window he'd propped open.

Unfortunately, the words blowing across the breezeway were in an unfamiliar tongue. Whatever the discussion's nature, it was becoming more heated, with the older man pacing the length of the balcony and gesticulating wildly.

In the dim street lighting, Winston could occasionally make out the new occupant's face: the younger man looked weary, as if he had been on the receiving end of this intense conversation many times before. In fact, he looked unwell.

Winston strained to make sense of the language they spoke, which sounded to him like a cross between Spanish and Russian, maybe Polish? He could occasionally make out a word that sounded familiar, like *comfortable,* but the context escaped him.

Suddenly, it occurred to him that he could use the translating app he had installed on his phone, the one he used to spy on two of his Spanish-speaking co-workers to make sure they weren't talking about him. Winston slid his phone under the small table next to his seat cautiously so that the screen's light wouldn't catch the men's attention.

To his great disappointment, much of the conversation was too low for his phone to capture, but one impassioned cry from the older man, *Ascultă-mă!* registered. Winston lowered the volume on his phone and bent over to press translate as he held the phone to his ear.

Listen to me! The app identified the language as Romanian.

His efforts to understand their debate was mostly useless, though he did feel a sense of smugness in uncovering the man's background. Winston could tell that the older of the pair was winning his argument out of sheer endurance as the taller Romanian looked wan, exhausted.

"*Trebvie să vânezi!*" the older man bellowed, his fist raised in the air for emphasis.

You need to hunt! The translation app buzzed.

Winston furrowed his brow, wondering if the translation was accurate. He looked across at the men again, and although he could not hear the stranger's response, he could tell the younger man was relenting.

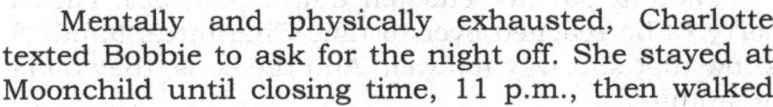

Mentally and physically exhausted, Charlotte texted Bobbie to ask for the night off. She stayed at Moonchild until closing time, 11 p.m., then walked back to her apartment, forgetting her promise to Tatiana to call.

Her phone buzzed with a text from Tatiana. Where you at? Am I picking you up tonight?

"Damn," Charlotte exhaled and then concocted an excuse. OMW. Stopped to get us chicken from Coop's. Be there in a few.

Her lie meant she now had to double back and grab some food, but Charlotte hadn't eaten all day, and she hoped the food would keep a lecture from Tatiana at bay.

Once she had the warm, aromatic bag of fried chicken with red beans and rice sides, Charlotte hustled back home. As she neared her apartment, she scanned the balconies and saw Vasile and Mr. Andrei heading back into his place. Despite herself, she shuddered involuntarily—and not because the air was turning crisp.

Tatiana pulled open her door almost as soon as Charlotte knocked, further shaking her.

"Not cool, girl. You're supposed to call me, Tatiana fussed.

"Shit, sorry," Charlotte groaned. "It's been a long couple of days." She slid into a leopard-print chair in Tatiana's living room and dug into the bag to hand Tatiana a Styrofoam box of chicken.

Tatiana sat down next to her on the couch and popped open her box. "Girl, yessss. I just smoked a fattie and *really* needed me some fried chicken. Mmmm." She took a huge bite of chicken breast and closed her eyes, relishing it. "Talk to me, baby."

"Detectives came by the store to ask about Pixie— the girl who died," Charlotte said.

Tatiana put her chicken down. "Oh, girl. I'm so sorry." She reached over to take Charlotte's hand. "I know that shit way too well. And the cops, they don't do nothin'."

Charlotte nodded silently.

"Snow, you givin' yourself time and permission to grieve?"

"What do you mean?"

"I mean you work all the damn time, even when you're here at home. You even let yourself think about this friend of yours and cry? Get mad? Break shit?"

"No," Charlotte whispered.

"You need to slow down for a few days," Tatiana advised. "World ain't gonna fall apart if you ain't at Jack's with your titties out."

"It's not that—I don't give a shit about the club," Charlotte said. "I mean, except I have to so I keep money coming in. My aunties, Mama—they won't listen to me about the shop. They act like it's still 1920, that they can get by on nickel flour and eggs. You know what I'm dealing with. I feel like I'm babysitting them all except Mama. And then Pixie—I keep thinking about her babies, Tati. They gotta go on without the person who loved them more than anyone else ever will. That's just not right, and I'm sad, and I feel—" she said, her voice breaking, "I feel like there's nothing I can do about any of this shit."

"Come here, baby, come here." Tatiana pulled Charlotte in for a hug. "I wish I had an answer. Life is *fucking* hard. You gotta take care of yourself. You always lookin' out for everyone else, but take time to be sad. That kinda shit will sour and hurt you."

"You're right," Charlotte said. "Maybe I'll take off a day or two, get my head straight."

"There you go, baby. Good thinking. You ain't no good to anybody if you're burnin' the candle at both ends. You even eat today? These red beans probably the best I've had in a long time."

Charlotte knew Tatiana was lying about the beans, but she tried them and was happy with the warmth of the comfort food. She realized, too, how ravenous she was, and ate voraciously.

"Okay," said Tatiana, licking her fingers, "These damn biscuits gonna give Miss Tati some for real thighs and breasts. Mmmm."

Charlotte laughed, grateful for the company and comfort.

"So, I gotta tell you what I been up to today," Tatiana said. "They—" she pointed her glitter fingertips upward, "They was up there arguing tonight."

"Who?"

"Him and the old dude. I couldn't hear too good and didn't wanna step out to listen, but I started doin' some researching."

"About?"

Tatiana rolled her eyes. "About what. About revenants is what."

"Yeah, I talked to Mama about that today. She told me about the connection with vodou, but she doesn't think that's what we got here. You get that sense at all—like Mr. Andrei controls him?"

"Nope. If anything, I think it's Vasile owns Andrei. But look," Tatiana said excitedly, pulling a printout from the table next to her, "I made a list of shit we can try. We got the garlic already," she pointed, handing the papers to Charlotte. "Now we just check off what works and what don't."

Charlotte glanced over the list. "Wolfsbane. Wild rose. Mirrors. Tati, where'd you get this?"

"Wikipedia," she answered proudly.

"Wikipedia," Charlotte repeated, "to repel a vampire."

"*Revenant,*" Tatiana corrected. "That's what Mama Sally said it was."

"Okay, wait. First of all, she isn't sure, she said. She's only going by what you told her."

Tatiana looked hurt and pulled the papers back. "Well, we gotta try something. You got any ideas?"

"We can't poison him with wolfsbane," Charlotte said. "Lemme look at what you got here. We haven't even waited to see if he reacts to the garlic and onions or the rosaries."

"Okay, I feel you. We'll wait on the big caliber." Tatiana looked upwards, lost in thought momentarily. "But we know he don't go out in daylight, so I checked that off. I don't care who you are—ain't no way you can avoid going out in the day for two weeks, especially when you moving in."

"Well, mark that off, but I don't think we have enough information on his comings and goings to say for sure. Hell, you and me are out mostly at night, Tati."

"You right. You right." Tatiana reached for a pencil and made a note on her charts.

"I'll make a sour jar with the wolfsbane. Let's go through your list and consider anything that won't actually kill someone."

"Deal," Tatiana said. "Look at us, being detectives. Bitch, with enough sleep, you and me can probably figure out who killed our friends."

A cloud of sadness hovered over the room again. "Yeah," Charlotte said despondently. "We'll see."

Chapter 10

Charlotte woke to Ghost nuzzling his head against hers. Grateful for the affection and silence, she stroked his cheeks and back while he purred loudly.

"Man, we *do* need a day off, don't we, minou?" She checked her phone for the time: 10:20 a.m. She'd finally gotten a full eight hours of sleep. "We not gonna do shit today, Ghost. We're gonna stay in and watch something stupid—reality TV, some shit like that. Lemme call the store."

"'Sup, little Mama?" Sylvie said when she picked up the phone at Moonchild. "When you comin' in?"

"I'm not," Charlotte said. "I need to get some stuff done here at the apartment. I been running nonstop."

"Okay, lemme let you talk to Cassie. She said she has something to tell us. Mama? I'm gonna put it on speaker."

"What?"

"It's Charlotte on speaker. You said you needed to talk to us."

"Where she at?"

"She's not comin' in today. Mama," Sylvie sounded exasperated. "You can talk to her."

"Hi, Tauntie Cass," Charlotte said.

"Why ain't you comin' in today?"

"I'm just—I need a break," Charlotte said.

"You definitely need a break, baby. We know you're hurting," Sybil interrupted. "We can manage just fine without you here."

"Hush," Cassie snapped. "You two been tryin' to talk over me from the day you was born. You gonna have to come in tonight, Charlotte. Mama says the coven is heading out to the cemetery, her included."

"What?" Sylvie and Sybil asked in unison.

"I'm just passing it along. Char, Bobbie said the girls ain't working tonight, just the ones who aren't with us gonna cover," Cassie explained.

"Wow, okay," Charlotte said. "Any idea what we're doing there?"

"She didn't say much. You know how she is. Just told me we need to go mourn your friend and gather for protection. I guess she'll explain when we get there. She said be here by midnight so we can go together."

"Anything she needs me to bring?"

"She said you'd know what to bring. She told me to have you text the girls, let them know."

"All right. See y'all then."

Charlotte hung up, sighed, and slid back against her pillows and rubbed Ghost's chin. "Well, boo—I guess we get most of the day off, at least. Let's find some trash to watch."

By the time Charlotte reached Moonchild, quite a few of the dancers were already present, their faces pinched with concern about being called in. Alyssa and Bobbie showed up not long after Charlotte, the latter's face clearly marked with the anguish of losing Pixie.

The witches continued to flow into the shop until about ten minutes after midnight, when Sybil shut off the open sign and hung up the closed and dimmed the storefront lights.

And the women spoke in hushed tones, waiting to hear from Mama Sally.

At 12:30, Cassie pushed back the beaded curtains and guided Sally, who was also holding a gnarled ash cane, to the waiting group. Charlotte grabbed Sybil's chair, placing it in front of the counter, so Mama could sit down.

Sally took her seat and wasted no time. "I'm sorry to call you girls out here so late. I can tell we are all here, save one—the bright light that was Pixie has been snuffed out by a monster. Miss Bobbie got to talk to her Mama and told her Pixie's friends will do everything we can to find out who's responsible." She reached for Cassie's hand. "And you all know we are more than her friends here; we're her coven, even closer than blood."

The women murmured in agreement. Charlotte searched the faces and saw profile after profile in anguish. A loss of one of them—but especially someone as well-loved as Pixie—affected all.

"Miss Alyssa agreed to collect funds for her funeral with a—something electronic."

"A GoFundMe©, Mama," Alyssa called out.

"Yes, so you all know what to do. That'll ease her Mama's burden somewhat. She needs to get her baby's body to Ohio, where the family's burial plot is."

"Yes, Mamas," and "Yes, ma'ams," resounded from the women.

"But I didn't bring you all here at this hour to tell you about the donation. Pixie's blood was spilled in *our* cemetery. Her Mama don't wanna hold a service here. We're gonna go to Holt together tonight to pay our respects, make sure her spirit is at ease as best we can, and protect our coven. I don't want *none* of y'all going out there alone. If you takin' the bus, you go in a group. Miss Bobbie says four of y'all can ride with her. I want you to look around the shop carefully before you leave. If you ain't made a ladder recently, get some string, beads, feathers. Charlotte, can you lock up and ride with Miss Bobbie?"

"Yes, Mama," Charlotte said.

"Cassie, Sybil, Sylvie and me are headin' out now. We're slower than you younger witches." Sally reached for Cassie's hand again and lifted herself up with her cane and Cassie's help.

Alyssa led the way, fussing about Mama as she loaded the precious cargo into her Cadillac. Charlotte gave the rest of the girls a few minutes to pick out items they might need. She checked her own back-pack to make sure she had the mandrake root and White Out in case they encountered any problems. Thinking of Pixie, she grabbed a jar, flashlight, and plastic bag.

"All right, ladies. Let's head out. Who's going with who? *Nobody goes alone.* You heard Mama. Have your drivers drop you a block or two from the cemetery so we don't all pull up at once," Charlotte called out.

With that, the girls split up into two groups, hail-ing Ubers or riding with Bobbie. Charlotte was re-lieved no one was taking the bus as they had learned Pixie took it alone to meet her death. Also, this meant everyone would arrive at the cemetery within ten min-utes, give or take.

The car ride to the cemetery was tense. Bobbie squeezed Charlotte's hand to reassure her, but Char-lotte worried about what they would find at Holt that the police might have missed. When they pulled up to the gates of the cemetery, Mama and her girls were standing patiently in the dark, looking so very out of place for the hour. Alyssa scanned the streets, relieved to see Bobbie's car approaching.

"I told the girls to get dropped off a few blocks over," Charlotte said. "Looks less suspicious."

"Like this don't?" Sybil laughed as she gestured at their group. Scowling, Sylvie shushed her.

"How are we gonna get Mama and them over the fence?" asked Jade Rose (real name Hoa Nyuyen), a beautiful Vietnamese dancer from a Terrebonne Parish lugger family.

Mama chuckled and dug in the heavy folds of her purple dress and overcoat. "We got plenty of ways in, baby girl, but this don't take magick." With that, she triumphantly lifted a heavy set of keys that clanked together under her tremoring hand. "Cassie?"

Cassie obediently took the keys from her mother's hand and handed them to Charlotte. Just as Charlotte unlocked the gate, the remaining girls of the coven arrived. If anyone happened to chance on them at this hour—which would not be unusual as cemeteries were popular with many local practitioners of magick and vodou—their group would simply look like a late-night tour outfit. The dancers were in sweats, yoga pants, jeans, and Cassie and Sylvie both had their official tour guide badges hanging around their necks.

Holding onto Cassie's arm and feeling the way with her cane, Mama led the girls in through the gate. Charlotte pulled it shut behind them, leaving the lock open but fixed so that it appeared locked. And then, silence: the women knew they were on hallowed ground, but they were also wary of the difficulty of navigating around the haphazard gravestones, borders, and personal items spread around the cemetery.

Using her cane as a divining rod, Mama moved around the gravestones nimbly. The group walked under soft blue light of the waxing moon toward the old oak in the center. Once there, Sally whispered a benediction to her lost son and grandchildren. Cassie looked at Honoré's grave, and her daughters noted the pang of grief that flashed across it.

"What is lost, so may it be found," Sally whispered. "Help us honor our sister and find where she bled her last."

As if on cue, the wind rustled through the oak leaves, and the Spanish moss shivered on its branches. Sally took in the air, listened to its message, and reached once more for Cassie's hand. Sightlessly, she turned and turned to assess the perimeter of the tree, reaching out with her cane to point at a spot some eight feet in front of her.

Charlotte looked at the faces of the women around her and was surprised to find Sybil's eyes were closed, pointing forward in the same direction as Mama's cane.

Hanging on a wooden cross with hand-painted lettering was a slim gold necklace. Nearest to the crucifix, Bridgette looked to Charlotte for permission, and Charlotte nodded. "Anyone bring a light?" Bridgette whispered. She reached for the necklace and held it out in front of her as the women gathered around her. Charlotte pulled the flashlight from her backpack and illuminated Bridgette's outstretched hand.

"It's hers," Sally confirmed, her voice causing some of the girls to jump. Alyssa looked to Bobbie for agreement.

"Let me see, Bridgette," Bobbie said. She held the necklace up to the moonlight to inspect it: a delicate gold necklace with two dangling figures of boys and their birthstones: pearl and sapphire. It had been a gift from Derek and her sons to Pixie on Mother's Day, and she had been wearing it faithfully every night at Jack's.

Overcome by the sight, Jade gasped, and the mood among the women fell lower than a Victorian grave. Charlotte felt a sickness in her stomach, one she had felt since the day the dancers had learned of Pixie's murder.

"We need to ask for clarity and protection," Mama advised. "All of us. There's something rotten in the city, and it won't stop hunting until it's full. Girls," she addressed the dancers, "You're young and vulnerable. I don't want *any* of you out alone at night. Miss Bobbie?"

"You bet," Bobbie said. "I'll drive your asses wherever you need to get to. Don't you make us come grieve for you like this—" Her voice broke, and she choked through her sobs.

"Sylvie, baby, can you lead the girls through a ladder?" Sally asked. "I think we can use both the ritual and the comfort."

"Of course. Girls, any string will work. If you need leaves or blades of grass, you can add them. Don't take anything from the graves, though. Bad juju."

Thanks to Charlotte's help and direction at Moonchild, the girls came prepared, pulling blessed feathers, beads, charms, and string from their pockets and purses. They watched Sylvie's actions as she knotted her cord and began the spell, which they repeated:

> One is for a loved one lost,
> Great our love, greater the cost;
> Two is for the threat unknown,
> Hidden in weeds overgrown;
> Knot of three, we tie for thee,
> Defiler of our sacred tree;
> By this knot of four
> Is our power restored;
> Five will reveal your evil in time,
> Knot of six we do thee bind;
> Seven we seal to keep us safe,
> Protect us from all anger and hate;
> Eight we tie thee down again,
> And seek we justice for our friend.

Charlotte tied her cord to a loop in her jeans and knelt down to feel the earth where Pixie had taken her last breath. She pulled the glass jar from her backpack, scooped up some of the dirt, and fixed the lid tightly. The women spent a few moments with their own offertory candles and chants at the spot where Pixie died, hoping to appease her spirit.

Suddenly, Sybil tapped Charlotte's shoulder and pointed to two flashlight beams moving up and down in the darkness, headed for the group. "Cops."

Charlotte stood up and eased her way behind Sybil and some of the other women.

"Well, good evening, ladies," said one of the policemen as he approached. "We got a call there are people in here that probably shouldn't be."

Cassie stepped forward and displayed her tourist badge. "Officer, we with Moonchild Metaphysical & Vodou. We have a tour group and permission to be here."

"Right. Who gave you permission to be here? We've had complaints from families about graverobbing. Y'all wouldn't be doing any of that, being a vodou outfit and all?"

"No sir," Cassie responded. "We got family here ourselves. The LeNoirs. They buried over there." She pointed toward the oak.

"You got your tour license on you?" the cop interrupted.

"We keep that at the shop. Nobody takes their license out on tours."

"Ma'am, it's after 1 a.m. I doubt there's anything good going on at a graveyard this time of night, except when the dead get to sleep undisturbed. We're gonna need to get some IDs and check your bags."

The women mumbled, both with concern and protest. The second policeman pulled Jade's ladder from her hand. "You wanna tell me what this is?"

"No, she don't," Charlotte said. She stepped from behind her aunt and blew a heavy dose of White Out into the officers' faces. The men coughed but couldn't avoid the potion's effects: they looked at the women, disoriented, and the women's faces grew more and more blurry.

"Let's go," Charlotte urged. "Get Mama out first." While the women rushed to the cemetery exit, Charlotte watched the officers kneel, then lie back to look up at the moon. The potion was working quickly.

"You're doing a good job," she told the men. "You're here after a noise complaint, but all you found out here was a possum rattling around. Once you come to, get outta here. This ain't a good place for anyone right now."

The officers moaned in agreement, and Charlotte hurried out of the cemetery, away from the death and danger, if only momentarily, to the security of Bobbie's car.

True to her word, Bobbie dropped the dancers off at their respective apartments. By the time Charlotte was climbing the staircase to her place, it was almost 3 a.m., but the sorrowful evening's events meant that she was wide awake.

Because it was also nearly the witching hour, the time of night when black magic is most potent, Charlotte pulled the jar of dirt she'd collected at the graveyard from her backpack and gathered the other materials she would need to create a sour jar.

While the communal ladder spell and fetishes the coven had made on the site of Pixie's final moments on earth was powerful, Charlotte felt a sour jar—a hex meant to disrupt the target's life or relationships— was also useful since she was in such close proximity to the man she felt posing a threat to Tatiana and her.

As she dug through her kitchen drawers for thread and matches, Ghost stepped into the room, mewled, and yawned. "Hey, baby," Charlotte cooed. "You gonna help Mama with this spell?"

Ghost blinked sleepily and watched as Charlotte unscrewed the jar of dirt, added a jumbled length of yarn, wolfsbane she'd taken from Moonchild, and then poured vinegar over these contents and resealed the jar tightly. Taking the jar out to her balcony, she grabbed a short candle from her altar on her way through her patio doors and sat down.

The city was quiet around her, and she was grateful for the stillness. Lighting a match, she ran the flame along the bottom of the candle and affixed it the top of the sour jar. Finally, she lighted the wick and watched the flame dance in the inky night, the wax melting over the sides of the jar to seal in the contents.

When the candle was almost entirely burned out, Charlotte heard the thumping of footsteps in the stairwell. She moved the jar under her patio table and held completely still. To her left on the street below, she saw Vasile duck into the shadows and head north up St. Peter. He seemed to glide under the cover of darkness, and within seconds, he had disappeared altogether.

"Now where are you going at this hour?" she whispered. Charlotte watched the candle's flame extinguish and walked over to place the sour jar next to the gate separating her balcony from Vasile's.

To her surprise, the pots of garlic and onions that Tatiana had placed there just days before lay on their side, their contents spilling out, the garlic desiccated beyond salvaging. Charlotte searched around her balcony and decided to place the jar behind a large fern, out of view and out of reach of any future tampering.

"Now," she said, "Let's see how you handle magick."

Winston was dreaming, his eyes fluttering back and forth under his eyelids. He was watching a woman in white slowly descend a darkened staircase, the parameters of which weren't clear.

As the perspective in the dream cleared, he could see her carrying something pale in her arms, like an infant.

But it wasn't an infant; it was a dead piglet—slaughtered—and its blood streamed from its lifeless body onto the front of the woman's elaborate lacy dress.

When she reached the bottom of the staircase, the woman rushed toward where Winston would have been standing had he been able to see himself in the dream, her black hair streaming behind her, her mouth gaped into a wide O, and she screamed with rage.

Right before the banshee reached him, Winston jerked himself awake, his heart thumping rapidly, a bass drum rattling his rib cage. He glanced around his room cautiously, fully expecting to see the nightmare lurking in the shadows.

The room was quiet, the only movement coming from Sophie's large tank, where the python was moving around slowly, tasting the air with her tongue. Winston watched her from his bed, placed his hand on his chest, and inhaled and exhaled slowly as his heart rate decreased.

He tried to recall details of the dream, but it splintered and sifted away from his mind rapidly, until all he could picture was the piglet, the dress, the blood, rushing toward him with the woman's mouth looking for all the world as if she were going to swallow him whole, like Sophie with rats.

Shuddering, Winston pulled his covers tightly around himself and watched Sophie hunt until his eyes once again grew heavy and he fell back to sleep.

Chapter 11

Although she had the mandrake in her backpack and had now taken to carrying her ivory white hilt (Legba) and ebony black hilt (Kalfu) knives in her boots, Charlotte was relieved to see Tatiana waiting for her in the entryway of Jack's at quitting time. Although Charlotte rarely used the knives—a gift from her father, who had purchased them for her on a tour to Haiti—she felt they would be appropriate, blessed should she need to use them on the evil stalking the city.

Dressed in a neon blue fake fur shrug over a flowy green dress with blue flowers that reminded Charlotte of a painting, Tatiana stopped her flirtatious conversation with Big John the doorman, and waved excitedly. "Hey, girrrrl, you ready?"

"Yeah, let's go," Charlotte said, yawning. "I'm ready for bed."

"Hey," Big John interrupted. "Y'all got a ride? Miss Bobbie says to make sure you all get home safe or call you a ride."

Tatiana batted her eyelashes seductively and gripped John's impressive bicep. "Why John, if you so worried about us, why don't you come walk us ladies home? You can be our muscle. Ain't that right, Snow?"

"No, ma'am," Big John said with gravity. "I gotta make sure all the girls get home safely. Snow, you need me to call you a ride?"

"Nah, man. I got it," Charlotte answered, waving her phone as evidence. "Thanks, though. Come on, Tati. Leave this poor man alone."

The pair walked out into the streets, using the front entrance as Bobbi had banned the girls from using the alleyway entrance behind the club, which they had done before Pixie's murder.

Once they were out under the streetlights, Charlotte noticed that Tatiana was once again holding several grocery bags in her hands. "What's in the bags?"

"Kalua and coffee. And salt."

"What?" Charlotte laughed. "Why salt?"

"I'ma show you," Tatiana said, "Once we get home. I got the coffee so you can sit with me for a while. Hey, you work Thursday? I gotta show and want you to come out. It's been a while."

For once, Charlotte was too exhausted from the previous evening's activities to protest. "Yeah, I'll be there, but I can't stay up late tonight—we were up late last night."

"Ooooh, girl, who is WE?" Tatiana asked, her brown eyes sparkling with curiosity.

"Oh lord, it ain't like that," Charlotte sighed. "Family. Went out to the cemetery last night. Mama's orders."

"Oh shit," Tatiana said. "Secret witchy stuff?"

"You see the news today?"

"Yeah, I caught some of it at the bar. What happened?"

"Cops found a body at Holt—it was one of our girls." Charlotte's voice broke. "We called her Pixie."

"Oh my god, I saw that!" Tatiana exclaimed. "I'm so sorry, baby." She pulled Charlotte in for a hug. "They'll catch the motherfucker. I promise you."

"I hope so," Charlotte said, wiping away her tears.

"Matter of fact, that's what I got the salt for," Tatiana said proudly as the pair walked up to her stoop. "Here,"—she pushed open her door and handed Charlotte two folding chairs, "Set these up and relax. I'm gonna make you some coffee." She placed the grocery bag with the salt down. "I got some biscuits I made this morning I'ma warm them up, too. Gimme just a minute."

"Thanks, Tati," Charlotte said, pulling one of the chairs open. She pulled open the second chair and sank down into it, listening overhead for any movement from Vasile's place.

Within minutes, Charlotte had a steaming, comforting cup of Kalua and coffee and a plate of warm biscuits for them both. She handed the plate of biscuits on Charlotte's lap and gingerly handed her both mugs.

"Wait, what—?"

"Shhhh," Tatiana placed her index finger over her lips. She leaned over to pull a box of kosher salt from the grocery bag. She punched a hole into the box of salt with her thumb and tiptoed into the dark hallway leading to the upper floors. In less than a minute, she returned, still on tiptoe, took her mug from Charlotte, and eased into her chair.

"Okay, what the hell was that?"

"Something I found online. You know." She pointed a glittery fingernail upward and whispered. "For the *revenant.*"

"Salt?"

"Shhh. Now we gonna wait."

By the time Tatiana went in to make the third mug of Kalua and coffee, Charlotte resolved to head up to bed. It was after 1, and the caffeine wasn't nearly strong enough to keep her awake. Suddenly, she heard the distinctive sound of footfalls in the hallway and found herself subconsciously holding her breath.

The footsteps stopped midway down the staircase, and then: nothing. Charlotte strained to listen for any sounds, but there was no movement whatsoever. Gripping her mug, she slipped to the side of the wall adjacent to the staircase and listened carefully. All of a sudden, Vasile's throaty laugh echoed in the stairwell.

"Really?" he mocked. "Salt."

Charlotte tried to compose herself, but her mug shook in her hands. She bent down quietly and set down the mug, pulling Kalfu from her boot.

"I know what you are," she hissed into the darkness, surprising herself with her false bravado. She backed up, bracing herself strategically against the wall in case she had to protect herself.

"Do you?" Vasile smirked, emerging from the void to loom over her. "Let me tell you a secret, Charlotte. I know what *you* are." He winked at her and stepped off the stoop, off into the city.

His arrogance made Charlotte hot with fury, and she realized she was frozen in place, too stunned to respond, until Tatiana came back out with the coffeepot. Looking at Charlotte's blank expression, Tatiana asked, "What is it? Did it work?"

BITCH WHERE YOU AT?!! Charlotte laughed as the text popped up on her phone and texted back, It's only 9:30 and ur diva ass won't be onstage till 11.

In truth, Charlotte had forgotten her promise to be at the Honey Pot for Thirsty Thursday Thots, a weekly drag event Tatiana emceed. Charlotte left Moonchild at 6, ready to spend a few hours at home tending to her dad's plants. She hopped in the shower, threw on some jeans, heels, and a backless long-sleeved tee and hopped in an Uber.

As Charlotte paid the $7 cover, Tatiana shuffled to the door, protesting, "Nah, she ain't need to pay! She's my guest."

"It's cool," Charlotte said. "Gotta pay to keep you in fine outfits like this. Let's see what you're workin' with here!"

Tatiana spun around proudly in a tight-fitting, sleeveless sequined hot pink gown and purple gloves. Her wig was long, and flaming red. Charlotte clapped her hands and shouted, "Jessica Rabbit! I haven't seen this one!"

"Doesn't she look fabulous?" another queen said as she passed by with an elaborate drink in her hand.

"Aww, thank you, Cali," Tatiana said, blowing the other drag queen a kiss. "Come on," she grabbed Charlotte's hand, "I reserved you a table."

"Really?" Charlotte said. "I can stay back here by the bar. You gotta make those tips."

"What, you not gonna tip me?" Tatiana gasped in mock horror. "Jake, Jake! Get my baby girl Snow here a drink," she yelled to the young, muscular barback. "What you want to drink? Wells on special, Long Islands, but don't order those 'cause they a pain in the ass to make."

Charlotte laughed. "Why even tell me the special, then? I'll just do a rum and Coke."

"She wants a rum and Coke—well or shelf? Never mind, he's not even listening. Lemme go get it for you." With that, Tatiana was off to the bar, leaving Charlotte to look at the stage.

Unlike many stages, the performance area at the Honey Pot also included a staircase from the second-floor dressing rooms that the queens often used to make a dramatic entrance. Since Tatiana was the headliner, the onstage set was hers and consisted of a vanity and two tall mirrors flanking either side. Charlotte relaxed in her chair, knowing she was in for an evening of fun—and she'd had too few of those in the last few weeks.

"Here you go, baby," Tatiana said, placing the rum and Coke on the table near the stage. "I told Jake to take care of you. I'ma go mingle," she kissed Charlotte on both cheeks, "but I'll keep checkin' on you."

"Not necessary," Charlotte said. "Thanks, Mama. Can't wait to see your act."

With that, Tatiana wiggled off in her tight, sparkling dress, leaving Charlotte to sip her drink.

The lights dimmed, and a queer comedian took to the stage to warm up the crowd. Charlotte felt the rum warm her up, and she laughed at the slew of jokes about being queer in New Orleans and dealing with well-meaning, but drunk, tourists in gay bars. Most of the barbs could easily be applied to her own experience working at the shop—the tourist naivete, the inane conversations, the misplaced platitudes.

Enthralled with the comedy, Charlotte didn't notice as someone approached her table from behind, and jumped when she heard a familiar voice whisper, "Good evening, Charlotte." Pulling a chair out, Vasile nodded to her and sat down as if invited.

"I'm sorry—what?" Charlotte said, knocking her drink over.

"We gonna need a fresher rum and Coke, and what can we get you?" Tatiana said, hovering over the table.

"I didn't mean to scare you—I have a really bad habit of doing that," Vasile said apologetically, wiping the spilled drink with napkins from the table. "I would love a martini, but only half a glass," he said to Tatiana.

"I got you," Tatiana said.

"Hold up, lemme come with you," Charlotte growled. She stood up and grabbed her friend's hand, ushering her toward the bar. Once they were out of earshot, she spun Tatiana around and stared into her eyes. "Tati, what the *fuck* is this?"

"Shhhh," Tatiana said. "You see them mirrors?" She pointed toward the stage. "We know the salt didn't do shit, but I figure we check him out here, in front of witnesses, and we safe."

Charlotte groaned, her shoulders slumping in defeat. "You could have asked me."

"I know, and I'm sorry. I didn't think about it until yesterday, and I left an invitation on his door. Let's just see what happens."

Lost for words, Charlotte shook her head and walked back to her table. "First time at a drag show?" she asked as she slid into her seat.

"Yes," Vasile said, watching the comedian finish his act. "I am very excited about this performance. We don't have this in the countryside, where I'm from. Is there anything I should know? I am grateful Tatiana invited me, and I don't want to embarrass her."

"You got cash?" Charlotte snapped. "'Cause it's rude not to tip. And don't be an asshole during the acts, and no getting onstage unless you're invited."

"Okay," Vasile said, clapping along with the audience as the comedian left the stage. "I will watch you."

"Rum and Coke, martini half...?" Jake interrupted, sliding their glasses onto the table in front of them. "Y'all good?"

Vasile pulled out some bills and handed them to the waiter, who looked confused. "Well, thank you, sir," Jake said and hustled back to the bar.

"Okay, you tip the bartenders and waiters at the end," Charlotte said, "Otherwise they gonna think you're flirting with them, which it's cool if you are, but most of these pretty boys here are just gonna hustle you."

"Ah, okay. This is good information," the young man next to her said seriously, as if he were an anthropologist learning about an entirely different culture. Charlotte felt her guard relax at his confusion, and she remembered that her suspicions of him were still unfounded, and he *was* the stranger in the city.

"Yeah, just ask me if you have any questions," she whispered as the stage lights dimmed.

The first act was a drag queen comedy sketch based on Judge Judy. The act was over-the-top, but it confused Vasile, who whispered to Charlotte, "Is this satire of your American judicial system?"

"I mean, yes and no," she said truthfully. Vasile looked at her in the eyes quizzically, and she realized her answer was no answer at all. He laughed at the extreme comedic exaggeration of the performers and clapped along with the rest of the audience.

After the act concluded, the lights remained dim, and pop music thumped into the happy crowd. Charlotte glanced at Vasile surreptitiously. He had dressed up for the event, it seemed, wearing a sports coat and a pressed shirt and slacks. Despite herself, Charlotte looked back at him for another glance. He had a five o'clock shadow, making him look darker and more handsome than she remembered from her few encounters with him in the shadows. His hair was a dark, glossy brown, with curls lapping at his collar line.

Charlotte found herself wondering what it would be like to run her fingers through his curls.

As if he could read her thoughts, Vasile caught her eyes and smiled. Charlotte felt herself blush and looked back at the stage. Out of the corner of her eye, she could see Vasile pulling a plastic, malleable flask from his coat pocket. He poured a thick, yellowish substance into his martini glass and stirred the mixture with his finger.

While few things in New Orleans surprised Charlotte, she made a mental note of what she'd seen, wondering what the concoction he'd made actually was.

"Can I get you another, sweetie?" Jake, shiny and beautifully tanned and muscled, interrupted Charlotte's thoughts.

"Yes, thanks," Charlotte said, surprised by how quickly she'd drained her drink.

"How about you, cutie?" Jake said to Vasile.

"Ah yes, please. Just half," he answered.

"Responsible, I like it," Jake laughed flirtatiously.

Vasile looked confused again, but he smiled politely and looked to Charlotte for help. His expression was so innocent and flustered that Charlotte covered her mouth to prevent herself from laughing. Looking into her eyes, Vasile looked for malice in her amusement, and finding none, smiled at her.

All of a sudden, the house lights went off altogether, and some members of the audience gasped. A spotlight beamed onto the staircase, and a dramatic piano prelude sounded loudly as Tatiana stepped into the spotlight, raised a satin-gloved hand, and sashayed down the staircase. Because she was a well-respected and loved performer, her descent was met with applause and dollars littering her approach to the stage.

As a performer herself, Charlotte was in awe of Tatiana's showmanship. The tall queen commanded her audience, captivating it. Charlotte pulled her eyes away from her friend only briefly to see how Vasile was responding, and their neighbor was on the edge of his seat with a huge, toothy grin on his face.

Once the music cued up, however, Tatiana ignored the stage to mingle with the crowd to lip sync Peggy Lee's "Why Don't You Do It Right." As usual she had done her homework, perfecting Jessica Rabbit's seductive moves as she moved from table to table, flirting with the audience, who was only too happy to toss bills in her direction.

"Oh, this is brilliant," Vasile said as Jake placed another drink in front of him. Charlotte watched, intrigued, as her neighbor downed his first drink and pulled the flask out to add more of the thick yellowish mixture to his vodka. "Just brilliant."

"Thanks," Charlotte whispered to Jake as he set another drink in front of her. She took a heavy draught from her own drink and found herself relaxing further. It had been far too long since she had enjoyed a night out, and despite her initial irritation at discovering Vasile was part of the evening, she found herself unwinding.

Tatiana slowly shimmied toward their table, singing, "If you had prepared twenty years ago." She sat on Vasile's lap, and the spotlight lingered over their table as she leaned into his face and sang, "You wouldn't be a-wanderin' now from door to door/Why don't you do right, like some other men do?"

To Charlotte's surprise, Vasile was completely at ease with the tall drag queen on his lap. His eyes shone with amusement, and he grinned widely, then tossed his head back and laughed. When Tatiana moved on to another table, Vasile turned to Charlotte and asked, "So now I throw the money?"

Charlotte smiled. "No, you should have handed it to her when she was over here. She'll be back."

"Ah, okay."

After the song ended, Tatiana shimmied up to the stage to emcee the remaining acts, which consisted of a dance-off, a comedy skit, and more lip-syncing performances. Jake brought several more rounds to Charlotte's table, but after his third, Vasile declined any further drinks. His face was flushed, and he leaned further and further in to ask about the performances.

"I guess what you got in your flask there is pretty strong," Charlotte said pointedly.

"Oh, no—it's the alcohol. I rarely drink. I have a condition—"

"Right. *Anemia.*"

Vasile smirked and continued to watch the stage.

"Okay, ladies and gentlemen and everyone in between!" Tatiana called. "I say we have us a good ol' fashioned Southern cakewalk, except we do that different here at the Honey Pot. Let's get us some fine lookin' manmeat up here! Whatchy'all think?"

The crowd roared in agreement. Vasile clapped and looked to Tatiana for an explanation, but before Charlotte could even respond, Tatiana was wandering through the crowd and pulling men from their seats to direct them onstage. Before long, she came to Charlotte's table. "Okay, baby boy, you, too," she said, tugging on Vasile's hand. He laughed and teetered up out of his seat, balancing himself by resting a hand on Charlotte's shoulder.

"All right, you fine, fine, men," Tatiana cooed as she led Vasile to the stage. "We gonna line up back here and have a beauty pageant. DJ, can you play us some pageant music?"

Realizing they were now on the spot, the men chatted with one another in line, protested lightly, and laughed at their predicament.

"Here we go," Tatiana said, waving a young, chubby man from the front of the line to the front of the stage. "Bobby Boy is a Kenosha, Wisconsin native whose highest aspiration is to make the cover of *Out* magazine." 'Bobby' laughed and walked to the front of the stage, using his best pageant wave. "He's hoping to find the man of his dreams here tonight, so get those dance cards ready, bitches. Right now, Bobby is a professional go-go dancer in Kenosha, and the bitch is gonna demonstrate his best twerk!"

The audience roared as Bobby laughed, shook a finger at Tatiana playfully, then bent over at the waist to twerk at the edge of the stage. His performance garnered him a joyous applause, and he pranced to the back of the line.

Charlotte watched Vasile onstage, surprised to see he was relaxed and joking with the other men in line. He applauded for his 'competition,' and Charlotte found herself admiring his looks once again. He was dressed the most elegantly and seemed so at ease with himself and his surroundings. Everything about him was attractive, and as Charlotte watched him, she nearly forgot the gnawing feeling she had that he was dangerous.

"Don't be fooled by the Armani suit," Tatiana said as Vasile reached the front of the line. "The sexy sultan is an Arabic playboy y'all can't handle." She waved Vasile forward, and he walked to the front of the stage. "Vasile is 6'3" of spicy shawarma goodness come to life. Y'all feeling hot up in here?" The crowd roared in appreciation. "He doesn't just own his own helicopter: he owns the whole airline."

Vasile looked to Tatiana and gestured in amusement and confusion, but she was momentarily distracted, watching the mirror next to her. She turned back to the crowd and cooed, "If your dream is a one-night stand with a man who will break your heart and leave you breathless, Vasile is the Arabic lion of your dreams."

Vasile whipped off his sports coat, tossed it onto his shoulder, and turned to wiggle his butt at the audience. The crowd laughed and clapped with appreciation, and even Charlotte couldn't help but laugh with them.

After all of the men had paraded out, Tatiana pulled a crown and sash from the vanity onstage and held the crown over each contestant's head as the crowd clapped for their favorites.

And after five rum and Cokes, Charlotte found herself on her feet, whistling and clapping for Vasile. When it was over, however, Vasile didn't take the crown, though there was no look of defeat on his face as he jogged back to his table with Charlotte.

"This is *incredible!*" he said breathlessly. "Maybe next I can come to your show? Is it anything like this?"

Charlotte laughed loudly this time. "Nah, not quite. They won't let you come shake your ass on my stage."

"Maybe I will show up sometime anyway," he said.

"Sure," Charlotte said, and her eyes met Vasile's. The pair looked at one another briefly, each as if seeing the other for the first time, and then looked away.

"Can I get you another drink?" Vasile asked. "I'm going to go find Tatiana to give her the tip now."

"Oh, right," Charlotte said, and reached into her purse to pull out some cash. "I don't need a drink, but give her this from me."

"I will be right back," Vasile promised and jogged back to the front of the stage to hand Tatiana, who was surrounded by fans and suitors, the money. As she watched her new neighbor, Charlotte felt the strong urge to pay her tab and bolt so she could avoid any awkwardness—if that were even possible at this point.

"Can I get you another, miss?" Jake interrupted.

"No, but I'll take my tab."

"Girl, no. I'll put it on his. Let's make him say he wants to split it on a damned date," Jake said.

"Oh no—no, this isn't a date. He's just—he lives next to Tati and me."

"Okay. He doesn't look like he'd mind it being a date," Jake said, winking at her. "I'll be right back with the tab."

As he left, Vasile returned and slid into his chair. "Well, Charlotte. What is next? Who will sing next?"

"Oh, that's the show," Charlotte answered. "After this, it's club music and dancing if you're into that."

Jake slipped the tab onto the table, and as Charlotte pulled it toward her, Vasile placed a hand on her arm and protested, "Ah, no, what is this? This is my pleasure, please." He looked to Jake for help, who smiled and pulled the tab from under Charlotte's hand to give to Vasile.

"Sorry, baby girl," Jake said, "This is a boy's world here at the Honey Pot." With that, he left to attend to other customers.

"I have money," Charlotte said. "And you didn't drink anything!"

"Please, Charlotte," he said, surprising her with the sound of her name from his lips. "I so rarely get to enjoy an evening among other... people. You would do me an honor."

Charlotte felt the light pressure of his hand still on her arm and felt the same strange attraction to him that she'd felt on her balcony the first time she met Vasile. She found herself unable to resist and nodded her assent.

"So what next? Shall I walk you home?"

"Y'all not leaving?" Tatiana said, walking to their table. Though her question was for her neighbors, her eyes were on Jake, and she blew him a kiss as he walked past her to the bar.

"I was just wondering myself what Miss Charlotte here would like to do."

"Tati, you killed it, as usual. And yeah, I think I better head home. I gotta work both jobs tomorrow."

Vasile stood and gallantly offered to pull Charlotte's chair back. "I will make sure to get her home safe, Tatiana," he said. "Thank you for inviting me. This was the most wonderful evening I have had in a long, long time."

"Okay, baby," Tatiana said, and took both of their hands. "Charlotte, you good, or you need me to come with?" She looked at Charlotte knowingly.

"I'll be fine," Charlotte answered. "I might set Vasile up busking, get him to make us some extra cash with his dance moves." The women laughed, and Vasile shook his hips gamely.

"All right, Mama. You text me when you get in. And you—" the queen pushed a well-manicured tip into Vasile's chest—"don't you pull no funny shit. I know where you live."

With that, Vasile (maybe vampire) and Charlotte (definitely witch) left the doors of the Honey Pot and into the dark streets under the amused, watchful gaze of the swelling moon.

The walk home from the Honey Pot likely would have been met with much more uneasiness, but as both parties were still flushed with alcohol, the conversation wasn't the tense small talk one would expect when one party suspected the other of being a blood-draining revenant.

Charlotte found herself questioning her own suspicions. Would a vampire really get onstage during a drag queen contest? Her turmoil was mostly internal, with Vasile asking more questions than she did.

"What is your other job?" was one such question, and it put her on the defensive when he laughed at the mention of vodou and metaphysics.

"So you are a sorceress," Vasile said, his dark eyes glimmering with delight. "We have quite culture of these in my Romania.

"Romania?" Charlotte said incredulously. "I thought you were an Arab."

"No, *Tatiana* thinks I am an Arab. She's wrong only by about some thousand miles, though." He glanced at Charlotte as they walked the few blocks to their building. Her hair was in two long, shiny black boxer braids. In jeans and the black top, she looked to him like an assassin—a beautiful one by whose hands many men would happily meet their ends. Since Charlotte had her hair up, Vasile would look at her neck covertly from time to time, wondering what it might be like to press his lips to it and inhale her scent.

Though attracted to the man escorting her home, Charlotte kept her eyes on the walkways in front of her. Traversing the night streets of New Orleans in heels was tricky. As they neared St. Peter's, she briefly stumbled over an uneven curb, catching herself on Vasile's arm.

"I'm sorry," she said, releasing her hand quickly.

Their eyes met, and Vasile drew in his breath, and despite himself, gasped, "You have comets in your eyes. How they burn!"

Embarrassed, Charlotte laughed and pointed overhead. "It's the reflection of the Hunter's moon. It'll be full soon, and you'll see folks here acting all kinds crazy. You might even act crazy. It's gonna be a big, pregnant moon this year."

Vasile looked at the silver threads of moonlight reaching out from the moon into the dark space around it. He seemed taken by either her words or the moon itself, nodded, and continued walking. When they reached the stoop to their building on St. Peter's, he motioned for Charlotte to walk ahead of him toward their doors.

"Thanks for getting me home safely," Charlotte said. "I better text Tati."

"The pleasure, again, is entirely mine," Vasile purred and stepped closer to her. "Thank you for a most memorable evening. Would you like to have a drink with me?"

Charlotte fumbled for her keys in her backpack, her hand brushing past the mandrake root. "I—I better not," she said. "Like I said, long day ahead."

Looking dejected, Vasile looked into her eyes again, and Charlotte felt that same strange yearning pulling at her. "Thanks for the drinks," she said, snapping from her thoughts, and turned her key in the lock. "See you soon."

Vasile smiled. "I certainly hope so. Good night, Charlotte."

When she reached inside and had double bolted the doors, Charlotte exhaled wearily as Ghost came running up to her. She stooped down to pet him, then pulled her phone from her purse as she heard a text notification.

WAIT UP FOR ME, BITCH!!! Tatiana had written.

I can't—too tired, Charlotte texted back. This was not a night to stay up late, drinking, and she had just turned down Vasile. After a moment, another text flashed across her screen.

YOU BETTER. WE GOTTA TALK ABOUT HOW THAT FOOL AIN'T GOT NO REFLECTION.

Chapter 12

Charlotte ate an egg and cheese sandwich on her walk to Moonchild, mulling over Tatiana's revelation about Vasile and the mirrors. Tatiana had showed up on her stoop piss drunk after 4 a.m. and even now was sleeping it off after keeping Charlotte up, insisting she'd looked for a reflection on the stage mirrors and found none.

"Why the fuck did you let me walk home with him, then?" Charlotte groused angrily, which provoked fat tears to drop down the drag queen's face, smearing her eyeshadow. She cried for another twenty minutes, proclaiming her love for Charlotte and insisting she hadn't meant to send her off. Ghost refused to join them, lingering only in the dark hallway to scowl at the pair for disturbing his sleep.

Charlotte was relieved when the tears turned to silent snoring, covered Tatiana with a blanket, and headed back to her bedroom.

The problem, now, that was running in Charlotte's head, was whether or not Tatiana's memory had been sound enough to remember a reflection or lack of one. For the moment, the question of Vasile's humanness was to remain unresolved.

The early walk and the sandwich helped Charlotte to feel more human herself after drinking the night before, although she anticipated a quiet day at the shop. As the waxing moon was pregnant with power, Charlotte would stay in the kitchen with Mama most of the workday, working on spell votives of varying potencies. She could smoke on the stoop, heat and pour wax and ingredients, listen to Mama's advice and stories, and enjoy the cooler weather.

The twins were still asleep when Charlotte got to the shop at 9, with only Cassie awake to let Charlotte in. "Wondered if you'd remember how to get up this early," Cassie said.

"I said I'd be here."

"Yeah, you did," Cassie said flatly. Charlotte couldn't tell if her great-great aunt was being sarcastic or not but ignored the comment either way. She walked to the back and could already smell Mama Sally's strong coffee wafting through the hallway. Mama was listening to 60s R&B, with Ray Charles's "Unchain My Heart" playing from her old radio, her hands happily tapping along to the music on the tabletop.

"Stugots," Mischief cooed, hopping back and forth on his perch.

"Well blessings, baby," Mama said. "You want some coffee?"

"Yeah, I think so," Charlotte said, kneeling to kiss her grandmother's hand and then her head. "Heya, Mischief." She rubbed the back of the parrot's neck—one of the few places you could touch him without fear of getting bitten.

"ARSCHLOCH," he cooed.

"He's pretty chill today," Charlotte said.

"Well—the girls aren't up and arguing, for one thing," Mama chuckled.

Charlotte poured herself a cup of coffee. "I see you got your recipes ready," she said, touching the yellowing paper under Sally's hands. "And we got our R&B going."

"Sure do," Mama said proudly. "'Course I still have all this in my head, but I keep it written down just in case my mind slips up." She chuckled to herself at the thought. "Now, when you gonna tell me about this beau you saw last night."

Charlotte blushed, and stammered, "You saw that, huh? Nothing gets by you. Ain't no beau, though. Tatiana invited our new neighbor to her show without telling me."

"Well, seems you had fun. What's he like, this new neighbor? All I can see is tall, dark, mysterious. Handsome. But that sounds like *la merde* the fortune-telling frauds in the square would tell you." Mama laughed at the idea.

"You're funny today," Charlotte said, desperate to change the subject. "Lemme get the wax pot, and we'll get cooking."

And so, the day did go well, the way Charlotte had hoped, until about 1 p.m., when the angry flurry of the twins' voices sounded down the hallway and drew closer until the pair stormed into the kitchen. Sybil had a packing slip in her hand and slapped it down on the table in front of Sally, who didn't flinch a muscle.

"Girls," she reprimanded. "You cannot bring that energy in here while we're working. You know that."

"Yes," Sylvie whispered respectfully, "But this is important."

"Is it?" Mama asked.

"We just gotta ask Charlotte to look at this," Sylvie said, plucking the slip from her twin's hand. "*Someone* ordered way too many oils, and since the company considers it a personal item, we can't return them."

"By too many," Charlotte said, turning down the wax and wiping her hands on a towel, "how much we talkin'?"

"Six hundred thirty-seven dollars," Sybil answered smugly, crossing her arms to smirk at her sister.

"*Vouzan!*" Sally yelped. "How do you spend that much on oils?"

"VOUZAN!" Mischief screeched triumphantly, the one curse he'd learned from Sally.

"Lemme see the slip," Charlotte said. Sylvie handed over the slip and glared at her sister. After scanning it briefly, Charlotte sighed. "Did y'all even read this?"

The girls looked at one another, sulking.

"I didn't think so," Charlotte said. "You're both in the clear. Your Mama placed the order by phone."

"Girls, get back up front and quit arguing with each other. Send your mom back here. Charlotte, you turn off that pot and go help them up there. I need to talk to Cassie alone." Mama's face was grim, and her family knew better than to protest. Charlotte set the slip in front of Sally, who ran her hand over it, absorbing what, Charlotte didn't know.

As she walked to the front, Cassie brushed against her in the hallway silently, her face twisted in a mixture or concern and childlike fear of getting into trouble. Not long after, angry voices echoed down the hallway until Cassie shut the kitchen door, Mischief punctuating the sound with "脳たりん！" (roughly translated as slow-witted person, from the Japanese).

Chapter 13

Because Tatiana was still at work, Charlotte took an Uber back to St. Peter Street. It had been a slow Thursday night at Jack's, but she stayed until 2:30 so Bobbie could let other dancers go, and she'd hoped to make enough tips to compensate for the money Tantie Cassie had lost at the store.

As she started to walk up the stairwell to her apartment, she heard a baby cooing, a hissed cursing, and a nervous jangling of keys. Charlotte hurried up the landing to find Andrei with a cherubic baby of about a year old tucked awkwardly under his arm like a football.

"What the *fuck?*" Charlotte fumed, pulling the baby from under Andrei's arm.

"Give him back to me," Andrei snarled.

Charlotte pulled the Kalfu knife from her boot and pressed it to the small man's carotid artery. "Back the fuck up, little man," Charlotte warned, and at this moment, Vasile opened the door to find his neighbor balancing a plump, tow-headed baby on her hip with one arm as she held Mr. Andrei at knifepoint with her other arm extended.

"Where'd you get this baby?" Charlotte snapped, keeping her eye on the small man. Oblivious to the danger, the baby giggled at the drama and pulled a large handful of Charlotte's hair and shook it up and down playfully.

"Prostule, ce ai făcut?" Vasile snarled, his voice shaking the wooden hallways and rattling down the stairs.

Charlotte edged her body along the wall, keeping the ebony-hilted blade fixed on Andrei.

"Charlotte, I am terribly sorry," Vasile offered. "There has been a misunderstanding."

Charlotte glanced at Vasile. He was slumped against his doorway, his shirt askew. He looked dreadful, his skin visibly yellow in the dim light of the hallway. His hair was limp and sweaty, and he shook like an addict deprived of heroin.

"Oh yeah?" Charlotte asked, her voice tinged with sarcasm. "I'm pretty clear on this baby not belonging to either one of y'all. You planning on eating it?"

"Vrăjitoareo!" Andrei spat in front of her boots. "What will you do with it, sorceress? Cut its throat and use its fat for your black magic? You think we don't know what *you* are?"

Ignoring the insult, Charlotte inched closer to the stairwell while the baby continued to play with her hair and the beaded necklace she was wearing, babbling *mumumum.*

"Charlotte," Vasile began. "I did not ask for this."

"I don't give a shit," she answered. "I'm taking it home."

"No need," Vasile said wearily. "Retrage-ți cuvintele, idiotule," he snapped at Andrei. The latter moved toward Charlotte.

"Nah," Charlotte said, glaring at Andrei. "You just tell me where to take her. I'll make sure she gets home safely."

Andrei shrugged. "I do not remember, and its mother must not love it anyway as I found it wandering in an alley."

"Can we continue this conversation inside?" Vasile said, shaking. "I fear we will attract attention, and—"

"Hah! You really think I'm going in there with you two?" Charlotte laughed. "Fuck off with that. You just stay back." She kept the knife aimed at the pair and slid down the stairs with her back against the wall. "Don't even think about following me," she warned Andrei. "'Cause I won't hesitate to find out how human you are."

Andrei spat again and cursed her in Romanian.

When she reached the bottom of the stairs and stepped into the streets, Vasile inexplicably stepped in front of her. His face was grim and wan.

"Charlotte," he pleaded, "Please, listen to me."

"I said step back," she warned, wishing she could remember the best ways to ward off a vampire and whether or not she had anything on her for protection other than the mandrake.

Vasile lifted his hands and stepped back. "I will not harm either of you. I promise."

"No, you won't," Charlotte said, emboldened, her voice raising. "What the fuck, Vasile? I mean, really? A baby? Can't you eat a tourist, or an Air BnB mogul or some shit?"

Vasile sighed, defeated. "I would not have 'eaten' this child. I assure you, Charlotte. Mr. Andrei is worried about me."

"Well, yeah. You do look like shit," she said. "But a baby, for fuck's sake. A *baby.*"

"I promise you, you misunderstand."

"Jesus. I let you walk me home," Charlotte said, her voice raising. "Would you have—"

"Enough," Vasile said loudly. "You know the answer to that."

"Do I? Really? Like I'm gonna take your word after this?" Charlotte said, looking at the baby on her hip. "You just stay away from me—you and that creepy friend of yours."

Suddenly, a voice interrupted their argument from the darkness. "I don't know what the hell is going on here," Winston said from his balcony, "but I'm calling the cops! It's three in the morning and *some* of us work normal hours."

"Shit," Charlotte hissed. "This is ridiculous. Hey!" she called up to Winston. "This asshole screwed up the stairway, and I tripped with my niece here."

"I'm supposed to believe that is your niece," Winston snarked. "And that you're out with her at 3 a.m."

"Please, I'm sure we can work this out," Vasile said wearily.

"You can work it out with the cops," Winston said. "I've had it with the freaks on this block and in this city." He turned and stepped into his apartment, closing his patio door with a firm snap.

"Well, this is a disaster," Vasile said, scowling. "Andrei will pay for this, I assure you."

"I'm taking the baby back," Charlotte said. "Just go back to your place and don't answer your door if the cops knock." She shifted the baby on her hip. "And don't come near me again. Ever."

With that, she headed off into her apartment with the babe, hoping her divining skills were still sharp enough to get the child back home.

Chapter 14

Charlotte would spend almost two hours of divining to locate the baby's house and deposit it safely back into its crib—and worse, she'd had to use Midnight Ink, a concoction she never sold and only used in extreme situations such as the one she'd found herself in. Made from the ink of the toxic blue-ringed octopus, Midnight Ink was one of the few potions Charlotte found only worked with ingestion, and as the octopus species used its ink less and less, she found it almost impossible to find the true item on the black market.

Knowing that carrying a white infant through the French Quarter at 3:30 a.m. would likely raise suspicions, she pulled the vial of Midnight Ink—marked with multiple crossbones and POISON! warnings—from her fridge and downed the contents. Grabbing a black hoodie and her backpack, she swathed the child, who was now sucking her thumb and nuzzling into her shoulder sleepily. Charlotte stepped back out into the streets, pushing her way past the now-arguing Vasile and Mr. Andrei, who didn't notice her slip into the night.

When she reached the end of the block, Charlotte tried to stem her anxiety. She wasn't the best diviner at Moonchild, nor even the best in the coven among the new girls. Charlotte pulled a heavy lapis lazuli crystal attached to a chain from her pocket and let the energy of the city pull the heavy blue stone in what she hoped was the right direction.

After many starts and restarts, the entire process took Charlotte nearly two hours, when she finally found the shotgun home of the baby off Elysian Fields. A first-floor screened window had been cut—by Mr. Andrei, no doubt, the liar—and Charlotte carefully lowered the sleeping baby into the window, setting it gently into its crib.

Exhausted, she found herself stumbling home, her stomach churning from the effects of the potion. She barely made it into her apartment and to her toilet before she threw up, her bile a dark reddish-brown. Her body shook, and she felt ice-cold. With a final surge of effort, she dragged herself to bed.

After a few hours of sleeping like the dead, and since Cassie and Sylvie had a full day of tours booked, Charlotte didn't head to Moonchild until 1 p.m. She hated to leave Sybil there to handle the store alone, but Charlotte's stomach still ached, and her head was still foggy from lack of sleep and toxins in her system. Also, she just could not take an argument this morning—the idea of listening to the twins argue or Cassie and Mama debate made her want to head back home and hide under her comforter all day.

"Oh baby, you look awful," Sybil said as Charlotte entered the doorway to Moonchild. "What have you done to yourself?"

"I don't even know where I'd start, Tantie, but I'm here."

"Let's get you some tea, have Mama fix you up," Sybil fussed, hugging her great-great grandniece. "If you feel better, maybe you can run register."

"Thanks," Charlotte sighed. "I can call Bridgette to come in if we get busy."

"I got her number," Sybil said. "You go get some tea."

Charlotte slipped past the glass beaded curtain, grateful that relief was in her immediate future. Mama Sally's strong restorative tea—one that Charlotte begged her to allow the store to sell—was an elixir for almost any self-induced poisoning, hangovers most of all.

"You burnin' the candle at both ends," Sally chided as her great-great-great granddaughter walked into the kitchen. "Best be careful or you're gonna look like Mama Sally by the time you're thirty." Sally chuckled at her own joke. "I knew you was coming. Water is about to boil, and I got your tea set up."

"Thanks, Mama," Charlotte sighed with relief, kneeling to kiss her grandmother's hand. Sally ran a hand over Charlotte's hair.

"Worried about you, girl," Sally said. "You always running. Now what did you do to yourself? You feel clammy. You not pregnant?"

"Lord, no! Why would you even wish that on me?" Charlotte laughed.

"BUTTANA," Mischief cooed.

"I saw a baby," Sally frowned.

"Not mine," Charlotte said. "Thank the goddess." The teakettle began to sing, and Charlotte poured the steaming water over the contents of Sally's concoction. She sat down with her grandmother and let the warm tendrils of steam soak into her pores. When it cooled, she sipped it cautiously, pleased with the sensation of the warmth hitting her empty stomach.

"You need to eat better, too," Sally fussed. "I can hear your stomach, child. Lemme make you some eggs, bacon, and grits."

"Nah, let me make that for us," Charlotte said, standing.

"Oh, sit down," Sally said forcefully, putting her hand on her granddaughter's shoulder to push her back into her seat gently. "Finish your tea and let someone take care of you for once, child. Once you feel better, we'll get to some light work. I need you to help me make a list for our Sabbat plans." She pulled a cast iron pot from the oven and opened the fridge to search for the bacon and eggs.

Charlotte sat back in her chair, feeling safe and loved. Her stomach rumbled as the bacon sizzled, but she could feel the tea begin to work its magic, and she relaxed as the toxin from Midnight Ink slowly began to leave her body.

Chapter 15

HEY, HO. GOTTA DATE N CAN'T MEET UP AF-
TER WORK. YOU BETTA GET AN UBER.

Tatiana finished her vodka and cranberry drink
at the Honey Pot and stepped out into the night. Her
phone buzzed in her hands, and she read the incom-
ing from Charlotte.

Bet. You be safe. <3

Overhead, the moon was full, luminous, sending
silvery beams through the crisp air and into the city
streets. It was the perfect night for a clandestine meeting at City Park, and a hot and closeted black man
named Dion matched with Tatiana on Grindr. They
chatted back and forth as she drank and worked the
crowd at the club, the discussion quickly moving to
where they could meet for the night.

Tatiana knew better than to meet random men at
her apartment; she'd made that mistake a few times
when she first used Grindr and had been robbed
twice. And while she enjoyed the thrill of casual sex
with strangers, she was furious about being robbed,
and vowed never to have men she couldn't track down
back to her place.

12:38. Tatiana had about an hour before her hook
up, so as she walked to the bus stop, she popped into
a tourist shop and bought two condoms. "Busy tonight?" the shopkeeper winked.

"You know it," Tati laughed, flipping her hair over
her shoulder playfully. Once she got into the bus, she

pulled out a compact and checked her makeup and hair. "Flawless, bitch," she announced to no one. "I'm flawless."

The ride was long enough to give her time to check her messages and confirm with Dion. Although Dion claimed he was single, Tatiana knew from past experience that hookups in public places at late hours generally meant that the party hiding something was either a politician, a preacher, or married. She felt guilty only about the last, although she fully understood the need to hide one's sexual preferences in the first two instances.

She wouldn't and didn't judge, having been shunned by her own Pentecostal family when she came out.

Tatiana hopped off the bus to walk to City Park. With its lush tree cover, the park was a popular hook up spot. While there were plenty of dark corners for all manner of questionable activity, Tatiana told her date to meet her in the trees off Roosevelt Mall, close to the Little Lake. This gave them a wide area to explore in case the first spot was occupied by other late-night carousers.

The moonlight illuminated the path, and Tatiana checked the surroundings. Although there were sometimes cops patrolling the streets, they seldom got out of their cruisers and into the tree lines. She dropped Dion a pin to send her location.

Be there in 20. Traffic. Dion replied.

Tatiana stepped into the tree line and sniffed her underarms. Digging into her purse, she pulled out a small bottle of sample perfume and sprayed herself— chest, neck, and under her shiny green miniskirt.

As she snapped the cap back onto the perfume, she was briefly aware of a shuffling of leaves on the ground and snapped her head around. "Dion?" she whispered.

Silence was the only reply. Tatiana slipped her underwear off and let it fall to her ankles. Using her heels, she deftly kicked it up into her hands and stuffed it into her purse.

Something rushed toward her so quickly and brutally that all 6'3" of her large frame felt like it had been hit by a New Orleans linebacker. She hit the dirt, the wind knocked out or her and couldn't find her voice. Tatiana could taste the dirt in her mouth. Whoever had her pinned was preternaturally strong, and despite her own size and strength, she struggled to move.

And then, the sound of teeth crunching into her skin—first her shoulder, and then her neck—crackled in her ear. The pain was excruciating, and Tatiana spat dirt of out of her mouth and tried to scream, but the force of the bite was too strong, so she could only gasp and look up through the trees, where the moon watched impassively, lulling her to sleep.

Chapter 16

Jack's Halloween Party—like so many other events in the quarter—was an important event. Bobbie sent out personalized invitations to high-dollar customers, who looked forward to claiming their favorite dancers and drinking overpriced alcohol at reserved tables.

For Charlotte and the other dancers, the party was an opportunity to make big money, and they wouldn't need to rely on Sucka Punch for tips. The girls were all dressed to kill, in nearly nude outfits or pasties with their costumes. Makeup and hair was flawless, and despite the pall of Pixie's death still lingering over them, they flashed brilliant smiles with all shades of lipstick and gloss.

Charlotte was finalizing her costume backstage when Bobbie stuck her head around the door. "Heya, Snow. Table 6 is asking for you. I told 'em they got competition. Ooh, you look great! Lemme help you with that."

"Thanks," Charlotte said, handing some bobby pins to her boss she was using to affix a delicate beaded headpiece to her hair. "Who's at 6? I walked through about 30 minutes ago."

"The lawyers," Bobbie said. "They're making bets about who's going home with you already."

Charlotte snorted. "They can keep dreaming." She stood and posed for Bobbie. "Whatcha think? Good?"

"I think you're gonna make us both a mint," Bobbie grinned, her eyes shimmering with delight. "Spin for me?"

Charlotte turned to let Bobbie take in her costume. Tatiana had helped her create a modern, vamped-up version of a Cleopatra bodysuit out of sheer netting, crystals, and golden viper embroidered into the netting that crossed her chest and ran down her torso between her legs and halfway up her back. Her black hair was plaited to the midpoint of her head and then left to fall over her shoulders, and her eyes had the heavy kohl makeup of Egyptian pharaohs. She was regal, stunning, and alluring all at once.

"Gorgeous, honey. Johnny got your track ready?"

"Yeah, I'm ready when Mandy's done. I'll head on back."

Bobbie squeezed her hands. "Go get 'em, Snow."

"You know it!" Charlotte said. "Can you send two of the barbacks behind the stage? Eric and that tall skinny one? They know what's up."

Bobbie gave her a thumbs up as Charlotte headed along the wall toward the stage, running her hands along her costume to make sure there were no pieces that would snag on her entrance. As she stepped up to the stage area, DJ Johnny caught sight of her, and his jaw dropped. He used his hand to pop it closed playfully, making Charlotte laugh. She pulled a rolled up carpet from backstage and unrolled it.

"Hey, let us help," came a voice from her left. Eric, followed by the new barback rushed to help her spread out the carpet.

"Thanks. Y'all ready, right?" Charlotte asked. "Don't be shy—flip it hard or I'm gonna fall."

Too stunned by Charlotte's beauty, the new barback couldn't even respond and stood dumbstruck until Erik nudged him. "Bro, you got this, right?"

"Yeah, sorry." The taller of the pair blushed. "We got you, Miss Snow."

Charlotte looked to Johnny and gave him a thumbs up as she lay down in the carpet and let the men roll her up gently. As M.I.A's "Bad Girls" began to thump from the club speakers, the men knew their cue and walked the rolled-up rug onto the stage, unrolling it rapidly so that Charlotte jumped up out of it dramatically and slid across the floor toward the pole.

The men in the club roared with delight. Charlotte felt their energy and wrapped herself around the pole, pumping her hips seductively against the metal. Lithe and graceful, she moved around the pole, emulating the movements of a snake, keeping her eyes on the men (and handful of women) in the crowd. The other dancers also found themselves struggling to pay attention to their customers, and the bartenders stopped midpour to watch Charlotte dance. Even without magick, she was beguiling, and everyone seemed lured by her beauty.

Cash flew onto the stage in a flurry, and Charlotte climbed the pole for her finale, sliding upside down from the rafters using only her thigh muscles, stopping gently when her hands touched the stage. She flipped her legs from the pole into a split and placed her head down to meet the stage as the song ended.

The crowd roared again, so that Johnny's announcement that Charlotte was available for private dances went unheard. Men called cocktail waitresses and dancers to them, handing them cash in the hopes that Charlotte could be bribed to come to their tables first. As she descended the stage, Charlotte looked to Bobbie, who held up six fingers and pointed to a crowded table stage right: the lawyers. Apparently, they had ponied up enough cash to merit first dance from Snow White.

Chapter 17

As Charlotte headed to table six, the lawyers—already rosy-faced with alcohol and smoking expensive cigars—gave her a standing ovation as she approached their table, and although she was all smiles and graciousness on the outside, Charlotte's mind was flush thinking about the cash she would make off of them that night.

Before the night was over, and after multiple lap dances and promises to stop at other tables, Charlotte figured she'd made $3000 without the cash the stage assistants had picked up for her after her dance. She tipped Johnny and the barbacks for their help and had Bobbie lock up her cash as Halloween was really not the night to walk around the city with a wad of cash.

When she finally made her excuses and escaped back to the dressing room, Charlotte unlocked her cubby and texted Tatiana excitedly to see if she was staying at the Honey Pot or heading home. As she changed clothes, she realized she hadn't gotten a response from her neighbor for a day or two—unusual for Tatiana, who was a relentless texter. She tried calling the number, but her call rolled over to voicemail immediately.

And then Charlotte began to have a sick, gnawing feeling in the pit of her stomach—one dangerously reminiscent of the way she felt hearing of Pixie's disappearance. She pulled on her jeans and Chucks, determined to head to the Honey Pot to see where her friend could be.

Winston stood in his living room rubbing his temples. His mother had insisted he leave the windows open as the apartment was "dank," and the sudden change in barometric pressure gave him a splitting headache. He had wanted to close them much earlier in the day, when he saw that a cold weather front and rain were in the forecast, but his mother would not *shut up* despite his protests. And so, the windows stayed open, and his head throbbed in agony.

Worse, the city was filled to the gills with VooDoo Fest tourists on top of tourists. Since it was the weekend, every single neighbor save the Romanian was out on their patios partying, music thumping from countless cheap stereo speakers, TVs, and iPad docks.

He heard kids squeal outside in the street and cursed to himself. In New Orleans, even kids stayed up late for parties. The high-pitched sounds of happiness pierced his eardrums, reverberating painfully in his head. There was no sanctuary for a man like him here in the city. He just hoped he would live long enough to leave it behind for the lighthouses of Rhode Island, listening to nothing but the Atlantic Ocean waves peacefully lapping the shore.

He checked the bathroom medicine cabinet for aspirin, but the bottle had expired sometime in January, which wouldn't have dissuaded him at this point, but it only held one solitary pill anyway. Winston scowled; he could leave for some kind of pain reliever and brave the idiots in the streets, or he could stay home and suffer and brave his mother's demands.

The streets it was. He checked the medicine cabinet mirror to make sure nothing about him could be construed for a costume or for someone who wanted to be approached. As always, he looked non-descript, even in his own eyes, and this pleased him.

The lateness of the hour meant his local market was long since closed. Winston braced himself for a walk closer to Bourbon Street, where shops would still be open and catering to tourists. He cursed the city, his mother, the weather, the tourists, the festival, his neighbors, children in general. As he walked north, he deliberately crossed the street or stepped into it to avoid other people.

This strategy was largely successful until he drew nearer to Bourbon. Suddenly, a gaggle of drunken women with glowing plastic cups and straws approached him, one of them deliberately blocking his path when he tried to avoid them by stepping into the street.

"WOOOOOOOOH!" she yelled in front his face, and it took all of Winston's remaining restraint not to grab her by the throat and squeeze the life out of her stupid, loud, spray-tanned body. "HEY TAKE A PIGDURE OF US!" She thrust a phone into Winston's hand and looked around for the other women in her party.

"Leave him alone, Michellllle," one of her friends slurred. "He looks busy."

"NO WAY, BRO!" Michelle yelled. "THIS IS PARTY CITY! RIGHT?" She said, struggling to keep her eyes open. "YOU KNOW WHAT I'M TALKIN ABOUT." She pressed a finger into Winston's chest. "PAR-TEE CITY!" At that, the women with her crowed with delight.

Michelle put her arm around Winston's neck and breathed an oppressive mouthful of stale vodka into his face. "Let's DO THIS," she urged. Winston pushed her off of him and scowled.

"OKAY, OKAY," she said, holding her hands up. "All ya gotta do is make sure we all look good and then click, ya got it? COME ON, GIRLS!" she bellowed to the others.

The group bunched together and asked one another about their makeup, hair, teeth. Winston watched them in disbelief. His head throbbed, and he resented the presence of a stranger's phone in his hand, but lifted the phone to take a photo. "WAIT WE AREN'T ALL READY!" Michelle screeched, pulling in the other women toward her. As they primped and posed, Winston lifted the phone and tossed it as far as he could over his shoulder, into the darkness.

"WHAT THE HELL?!" Michelle screeched, running past Winston to follow her phone. Winston continued forward, past the group, who were cursing at him. He couldn't help but smirk at their anger, and even their screaming at him, making his head pulse in anger, couldn't diminish the brief sense of elation he felt at having thwarted their photo opp.

As he headed through the quarter, Winston felt oddly invincible. A man passed out in a doorway tried to grab at him from the dark, surprising him briefly, and he kicked the shadowy lump out of his way. With his newfound power, Winston found his headache dissipating slightly.

Something caught Winston's eye near St. Ann's: her face illuminated by the streetlights, his neighbor was frowning and hurrying down the street. Winston forgot his headache and decided to follow her in the darkness. As annoying as she and her friends were, he was surprised she wasn't hosting a loud party on her balcony as the whole block seemed to be doing.

He trailed her for several blocks, the large number of drunken and loud tourists helped conceal his snooping. It occurred to him that although he had lived across from her for years, Winston had always just seen her as a fixture in the neighborhood, like the few horse hitches left in the city, remnants of an older time. He hated her but didn't know exactly why he hated her—except that she was emblematic of the city itself.

After a few blocks, she dipped into a gay bar, the Honey Pot. Winston wasn't familiar with the place personally as he found sexuality unnervingly disordered in itself. He wondered what she was doing in the place as it was known for catering to gay men, but he guessed that she was likely selling marijuana there— he had reported her apartment drug operation to the police multiple times with no results.

"Well, hey, cutie," a voice called to him from the shadows. Winston found himself seething; he knew he was anything but cute.

"What are you up to? Where is your costume?" An androgynous young man dressed in a shimmery, elaborate, and multicolored butterfly costume, stepped out of the darkness. "You lookin' for some fun?"

Winston closed his eyes and felt his headache slowly throb in his temples again. He realized he should have stayed home and gone to bed, ignoring the plaints of his mother. It was too late, really, to be out looking for aspirin. He began to question what his motives even were, out on Halloween, under a full moon, subjecting himself to people, every one of which he loathed.

Unaware that she had been followed, Charlotte stepped into the Honey Pot to a packed crowd dressed in their Halloween finest. As with Mardi Gras, the locals took costuming seriously, and the bright costumes in the club were stunning. While she walked through the drunken and flirtatious crowd, Charlotte felt anxiety rise in her as she looked for Tatiana's tall figure.

Trying to locate Tatiana proved to be a fool's errand with the madness of the crowd, the masks, the dim lights, and the loud music. Frustrated, Charlotte headed for the bar and pushed her way to the front.

"What can I get for you?" a bartender dressed as pirate asked her.

"I'm looking for Tatiana," Charlotte said loudly.

The bartender cupped an ear and leaned closer.

"Tatiana," Charlotte yelled. "The tall black queen?"

The bartender looked confused and shrugged. "Sorry, not sure. What can I get you to drink?"

Frustrated, Charlotte mouthed "No thanks" and moved away from the bar to scan the crowd again. She sighed heavily and headed toward the exit. From a corner near the door, a younger gay man dressed as a pink kitten came running up to her and grabbed her arm. "Snow!" Charlotte searched the beautifully made-up face but couldn't place it.

"It's me, Jake."

Charlotte took him by the hand and led the waiter outside. Once out of range of the noise in the club, Charlotte turned to Jake and asked, "Jake, where the hell is Tati? She hasn't responded to my texts for two days."

Jake's eyes welled up with tears, making the crystals he had affixed to his eyelashes shimmer under the streetlights. "Oh my god," he gasped. "You haven't heard?"

"What's going on?" she demanded.

"I'm sorry—the police took her phone and told us to let them contact her family..." he drifted.

"What *happened*?" Charlotte yelled.

"She got jumped at City Park three nights ago. She's at UMC." Jake's voice broke. "It's not good, Snow."

Shocked, Charlotte leaned back against the club wall. "Why the fuck haven't the cops come to her place? To talk to her neighbors? To me?"

"Fuck the cops," Jake said. "You think they care about our community—about a black drag queen?"

Charlotte looked up at the night sky, where the luminous Hunter's moon hung heavily over the city.

"*We* care. We're her family—and we're much stronger than whoever did this to her." She gave Jake a tight hug. "Lemme give you my number," she offered. And after exchanging numbers, Charlotte ignored her promise to be cautious and dashed to Moonchild to wake the only women in the city she knew who could help: her coven.

By the time Charlotte reached Moonchild, it was nearly four o'clock. She debated waking up her aunts and great grandmother, but she knew none of them would be able to see Tatiana until 8 a.m., if at all. She settled into Sybil's plush chair in the front of the store and closed her eyes, slipping into a fitful slumber.

When Sally came in on gentle cat paws and covered Charlotte with a blanket, the latter didn't stir, her body so overcome with weeks of anxiety and exhaustion. Although she would only get about three hours of sleep, Charlotte rose to the smell of Mama's strong coffee and eggs. She jumped with a start and looked at her phone. 7:22.

"Mama," she called, as she ran to the back. "Mama, thank god you're awake."

Mama nodded and continued to put together some egg sandwiches. "Have some coffee, baby," she said. "And we'll head out."

"You know, then."

"Yes, and Miss Tatiana is gonna need everything we got. Even then, may not be enough." Sally packed some items from her talisman and herb drawers into her purple bookbag.

"What should I bring?" Charlotte asked helplessly. "I don't know..."

"It's okay," Mama said, gently stroking Charlotte's hair. "You'll know once we get there and we can have Sylvie bring us what you need." She turned to the counter and reached overhead for her cabinets. "I can use your help finding some boxes for our breakfast."

"Gówienko," Mischief cooed to himself, preened his chest, and tucked his head back into his chest.

Charlotte texted Sybil and Sylvie both to let them know where Mama and she had gone and requested an Uber. Within 15 minutes, Mama and Charlotte were walking through the double doors of the University Medical Center and taking the elevator to the ICU. They had to wait another ten minutes before they could see Tatiana.

"I'm glad to see Miss Tatiana has some family visiting," the nurse on-duty said as she walked them toward Tatiana's room. "Just remember this can be traumatic for families, but try to stay positive as the patient can often hear you."

"Thanks," Charlotte said quietly.

Even with warning, however, Charlotte gasped when they entered the room. Tatiana looked grey, as if she had been in water for days. A tube ran down her throat, taped to her dried lips. Her upper torso was wrapped in a bandage that crossed over her left clavicle and neck. An ugly set of stitches crusted over with dried blood peeped from the top of the bandages near her neck. Her eyelids were several shades of purplish-blue.

She looked nothing like the vivacious friend Charlotte loved.

"You have some visitors, Miss Tatiana," the nurse said cheerfully as she checked the IV bags hanging behind Tatiana. Then, to Sally," I'll try to see if Dr. Seok can come update you all. He usually starts his rounds at 9. I'll see if I can rustle up some coffee for you."

"Thank you," Sally said, keeping her eyes on Tatiana's broken body.

Once the nurse left, Charlotte let a sob escape her lips. "Keep yourself together, girl," Sally warned. "We have work to do. She needs you to focus so you can help her. You get me?" She set her purple bag down on one of the chairs in the room and started digging through it.

"Charlotte, you hear me?"

Charlotte tore her eyes from the ghastly sight in front of her. "I hear you. Who the *hell* did this to her, Mama?"

"We not gonna worry about that right now, my baby," Sally insisted. "We gotta pull her back from the other side first." Sally pulled a bag of cornmeal from her bag and poured it onto the floor at the foot of Tatiana's bed. Next, she drew a bag of wood ash and poured it into the center of the cornmeal. "Take this," she said, thrusting a sacred rattle into Charlotte's hands. "Keep it moving until I tell you to stop." Finally, she pulled a green votive from her bag and lighted it on the perimeter of the grainy mixture.

Charlotte took the rattle and shook it rhythmically from left to right, the way she had seen Mama do in their rituals. She found the *tok* sound reassuring, giving her something familiar to do that felt helpful.

Her opaque eyes looking into the beyond, Sally began tracing the serpentine veve, or sigil, of Damballa in the ash and cornmeal mixture at her feet. "Great Damballa," she whispered, "Great serpent and creator of heavens, earth, and life-giving waters: listen to your child Sally. Help and protect our Tatiana, who even now is walking to the valley of Death with the Baron. It is not her time to dance with the dead, Damballa. Let her follow your path to shed her old skin and be renewed once more in your embrace. Spare her, and your children will teach her to honor you for the rest of her days."

With that, Sally pulled a bottle of rum from her bag, took a large draught, and sprayed it through her lips onto the votive until the flame extinguished.

"Okay, help me up, child," Mama said, reaching out her hand.

Charlotte grabbed her hand, hoisted her up, and quickly packed the rum and the candle into Sally's bag as the nurse walked back in with Dr. Seok, a slight, efficient-looking man who looked like he had every moment planned to the nanosecond.

"Sorry," Charlotte offered, "I spilled my grandmother's purse." She scooped the ash and cornmeal mixture toward herself and swept what she could into Sally's bag. The nurse sniffed the lingering smoke scent in the air, opened her mouth as if to reprimand them, but was thwarted by the doctor.

"Good morning," Dr. Seok said, extending his hand to Sally. Realizing she could not see him, he placed his hand on her shoulder. "I'm Dr. Seok. And you are the patient's...?"

"Grandmother," Charlotte interjected. "We only just found out."

"Well, let's step outside for a moment," the doctor offered, motioning toward the door. Charlotte took Sally's hand and led her out the door and into the hallway to a bench.

"I'm terribly sorry about your granddaughter," Dr. Seok offered as he looked over his notes. "I'm sure the police have been in contact with you by now."

Charlotte seethed inwardly, and Mama squeezed her hand. "Thank you, doctor," Mama said. "We all praying and hoping for some answers. What can you tell us about her injuries?"

"Right," the doctor answered. "I must say, I'm confused about the extent of her injuries, Mrs....?"

"LeNoir," Mama answered.

"Yes, Mrs. LeNoir. It looks like she was admitted here to us with extreme lacerations and head trauma.

I've never seen anything like this in the New Orleans area." Charlotte watched Dr. Seok's face as he seemed to be struggling to find an instance where he had seen a case such as Tatiana's in his training. "We have her in a medically induced coma for now, to try to protect her brain. There's an enormous amount of swelling, and we are concerned about her heart as well. We have had to resuscitate her three times in as many days." The doctor flipped through his notes.

"I don't want to give you any overly optimistic news," he said grimly. "Her condition is as serious as it gets here, particularly in the case of someone so young. I would advise you call in any other important family members or friends, both for her morale, but also in case..."

Sensing her granddaughter's tension, Mama squeezed Charlotte's hand again. "We understand," Sally responded gently. "Thank you, doctor."

With that, Dr. Seok gave a curt bow and continued down the hallway to his rounds. The nurse nodded her head toward Tatiana's room. "I'll have someone in here to clean this up," she said, "but please, please do not smoke around the patient."

Charlotte nodded and watched the nurse leave.

"Come, baby," Mama said, "We've done all we can today. Now you gotta go home and think about what you've seen here and what you can do for her."

As they walked out of the hospital and hopped into a car, Charlotte remained silent, ruminating on all of the ingredients, herbs, and spells she knew and had taught herself. She ran through everything she had learned through the years, and her mind raced with images of plants, fungi, roots. The answer was there, and she knew she had to find it before it was too late.

Chapter 18

Standing near the window, Charlotte watched as raindrops trickled down the windowpanes of Tatiana's room. She had puzzled over her notebooks for the past 24 hours, hoping to find some remedy for her friend.

Tatiana's condition hadn't changed, and it didn't take Sybil or Mama's foresight to see that the likelihood of the queen's surviving her attack was improbable. For her part, Charlotte was drained, lulled by the rain.

A nurse interrupted Charlotte's despair with, "Miss? There are other visitors waiting." Behind her, a sober-looking Jake from the club, a slightly toned-down Missy Sippi, and several other coworkers from the Honey Pot.

"It's okay, baby, take your time," Missy said as she stepped into the room. "We'll wait."

"I'll be done in a few minutes," Charlotte said to the other visitors, who nodded silently and headed toward the bench to wait their turn.

"Any good news?" Missy asked.

Charlotte shook her head glumly. "No, no change."

"I still can't believe this," Missy said. "First Ricky, now Tati..."

"You think they're related?"

Missy looked at Tatiana's broken body in front of her. "I don't know. Cops haven't told us shit, but that's a hell of a coincidence, don't you think?"

"What about the media?" Charlotte asked.

"What about 'em?" Missy drawled.

"You know what it's like here," Charlotte said. "If you're black, or poor, or trans, or gay, you gotta fight to get help. If the cops won't do it, shame 'em."

Missy looked at Charlotte seriously, considering her words. "You have an excellent point. I'll get the girls on it once we've finished visiting her." She moved to squeeze Tatiana's hand. "Good thing you can't see yourself, honey," she said to Tati. "I wonder when the swelling will go down—she just doesn't look like her elegant self."

"Let me know if y'all need any help," Charlotte said. "I'd better head out and let the others visit. Anyone get in touch with her family?"

"I know Jake tried," Missy said. "Not sure he got any concrete answer."

The rain picked up outside and drummed on the window. Missy looked at it, and thinking aloud, mused, "Rain and a full moon for Halloween. Hope that keeps the crazies indoors."

A flame ignited under her weariness, Charlotte stared at Missy.

"You okay?"

"Yeah, I gotta go. I just thought of something." As she stepped out of the room and into the corridor, Charlotte moved in a daze, barely acknowledging Jake's hug. When she left the hospital, she darted into an Uber, her hair damp from the downpour.

The moon. Water. Alchemilla. She whispered to herself. *Plumajillo.* She repeated the words to herself as a mantra on the ride home, a devotion punctuated by the relentless drumming of the rain on the car. Suddenly, Charlotte felt slightly less helpless.

The rain refused to ebb when Charlotte headed to Jack's around 10 p.m. Her mind preoccupied with

Tatiana's injuries, she'd hoped for a slow evening after spending most of the day working on an elixir for her friend.

She was completely exhausted, mentally and physically, and wished she could have just crawled into bed to fall asleep listening to the rain.

As she walked up the steps, Charlotte could hear that the club was more packed than it should have been for the rain and day and hour. After changing from her street clothes into her dancing outfit, she stopped Jade in the hallway. "Why's it so packed?"

Jade rolled her eyes. "It's not—it's just these loud-ass Tulane frat boys here for a birthday party. They're already sauced and getting handsy. One kept singing 'Little China Girl' to me. And they're cheap tippers."

"Ughhhh, I don't have time or energy for this shit right now," Charlotte groaned.

"I know. We're all just trying to stay away as long as possible and switch out so no one gets stuck with them. Make them buy you shots, at least. Assholes."

"Maybe I'll just walk the floor and try to stay out of reach."

"Good luck. Let me know if you need any help."

"Thanks, boo," Charlotte said, giving Jade a hug.

As she walked into the club, Charlotte cased the crowd. The fraternity was front and center, making as much noise as possible to get attention. Sprinkled throughout the floor in pairs or alone, a few men sat around the poles. The overall mood of the club was tense; large, boisterous groups of men weren't typically a good vibe for the dancers or the other customers.

"Hey, Charlotte." Bobbie slid her arm into Charlotte's and surveyed the club with her. "Kinda got a mess here tonight."

"I see—Jade filled me in."

"I told the newer girls to stay away from table 8 altogether. I've already had DeShaun warn them once." She motioned to the corner where DeShaun, all 6'6" muscled of him, was watching the group with his arms crossed, his expression blank with the dull calm of a man who expected trouble but wasn't menaced by it at all. "I'd like you to rotate with the more experienced girls—Bridgette, Jade, Mandy. If they fuck up again, we'll kick 'em out."

"I'm on it, B," Charlotte said, her eyes narrowing. She walked around the perimeter of the table to a pole diagonally across from the party so she could dance and observe the frat boy table for a song or two.

The party was keeping the cocktail waitresses busy running back and forth, ordering rounds of shots and individual drinks. Charlotte started her job at Jack's as a cocktail waitress and had learned to get all the orders before heading to the bar. From her perch, she could identify who the biggest problems at the table were. At the far end, reaching out to grab dancers and cocktail waitresses' hands, was a steroid jock who looked like he thought he owned the club. His long-sleeved t-shirt was intentionally two sizes too small, and he barked like a seal at his own jokes. Next to him, and almost equal in size, was a slightly smaller man whose face was bright red from booze. He would nudge the jock and point out dancers, slap his leg, and laugh at any of his frat brothers getting a lap dance.

Neither of them, to Charlotte's mind, looked like they were respectful of dancers or women in general, and their antics were fueled by the other men in their group who were also trying to show off for their peers. Bridgette was currently dancing for one of the party, and her pinched expression was one of tedium and frustration in equal amounts.

The smaller of the two men suddenly noticed Charlotte dancing and gripped the steroid jock's arm. The pair watched her dance lustfully, quietly for a moment before the larger one called for a waitress and pointed to Charlotte.

The waitress, a slight girl with tattoos all over her arms and chest, approached Charlotte almost apologetically. "Hey, Snow, those boys over there are asking you to come to their table."

Charlotte leaned down and smiled at her, then looked up to meet the jock's eyes. "Tell him I'll come for $20," she said. "Anything less isn't worth it. Besides, I like this song."

"Okay," the waitress answered nervously. Charlotte watched as the waitress walked back to the table and relayed the message to the two men. The larger of the pair laughed arrogantly and looked at his buddy for advice. Finally, after some negotiation, he handed a bill to the waitress and sent her back to Charlotte.

"Hey," she called up to the platform to Charlotte. "He said he'll give you a $10 to come."

Charlotte stopped dancing, pulled the bill from the waitress's tray, and tucked it into her G-string. "Tell him I'll come when he gets the rest of his allowance," Charlotte smirked.

"Really?"

Charlotte looked at the man again and shrugged. "Sometimes you gotta train 'em, baby," she said.

The waitress bit her lip and looked over at the table. "OKAY..." she said, but the inflection ended with a question, as she didn't understand what Charlotte was doing and doubted it would work.

After another round of negotiations, the waitress returned again, triumphantly this time with $100. Charlotte smiled at the men, picked up the cash from the tray, and handed the waitress a twenty from her waist. "Here you go," she said. "That's your cut." She stepped down off the pedestal and walked toward the table.

"You're a damned diva," the man barked at Charlotte as she approached, motioning toward his lap. "That should be enough for dances for all of us."

"Can you get a girl a shot?" Charlotte said as she slid into his lap. "What's your name?'

"Chase," he answered, ignoring Charlotte's eyes to look at her breasts and thighs. "Damn, you're hot."

"Hot, but expensive for a *stripper,*" said the smaller of the pair condescendingly.

"How much do you pay for non-strippers?" Charlotte asked nonchalantly.

"Bwahahaha!" Chase howled and put his arm around Charlotte's waist. "Hey, I like her already, Ben! What you want to drink?"

"I'll take a whiskey, neat."

"Top shelf, I bet."

Charlotte shrugged. "I like the well enough."

Chase looked around for a waitress and snapped his fingers at her. "Can we get a few whiskeys here?" he yelled across the club.

"I'll get your waitress," the girl said, barely concealing her annoyance with the coarse behavior.

"You want a dance now? Song is starting," Charlotte said.

"Aww, you that eager to get away from me?" the man asked, shaking Charlotte slightly with the huge bicep he had wrapped behind her back.

Charlotte smiled without responding.

"I like a girl with a mind for business," Chase offered. "I'm a business major."

"Oh?"

"Yeah. I gotta be ready to take over the family business one day soon. So how'd you end up stripping?"

The smaller of the two with the red face laughed derisively at his friend's attempt at conversation. Chase side-eyed him.

Charlotte smiled enigmatically. "It's good business, Chase—depending on the customer."

Chase laughed huskily. "Hah! Got me there."

"Y'all need something?" The cocktail waitress with the heavy tattoos approached Charlotte and the men.

"Yeah, we need some whiskey shots," Chase said self-assuredly. "Get my girl—what's your name, darlin'?"

"Snow."

"Snow? Okay. Get Snow here as many as it takes to make her find me attractive."

Charlotte struggled not to laugh at the waitress's expression, which said *We don't have that much alcohol here.*

"Okay, so no answers about the stripping. Are you 'putting yourself through school'?" Chase smirked, using air quotes.

"Nah," Charlotte said. "I just like the money."

"Why, Snow?"

"Really, Chase?" His friend sneered. "She's a coke-head."

The waitress returned with a tray of shots, and before being offered any, Charlotte picked up two glasses and shot them back to back, winking at the red-faced troll next to her. Charlotte's confidence and fake flirtatiousness, coupled with her beauty, stopped the man's laughter, and he reached for his own drink, awkwardly avoiding her gaze.

The music changed again, and Charlotte handed Chase a glass. He smirked drunkenly. "Thanks, babe." After he took the shot, Charlotte began dancing for him, and like so many men who acted brave, he actually froze up as she gyrated on his lap aggressively, looking him in the eye. He tried to laugh, but he was utterly captivated by her and couldn't break free of her gaze.

Charlotte was counting the moments when she could escape the table and hide behind the bar, in the back, at another table with a shyer customer who wanted to talk more than grope. She was pretty sure that Chase and his friends considered a hundred dollars high end, so she knew trying to squeeze any more out of them would be difficult. She'd already read the table and put them at $20 dances, no tips. As the song ended, she swung a leg off Chase's lap and ruffled his hair.

"All right, you boys have fun," she said.

"He gave you a hundred bucks!" his friend protested.

Charlotte refused to dignify the cheap outburst with a response. Chase grabbed her hand.

"How much for—something more hands on?" he asked.

"Not sure what you mean," Charlotte said warily.

"Sure you do," he winked at her. "You said you like money."

Charlotte could sense where this was headed. She looked over her shoulder for DeShaun, who was scanning the tables impassively.

"Nah, man," she said, pulling her hand away. "This ain't that kind of club, and I ain't that kinda girl."

"Yeah, right," the red-faced frat boy next to her said. "You're a stripper. Like all of a sudden you got morals?"

"All right, you boys have fun," Charlotte said, backing away. Chase reached for her again, gripping her wrist and pulling her to him, his face screwed into a blend of anger and fear of rejection.

"We're not done with you, Snow," he slurred. "Come on. Be nice. Be a good girl, huh?" With that, he tried to pull Charlotte toward him by her waist, and since she was on heels, she stumbled forward, her hand landing squarely in the middle of his chest.

"Fuck off," she hissed, pulling back from him. Chase grabbed her wrist and tried to pull her toward him again, but like a bolt of lightning, DeShaun was on him and pulled him from his seat.

Chase released Charlotte's wrist, and she stumbled back away from the table and out of range. "The fuck, dude?" Chase said. "What did I do? What did I do?" DeShaun ignored his pleas and pulled him toward the front, with Ben following close behind, too intimidated by the large bouncer to make a move. Charlotte followed the trio to the front, Bridgette high-fiving her as she walked past the dancer.

"Bro," Chase protested drunkenly as DeShaun ushered him out the front, "Be cool, bro. I didn't hurt her."

"You already got warned," DeShaun said flatly. "You can come back another day, when you're sober. Can't be rough with the girls here."

"This place is a fucking joke," the red-faced man protested. "One hundred dollars for a lap dance?"

"You're welcome to try any of the other clubs here," DeShaun said. "Good night, gentlemen." He pushed the smaller of the pair out after Chase. After the commotion ended, Charlotte approached the bouncer.

"Thanks, D," she said, giving him a hug.

DeShaun chuckled. "We all knew they wouldn't last. Now I gotta watch the rest of them kids until they pass out or get kicked out. Some people's children. You stone cold, though, Snow. Respect." He put out his fist and bumped it with Charlotte's.

The remainder of the evening was pleasantly dull. Warmed by the two shots, Charlotte made the rounds at the club, gave a few more dances, and then checked out around 1 a.m. She changed into her street clothes, made sure she had her backpack and mandrake, and stepped out into the night.

The rain had abated enough for Charlotte to walk home, and she was happy she'd worn her thick, studded leather boots. And although she'd promised her family that she would be careful, she elected to walk home, tucking Kalfu and Legba into her boots before she left. It was a Monday, after all, and the rain would keep most people in.

Her trek home was relatively short, and the crisp October air gave Charlotte a renewed sense of energy.

She suddenly felt a surge of hope since it was now October 31, a sacred night for her coven, and perhaps Tatiana's best chance for survival. She would go home and sleep late, Charlotte decided, revisit her elixir, and then head to Moonchild.

The moon overhead guided her way, and she felt strangely reassured.

Her elation wouldn't last long. After three blocks, Charlotte realized she was being followed: she could hear deliberate footfalls drawing closer.

Deciding that leading whomever it was toward her apartment was dangerous, Charlotte bypassed her street and headed toward Decatur, toward Washington Artillery Park. She darted across Decatur into near darkness, past the amphitheater and toward the river. Kneeling down quickly, she just managed to pull the two knives from her boots and stand back up to face her pursuer.

"Well, hey, Snow," Chase said menacingly. His smaller friend stepped up from behind him. "We thought we'd see what you were doing after work."

Charlotte could smell the alcohol wafting from the pair in the breeze, spoiling the cleansing rainy smell of the late October night. Although she couldn't see their expressions, Charlotte knew their faces would be cruel, hardened.

"I don't do shit after hours," she snarled.

"Yeah, you said you don't do shit in the club, now after hours," the smaller man said. "But I call bullshit. You sure took his hundred fast enough."

Chase stepped forward toward her. "I mean, no offense, *Snow*," he said, "But you left us high and dry, you know?"

"Huh," Charlotte said. "And you think I owe you more."

"Oh, I know you do," Chase said, taking another step forward.

Charlotte sensed something else in the shadows and tried to read the wind, but it answered *nothing*.

Although she was bluffing her bravado, Charlotte felt cornered and questioned her own judgment, cursing herself for not gauging how many people had actually followed her. She'd been jumped before, but it had been for money, and she'd given that up quickly. The intentions here were much more sinister, the threat much graver. She felt a wave of fear rush over her, and she shuddered as she crossed the knives behind her back.

As if by magic, a tall figure stepped from the shadows. "Now what is this?" a familiar voice growled. "Nothing good comes of a party in the streets this late. I sense you men are taking your heart in your teeth, as we say in my country."

Despite herself, Charlotte felt her shoulders relax as she heard Vasile's deep accent.

"Fuck outta here," the smaller man said.

Chase flexed his arms and stepped forward drunkenly challenging the stranger. "Hey, man. Fuck off before you get fucked. She owes us money."

Charlotte laughed. "I don't owe you *shit*." She glanced at Vasile in the moonlight and was shocked to find he looked even worse than she remembered. His face was glossy with a sick-looking sheen, his eyes sunken.

Vasile stepped in front of Charlotte and motioned for her to head northwest. "There's a cab waiting for you," he said, "You'll find it next to the police car there."

Charlotte couldn't tell if he was bluffing or not, but Chase and his friend stepped back and looked back toward Decatur to check. Without any hesitation, Charlotte walked briskly away from the park, keeping her knives in plain view at her sides. Once she reached the street, she broke into a sprint and ran home, checking over her shoulder as she ran.

Back at the park, where the full moon danced on the waters of the Mississippi, Vasile approached the men calmly. "Gentlemen, a word?"

Charlotte waited up, hoping she would see Vasile return home, but as the hours passed, her eyelids grew heavy, and she dragged herself to bed. She fell into a heavy slumber and slept like the dead, not rising until Ghost demanded food.

After showering and carefully packing her backpack with items she would need for the sacred evening, Charlotte headed to Moonchild through a light drizzle. By the time she got there at noon, the store was already bustling with clients ready to take a Halloween vodou tour or purchase materials for their own Samhain. Candles, potions, animal skulls, charms all flew off the shelves, putting Cassie into a better mood than usual before she left with Sylvie to take tourists from across the world to visit Marie LaVeau's grave, where they would leave coins or other offerings to the city's vodou queen.

"We still closing at 6?" Charlotte asked Sybil as they helped customers.

"Last I heard, yeah. You okay? I had a strange dream about you last night—you were by those cannons at Washington, hiding from someone."

Charlotte didn't know where to start and decided on saying nothing at all. "I'm good," she said at last. "I just wanna make sure I have time to drop off something for Tatiana."

"I'll go with you, baby. I know that's hard, seeing your friend..." Sybil paused to decide on the right word. "...close to death. I've been alive so long and seen so much of it myself, and it just don't get any easier."

Charlotte's eyes teared up, and she hugged her aunt tightly. "Thanks, Sybil. I definitely need the company. Not gonna lie."

"You know I got you. I'm gonna order us some po-boys, check on Mama. You good for a few minutes?"

Charlotte rolled her eyes and laughed. "Since I was seven."

The hours passed quickly, and even Mama Sally was busy with readings as her most select customers understood it was one of the most important days in the world of magick, and Sally was considered the current authentic reader in the city. By the time Sylvie and Cassie returned from their tours, the shop had made thousands altogether, and despite the underlying tragedies of Pixie's murder and Tatiana's attack and precarious condition, the LeNoirs couldn't help but feel hopeful, that their actions that evening could alter the effects of the evil they felt closing in. The rare full blue moon would be overhead, making the coven's power even stronger than usual. Sometimes even the most fragile flower can grow through the harsh soil of sadness.

Charlotte stepped to the back to give Sally a kiss, and the latter hugged her heartily. "You got some sleep," she noted.

"SHARMOOT!" Mischief screeched joyfully.

"Oh, hush, you," Sally chided. "And you got something else," she cackled knowingly.

"I think so," Charlotte said. "I guess we'll see. Sybil and I are heading to the hospital now, but we'll be back before long. You need me to get anything?"

Mama pulled a stack of bills from her purple apron and felt through them, pulling five out to hand Charlotte. "Stop at Black Sam's, baby. He's holding some Clement Rum for me."

"This is five hundred, Mama."

"I know that. And tell him to throw in some cheaper shit for us. The Clement is for the loa. Make sure the expensive one is sealed—pop it yourself in front of him before you give him the cash."

"Sure," Charlotte answered. "Anything else?"

"No, I got etouffee for us from the Reynard's. They brought it fresh today before their reading. Now don't forget what I told you about the rum. That should leave you with about three bills for extras. And you and Sybil take a car, eh? I don't have to lecture you about how dangerous this evening is."

Sally's last words were so poignant that Charlotte couldn't help but wonder if she meant the remainder of the evening, or if she knew about what had happened at the park in the wee hours of the morning. She looked at Mama's face for a clue, but Sally was busy smoothing the rest of her cash and organizing it, her opaque eyes revealing nothing.

Charlotte kissed her on the top of her head, and stuffing the money into her backpack, headed to the front to gather Sybil.

"She doing okay?" Cassie asked when Charlotte reached the front.

"Yeah, said someone brought us etouffee. I'll be back. I'm goin' to the hospital to drop off some medicine for Tati and grabbing some rum for tonight. Y'all better save us some etouffee. You ready, Sybil?"

"Why Sybil?" Sylvie asked.

Charlotte sighed. "She was here and offered, Sylvie. You wanna come, too?"

Sylvie looked toward Cassie, anticipating her mother's objection. Thumbing through money at the till, Cassie didn't look up. "Go on, all of you. Get outta my hair so I can get this counted and locked up. Talk so damn much that I gotta recount."

Like permanent teenagers, the twins rolled their eyes and headed for the door. "We'll be back soon. Gotta stop for rum for Papa Legba," Charlotte said.

"Don't let the girls drink any, or they'll fight through All Saints," Cassie warned. "Wear me out."

Charlotte nodded and hailed an Uber before stepping outside with her aunts. They were covered by the
overhang of the upstairs porch, and the rain misted
down around them as a gray-blue twilight began to
descend upon the city.

Sensing that their great-great niece was anxious,
Sybil and Sylvie were unusually quiet on the ride to
UMC. They followed Charlotte quietly up the elevator
to the ICU, where a nurse led them to Tatiana's room.

"It's generally only two at a time, but I'm a let you
two count as one," the nurse told the twins. "Have you
been here to visit before?"

"Yes," Charlotte interrupted, before her aunties
could interject. "We know the rules."

"Great. She's had quite a few well-wishers today,
so it might be good to keep it under thirty minutes.
Visiting hours are over in an about an hour."

Charlotte nodded her head and stepped into the
room, where Tatiana was still prone, bruised, and unconscious, but half of her room had been decorated by
her friends, with balloons and streamers in Halloween
colors across from her bed.

"Mon Dieu," Sylvie whispered. "It doesn't even
look like her."

"Sssst!" Sybil hissed. "She can still hear you. Don't
be antété."

Charlotte ignored the pair and dug through her
backpack to extract a small vial. Composed of moon
water gathered from the Bogue Falaya springs, Charlotte had concocted a potion of Frankincense resin,
nettle, alchemilla among other things. Looking at Tatiana, she held little hope her elixir would even work,
but it was the last gift she had to offer her friend.

"Watch the door," she whispered to her aunts,
who stopped arguing to move to the door and act as
sentries.

Moving quickly, Charlotte pulled an empty syringe from her backpack and poured the contents of

her vial into it. Behind her, Sylvie and Sybil looked at one another silently, their eyes wide.

Unhooking the saline, Charlotte quickly squeezed the potion from her syringe into the catheter leading to Tatiana's arm and then reconnected the catheter to the saline pack. She threw the syringe into the medical waste and bent over to kiss her friend's forehead.

"We're fighting for you, Tati," she said. "Come back to us."

Sybil and Sylvie approached the bed, each laying a hand on Tatiana's legs. "Come back to us," they echoed. Grateful for their presence and guidance, Charlotte took her aunts' hands and prayed her mixture would work.

Winston's bowels were a wreck, and the celebratory sounds in the streets did nothing to temper his discomfort. He spent the majority of the day either in the bathroom or in the bed, curled into a fetal position.

He hadn't felt sick like this in a long time, not since he had learned which dives in the city to avoid and how to properly sanitize his hands after handling Sophie and her rodent dinners.

He ran through what he'd eaten the last two days, but he'd packed his own lunch yesterday: leftover canned soup and crackers, ham sandwiches at home. He'd long since abandoned cooking larger meals since his mother had no appetite to speak of.

After another agonizing session on the toilet, Winston scrubbed his hands and went to the kitchen for water. He had once read that when a person is thirsty, it's too late and dehydration has already set in. He tried to stave off thirst after his first sprint to the bathroom, but he could tell he was still dehydrated.

After guzzling nearly an entire liter of water, Winston decided he would feed Sophie and grabbed a dead mouse packet from the freezer. Something about her movement when she was feeding or moving through her terrarium calmed Winston, and he hoped he could fall asleep watching her.

Animals—even arachnids—can act odd during full moons. Ungulates on the savannahs of Africa, for instance, don't graze openly. In turn, larger predators like lions have to hunt and eat during the day when the prey is available. Corals release larger amounts of sperm and eggs under moonlit nights. Domestic pets tend to get into more accidents during full moons. Scorpions find more prey and hunt more under moonlight. Humans, of course, are also part of the animal kingdom, and a study from the National Criminal Justice Reference System examining lunar patterns and human behavior determined that humans also engage in an increase in violent behavior under full moons.

Of course, Winston hadn't considered lunar influences on animal or human behavior as he snipped open the packet containing the mouse and moved as mechanically and precisely as he always had. Unfortunately, patterns are something even reptilian brains can follow, and the moment Winston carefully opened to lid to Sophie's habitat, she struck at his hand, gripping his pinky, and coiling herself around his arm.

Winston screamed in pain and stumbled backwards, barely catching himself as his left heel hit his bedpost. He grunted at this fresh pain, righted himself, and stumbled toward the terrarium, sucking in his breath as Sophie tightened her coils around his hand and wrist and digging her spiny teeth into his hand and pinky. His impulse to pull his hand forward, away from the source of the pain, only increased the pain as the snake's backward-facing needle-like teeth dug further in. Winston howled anew and waved his arm up and down, trying to shake Sophie's grip.

Suddenly, and to his horror, Winston felt his bowels rumble angrily. "Nooooooo," he moaned, and he struggled more urgently to release his hand and finger from Sophie's mouth. Impassive, Sophie shifted her coils, ready for the dying throes of the beast she'd subdued.

Hoping to delay the inevitable, Winston contracted his sphincter muscles, his intestines rumbling more urgently. He quickly unwrapped her, tail first, and lowered his hand into the terrarium. With his left hand, he held onto the tail Sophie was trying to twist around his arm again and pried the dead mouse from his hand. In her haste to eat, Sophie had missed the mouse entirely and was gorging on his little finger.

The dead mouse didn't entice her at all, and Winston grew more desperate. He handled Sophie more roughly than he ever had, hastily trying to unwind her coils from his arm and hand. He felt her muscles contract around his hand once more, and she tried to swallow his finger, her teeth again ripping into his flesh.

"Christ!" Winston yelped. Again, his instinct was to pull forward, and again his hand and finger were further mangled. In an impulsive move to get her to release him, Winston yanked his hand and finger forward as he pulled Sophie's midsection the opposite direction. The movement in two directions seemed to confuse the python, but she only let go of Winston's finger after ripping off a large section of his flesh, shaking the finger violently and snapping a bone in his hand audibly.

Winston tossed Sophie into her home and slammed the cover shut with his left hand, cursing to himself. Bent over and clutching his guts, he rushed to the bathroom, but to his despair, it was too late, and he relieved himself in the hallway.

Something about the humiliation of it all made Winston laugh furiously until he was in tears, and he cursed Sophie, his life, his mother, the city until he finally fell asleep to the sounds of loud Halloween revelry outside.

By the time the coven reached Holt cemetery, the rain had turned from a light mist to a steady, rhythmic stream—just as Mama Sally had predicted. True, also, was that the mood wasn't as light-hearted as previous years and focused on the remembrance of family and friends that had passed.

"Rain is good," Mama smiled, lifting her face to the sky. "It'll keep the police and fakes away. We can work without trouble."

She was right, as always. On clear Halloween eves, the witches of the LeNoir coven often found themselves having to compete for space with a host of lesser groups—from Wiccans, to graverobbers, to teenagers looking for a Halloween thrill. Tonight, however, the cemetery was quiet, darker than usual under the rainclouds. The moon would occasionally show her incandescent face, sailing in and out of the darkness through the rain.

Mama held onto Cassie's arm as the party made its way to the oak in the middle of the cemetery, where they could seek some cover from the rain under its branches and leaves. The Spanish moss clinging to the branches whispered and swayed in the wind, witnesses to the ceremony it was about to witness.

"Come, come," Mama urged. "The hour is now, and the gods wait for no one, priestess, witch, or king." She knocked on the oak and called to Papa Legba as the other women lighted candles and placed them in the thick roots of the mighty oak. While Mama called to Legba, Sylvie spread flour onto the damp earth near the roots and began to draw Legba's sigil into the flour.

Through the candlelight, Charlotte could see the dark earth appear through the stark white flour.

Sybil and Cassie made the sign of the cross, and the rest of the coven followed suit. Where the women generally did not identify themselves with any specific god or goddess in their day-to-day lives, tonight, the majority wore scarves of red, including Mama, in homage to the loa Papa Legba.

Moving seamlessly, Charlotte led the other members of the coven through the drawing of the sacred circle around the tree, protecting them from any outside forces that might want to harm them. It was a task they undertook with great care and solemnity—more so, Charlotte felt, than they had demonstrated in years past. As they moved in the circle, Cassie and her daughters began to shake rattles partially constructed from the vertebrae of cottonmouths Mama had killed on her escape from slavery as she tried to protect her babies in the harsh environs of the swamps.

As they shook the rattles, Cassie and her daughters also lighted votives in front of the family markers—Apollo, taken by the Spanish influenza of 1917; Honoré, gone far too soon and weighing on Cassie's heart; Moses and Armand, who lived long lives by non-coven standards. Charlotte lighted a candle for her mother, Melissa, who she never knew but had such a lasting impact on the family.

And then, they waited for Sally to begin. It was her 173rd Halloween, one which she knew demanded all the strength she could give to her coven.

"Tonight, mes bébés," she said, "Forget any hate in your heart. There's too much evil around us, and we will not meet its power with our own desire for revenge. We call on Papa Legba to guide us. Tonight, we use only white magic and keep our souls clean." She paused, and the women answered, "Yes, Mama."

"Tonight, we will make offerings to our ancestors and to the gods and ask that they forgive us our faults and lead us to a path that will keep us safe from harm."

As Mama spoke, Cassie and the twins kept the rattles whirring, and the effect of Sally's words and the rhythmic sounds of the rattles and rain had a hypnotic effect on the coven, many of whom began to sway or shake. Mama motioned to Charlotte, who moved toward her great-great grandmother and kneeled to pull the rum she'd been sent to purchase from her backpack. She handed the expensive Clement to Sally and then pulled other bottles from her pack to pass along to the other women.

Sally opened the expensive rum, took a swig, and spat it toward the tree and sigil, calling to Legba to accept her offer. "Venez, venez, Papa," she called, her unseeing eyes facing the tree. "Come to us and accept our offering." Sally took another drink and swayed, calling to Legba again. The snake rattles buzzed as Charlotte took a drink of rum and looked at her sisters, who were also passing the rum bottles, drinking, and calling to the loa.

As the Spanish moss waved above her, Sally motioned to Cassie, who handed her mother a small jar of honey. Sally held the jar high and then poured it onto the roots of the oak, another offering. Save for the women whispering and chanting, the rainfall, and the rattles, the gods were silent.

Then, the winds shifted, and the rain subsided slightly. Sally's body began to tremble, and Charlotte could feel the static in the air. Something abruptly joined them and took over Sally's body, and she began to hiss and sway, her movements mimicking that of a serpent.

Sylvie looked to her twin sister, confusion crossing her face. "Damballa," Sybil whispered. "The snake, giver of life."

While Sally had summoned Legba, it was Damballa who had chosen to come to them. Charlotte watched her aunties' faces, searching for any sign of worry, but they looked unexpectedly calm. Charlotte could not remember a time when an unsummoned loa had appeared at their conjuring, but she guessed from her aunts' expressions that this was not unfamiliar to them.

Possessed by the loa, Mama swayed in the wind, like a cobra dancing before a snake charmer, and only she knew what message the god was granting the coven. The rattles chattered as she moved back and forth, and her faced looked troubled, though the moment passed quickly. And then, it was over. She reached out and slumped onto Charlotte. "Thank you, Damballa," she whispered. "We hear you, and we know what you want. Cassie—" she reached her hand out to her daughter. "We need to honor him with the offering."

Cassie nodded and pointed to a box near Sybil, who brought the box to her mother. As Cassie bent down to open the box, Sally stopped her.

"Not tonight, baby," Mama instructed. "Damballa wants Charlotte to give him the offering."

Charlotte looked at her family quizzically but said nothing. She approached the box, kneeled, and opened the flaps to find a large, healthy, shiny black rooster.

"Damballa says you should use Legba, girl—that you honor them both with this gift," Mama said. "He says you'll know what he means."

Charlotte nodded and pulled the ivory hilt Legba from her boot. Lifting the rooster by the neck, she looked at her family. Sybil nodded, and Mama placed a warm hand on her arm, guiding her as she drew the blade across the bird's neck. The animal's blood flowed onto the tree and its roots, some of it hitting candle flames, making them hiss with pleasure. Charlotte looked at Mama, who smiled serenely, proudly.

Cassie motioned for the bird and returned it to the box. "Gumbo tomorrow," she said, and Charlotte smiled at how seriously her aunt delivered the sentence.

"The moon is strong and potent tonight," Mama said loudly. "Now, children, cast your spells, work your charms. Let's leave sadness behind and find solace in what we have gained tonight."

The women moved quietly in the darkness, some casting spells of protection, others whispering chants for Pixie, and Charlotte gathered herbs and cemetery dirt under the moonlight, hoping for a better tomorrow.

After stopping for coffee, Charlotte headed to Holt Cemetery the morning of November 1 to meet her aunts and great-great grandmother to clean the family graves and leave offerings for them as well. Charlotte loved the occasion and had since she was a child because her aunties told stories about the dead, keeping them alive in Charlotte's mind and their own. Cassie was the one bleak spot, suffering quietly as she tended her long-lost daughter Honoré's marker.

The rain had passed, and Sally helped Cassie in her work under the gray, cloudy sky, laying her hand on her daughter's shoulder and whispering comforts. They left food and performed small rituals to honor the LeNoir dead, but the events were quiet, in stark contrast to the rum-and-blood-soaked offerings of the night before.

"Make sure when I go, you all put me here with my babies," Mama instructed, as she had done every year for as long as Charlotte could remember. "We are more powerful together, even when we pass."

"Of course, Mama," Sylvie said. "What other cemetery would even have you?" The women laughed warmly, and the mood was a brief respite from the tragedies they had suffered in the past, distant and near. Charlotte savored the damp smell of the earth, the food, the wet wood of the oak, feeling safe and loved.

Her phone buzzed in her jeans pocket, stirring her from her thoughts.

"Ur gonna need 2 come 2 the hospital." It was Jake.

"Hey, is it okay if I go?" Charlotte asked. Her face pinched with concern.

"Of course, baby," Mama smiled. "We'll see you back at the shop. Cassie got that rooster plucked, and this is gumbo weather for sure."

"Thanks, Mama. Love y'all." Charlotte hugged them all and rushed to hail a car.

By the time she reached the hospital, Jake was waiting near the entrance for her. "Come on," he said. "I'm glad I got your number." Charlotte followed him to the elevator, fearful of what was to come and too frightened to ask. She had seen the numbers and doubt crawled across her skin, leaving goosebumps in its place.

As they rounded a corner, Charlotte realized the surroundings had changed. Before she could ask, Jake had led her into a room.

"Hey, bitch," a familiar voice croaked. There in the center of the room, was Tatiana. Although she looked awful, she was leaned upwards, with a TV on the wall playing *The Price is Right*.

Surprising even herself, Charlotte burst into relieved tears and rushed to her friend's bedside, reaching for her hand. "Tati, oh my god."

"Awwww, don't be like that, baby. Don't cry. Ms. Manhunter is gonna be just fine."

Charlotte searched Jake's face for an explanation. "Sorry," he said meekly. "This queen didn't want me to

tell anyone but you yet. She wanted to surprise you."
He brought Charlotte a box of tissues.

As she sank into a chair next to Tatiana, Charlotte
wiped her eyes and looked her friend over. While still
bruised, her hair still crusted with dried blood, Tatiana's color was no longer drowned-corpse gray.

"What day is it?" Tatiana asked.

"Wednesday. It's the Day of the Dead, Tati. Only
you would come back from the dead today."

"Oooh, girl," Tatiana winced in pain. "You givin'
me a new costume idea. I need some bright colors in
my life."

"We can definitely do that," Charlotte smiled
through her tears. "We gotta get you some flowers up
in here."

"As soon as Miss Thing gives me to go ahead, I'll
let the queens know," Jake said. "You know they will
drag this place up so much the glitter will be here until the Second Coming."

"I ain't gonna be here that long," Tatiana promised. "Don't let them hoes in here until I look better. I
bet my hair is busted."

"You look beautiful," Charlotte said, squeezing
her friend's hand.

"Don't you lie to a bitch, now," Tatiana huffed. "I
don't even wanna look in a mirror."

"Well, hi, Miss Tatiana," a nurse sang as she
walked into the room. "Just came to see if you need
anything."

"Water, please, baby. My throat is so sore. And is
that doctor ever gonna change the pain meds?"

"Yes ma'am, just waiting on the pharmacy." She
stepped around to check Tatiana's saline and looked
at Charlotte. "Your friend here just came back from
the grave, from what I hear."

"Yes," Jake interrupted. "They were telling us yesterday in ICU to think about calling a minister for last
rites, then she just surprised us all."

"You are certainly blessed," the nurse offered cheerfully. "I think we have to hold off on solids until the doc sees you, but he did okay some ice chips. I know you need that after getting those tubes out."

"Thank you, baby," Tatiana rasped.

While they spoke, something on the television caught Charlotte's eye, and she stood up, inching closer to the set. The noon news broadcast had just started, and the lead story flashed two familiar faces— the driver's license photos of Chase and the smaller man who had stalked her from Jack's to Washington Park. Charlotte pushed the volume button higher.

"...asking for help in identifying the person or persons responsible for what police are saying was a 'ritualistic' slaying in Washington Park sometime in the early morning hours Monday on Halloween. Chase Souder and Ben Bernard, both students from the University of Tulane, were found by a man walking his dog..."

Dazed, Charlotte stared at the screen wordlessly and found herself once again thinking about Vasile.

The clouds slowly dissipated as Charlotte returned to Moonchild, where her aunts were ladling steamy rooster gumbo into bowls. So, too, had Charlotte's mood shifted, so much so that Mama remarked on it right away.

"There's my baby," she smiled. "Good news on the wind, eh?"

Cassie handed Charlotte a bowl of gumbo with a scoop of rice in the center.

"Thanks, Tauntie," she said, and leaned against the counter, letting the warm smell of gumbo waft into her nostrils. "Y'all, Tatiana is coming through. She was talking when I got there."

"Of course she is," Mama smiled. "I knew you'd find the potion you needed."

"I'm not sure if that's it, or her strong will," Charlotte acceded.

"Both," Sally reassured her. "Don't you underestimate yourself, girl. You work too hard for that."

Charlotte took a spoonful of gumbo and chewed it in quiet contemplation. The store was still, a starkly different scene from the madness of the day before. Sylvie and Sybil were quieter than usual, their disagreement about who was going to clean the gumbo dishes more subdued and more hastily settled than usual.

Charlotte couldn't remember the last time she felt the hopefulness she held onto there with her family, and she savored its warmth as she did her Aunt Cassie's cooking.

"You working tonight, babe?" Sylvie asked.

"No, and you know what? I think I'm gonna celebrate, have some of the girls over."

"That's a good idea," Mama said. "All of you work too much—but you especially, Charlotte. It's not healthy. You too young to be married to work."

Charlotte nodded, finished her meal, and stepped off to text her friends to see who was off for the evening. Her mood elevated, she cleaned and straightened up the shop cheerfully while Sybil and Sylvie flipped radio stations between jazz and old R&B, squabbling about who was in charge of the front of the store until Cassie interrupted and put the station on gospel music, warning the twins not to touch the dial again.

On her way back to her apartment, Charlotte picked up a case of beer. She showered and changed into a warm off-the-shoulder sweater dress. By then, Brigette showed up with a bottle of tequila, and Monique and Chantelle—who managed to find a last-minute sitter for their kids—followed closely behind, excited for an impromptu night out together.

"Hey, Heyyyyy!" Chantelle sang as they entered Charlotte's apartment. "We brought tequila."

"Oh lord," Brigette said. "So did I."

"Y'all are up for a hurting," Charlotte said as she walked in the room with a plate of chips and dip. "I'll cut up some lemons. Which one of y'all is on baby duty tomorrow?" She joked with Monique.

"Neither," the tarot reader smiled. "My Mama agreed to let the kids spend the night, so Chante and I are in the clear."

Chantelle wrapped her arm around her wife's waist. "We never get to sleep in, so I'm about this party. Lemme help you with them lemons, Charlotte."

The evening passed quickly, with the women drinking beer and taking shots, gossiping, and dancing. Eventually, the party moved out to the balcony to smoke and wind down for the evening.

"I haven't seen you cut up in a minute," Brigette said, smiling at her friend.

"Snow is always on that hustle," Monique laughed. "She's gonna run this town before long. Watch."

"If all success took was losing sleep and my mind, I got it," Charlotte said. "I just got a lot going on."

"Yeah, you got a lotta people depending on you, Mama," Chantelle said.

"True," Charlotte said, exhaling a large puff of Kush. "Just gotta push through. It's all any of us can do."

"I'll drink to that," Monique said, and poured another shot into the women's glasses.

"I'm gonna be late to the store tomorrow," Charlotte laughed.

"Babe, I bet they can handle a day without you there," Brigette said. "Sleep late—hell, take off the day for once."

Charlotte looked at her friends' earnest faces around her and realized this was probably the most open way anyone had ever told her to take care of herself in a long time—perhaps her own fault since she rarely slowed down long enough to listen to advice.

"Maybe so, B. I don't think I'll have a choice with all this tequila and Kush."

The women laughed, their cackles raising up into the night sky, chasing the moon. As their laughter died down, Charlotte heard the familiar creaking of Vasile's patio door and leaned forward to see the Romanian step onto his balcony. He looked toward her and lifted his hand in an apologetic wave.

"Who's that?" Brigette stage whispered.

"New neighbor," Charlotte said. "Gimme a minute." She gingerly stepped over her chair and headed toward the locked wrought-iron gate separating the two patios.

Even in the dim light, Charlotte could see that Vasile was changed. His skin no longer had the yellowish-gray pallor, and the dark circles had disappeared from around his eyes. There was color on his cheeks, and he moved with much more energy than she had seen the last few days.

"Hi, Charlotte," he said. "I'm sorry to disturb you, but I just wanted to make sure you were safe after—" Vasile searched for the right words. "After the other night at the park."

"I'm good, yeah," she said. "I appreciate it." She searched his face for some explanation.

"Who's your friend?" Monique yelled. "Bring him on over!"

Charlotte waved her off. "I owe you."

Vasile smiled, his white teeth gleaming in the moonlight. "Hah, not necessary, I promise you. In Romanian, we say, 'a scăpat de dracu' şi a dat de tac-su'—you escaped the devil to run to his father." He winked at Charlotte, and she felt a strange longing rush through her body.

"I'm serious. I owe you. But hey, I gotta ask you something," she said, her words slurring. The tequila and weed were making her warm—and bold.

"Oh?"

"What happened to those guys after I left the park?"

Vasile looked at Charlotte, and she saw a glimmer in his dark eyes. "What do you mean?"

"Vasile, I saw them on the news today—they were killed not long after I left you. That's what the cops say anyway."

Vasile broke his gaze and looked down the street. "That is... unfortunate, I suppose."

Charlotte burst out laughing. "Unfortunate?"

The Romanian smiled, approached her, and wrapped his long, elegant fingers around the wrought iron. "I am just relieved you are safe," he said. "I am at your disposal for the reckoning of your account." He smiled at his own joke. "Good night, Charlotte. Enjoy your evening. Good night, ladies."

Charlotte watched as he walked back into his apartment, shutting the doors behind him. She realized after he was gone that she had been holding in her breath as he had approached her. She flushed with embarrassment and returned to her friends, accidentally knocking over the sour jar she had hidden behind a pot. Chantelle stopped it from rolling off the porch and picked it up.

"Sour jar, Snow?"

"Yeah," Charlotte answered. "I don't think it's working, though."

"Pfft," Brigette said. "If yours won't work, there's no hope for any of us."

"Magick's not foolproof," Charlotte said, steadying the jar back behind the plant. "Just insurance."

"That's about the only insurance a bitch can afford these days," Monique cracked. "'Specially with kids."

"Ain't that the damn truth," Chantelle agreed.

"If you're done flirting, let's get back to the tequila," Monique said. "And who wants a shot?"

"Hey, Pops!" Charlotte grabbed the phone and turned on her video.

"Well hey, baby girl," Andre said, his face breaking out into a huge grin. "How's things in the Big Easy?"

Charlotte didn't know where to start and wondered if her dad even needed to know all the events of the few weeks. Deciding he would likely worry, she decided to keep it light.

"Good, good. We banked on Halloween, as usual."

"You smoke all my Kush yet?"

Charlotte laughed. "Not even close. I work too much to smoke out all the time."

"You get any Endo going?"

"Next week, Pops. The plants need another week before they're full. Lookin' good, though!"

"All right. Make sure you're layin' in bed if you smoke it. It'll put you on the floor." He smiled and gazed through his camera lens. "You lookin' a little ragged. You okay?"

"Yeah, just trying to shake a hangover. I had the girls over last night, and they brought tequila."

"Ooofff, no. That's why I don't mess with alcohol. Stick to the natural stuff, baby. How's the fam? I tried calling the store a few days ago, but Cassie said Mama was asleep, and she was busy with customers."

"Yeah, it gets busy end of October. You know that, Daddy."

"Well, tell them I said I miss them. We got three weeks in Seattle and Portland, and then I'll be heading back."

"I can't wait to see you," Charlotte said. "There's so much going on."

"Oh yeah? What's up?"

"I got a new neighbor."

"All right. What're they like?"

"European guy. Romanian." Charlotte struggled to find a way to explain who or what Vasile was.

"He cool?"

"Yeah. To be honest, he helped me out Monday. Some assholes followed me from the club and tried to jump me."

Andre's face clouded over with fury. "Do what?"

"It's okay—I just was stupid and didn't get a ride."

"Look, Charlotte, you know I ain't never been one to lecture you, but—"

"I know. I *know*. It was stupid. But I'm glad Vasile was there."

"Well, thank him from your pops. I owe him some weed and barbeque. Something."

"Yeah, I'm trying to think of a thank you. I mean, I had the knives you gave me, but still."

"Weed is always appreciated," Andre laughed.

"I don't think he's a smoker," Charlotte said pensively.

"Huh. He straight?"

"Yeah, I think so."

"Well, get some of your girls to give him some dances at Jack's and hook him up with some drinks. I bet that's appreciated. I know I'd like it," Andre laughed, and his laughter was so infectious that Charlotte couldn't help but laugh with him.

"I'll figure something out," Charlotte said.

"I better get going," Andre said. "I'm supposed to drive this next leg, and they're waiting on me. Love you, baby. You stay safe, hear? And don't walk home alone at night."

"Yeah, Pops. Love you right back."

After she hung up the phone, Charlotte thought about her father's suggestion. Vasile *had* enjoyed Tatiana's show and wanted to see Jack's. Maybe the idea wasn't so crazy. She grabbed a piece of paper and a pen and scrawled a hasty invitation to Jack's Friday as her guest, when the club would be packed and fun.

As she stepped out onto the stoop and in front of her neighbor's apartment door, Charlotte briefly held some reservations about her idea. She folded the note in her hands, wondering if this would be a good enough thank you for Vasile's coming to her rescue.

Ugh, just go on with it, Charlotte told herself. She slipped the note under the door, her decision made.

Chapter 19

When Charlotte left her apartment Friday morning, there was a note tucked into her door on thick stationery.

"Hello, Charlotte," it read. "Thank you for your invitation. If I finish work early enough, I would be honored to be your guest. Please let me know if I need to bring anything other than money. V."

Charlotte tucked the note into her backpack and smiled to herself. While her motivation for inviting Vasile was to keep an eye on him and see what the other dancers in the coven thought of him, she was also happily surprised her neighbor would let her thank him for his help.

Because she would be in heels at Jack's all night, Charlotte grabbed a car to take her to the hospital to check up on Tatiana. She picked up two poboys on the way, oyster for her friend. By the time she got to the hospital, the poboys were still warm.

"Ohhhh, girlllll, is that what I think it is?" Tatiana yelled as Charlotte walked into her room. "I knew I smelled something good."

"I figured you were sick of hospital food, even after a day," Charlotte said, handing her the bag. She pulled up a chair and took in the room. Within one day, Tatiana's room was bursting with flowers and colorful balloons from well-wishers. "Wow! Who sent that huge bouquet?"

"Oh, girl, that's from Mr. D. He was really worried."

Tatiana, too, looked even better than the day before. She was sitting up in bed and had applied fake lashes and makeup. She had a colorful head wrap on and a silk robe with red poppies scattered across her dull blue hospital gown.

"Well, damn," Charlotte said, kissing her cheek. "You're all fixed up and looking fine!"

"I can't take these ugly gowns and surroundings," Tatiana said, biting into her poboy with relish. "I'm gonna have to sneak out if they don't release me soon."

Charlotte laughed. "I know it ain't one of your virtues, Tati, but try to be patient. Your body needs to heal."

"I *know* that," the queen sighed. "But they ain't doin' nothin' for me here I can't do at home—except serve bland, overcooked food."

"Girl, I have missed your humor," Charlotte said. "Just let the doctors make sure you're good. You were... we didn't think you'd make it, Mama."

"So I heard. You know I dreamed about you, baby?"

"Oh yeah?"

"Yeah. I'm not sure what day—they kinda all blurred together while I was out. But you was dressed in all white, like an angel. I could see myself asleep on the bed. Whatcha call them things when you can see yourself asleep?"

"What, like out-of-body experience?"

Tatiana took another bite of her poboy. "Damn, this is so good. Yeah, that's it. I was watching myself in a movie here in the hospital, dying."

"Well, we are all grateful you didn't, Tati."

"Girl, me too," Tatiana laughed. "Anyway, you looked like an angel and came to me, held your hand on my wrist. And it burned, Snow. I don't know how to say it, but it's like some energy came from you to me, and I felt it turn my blood from cold to warm. Not long after that—or shit, I dunno—I felt myself choking. I could feel the tube in my throat and pulled it out. That's when the nurses came in, and I started to come out of the dark, you know?"

Charlotte felt her eyes tear up. "Well, if I had any part in bringing you back to us, Tati, I'm grateful."

Tatiana washed down the remainder of her poboy with a bottle of water on a table next her. "Me too, Mama. I know you were here with me. Jake let me know you and your aunts came to see me."

"They did. Mama came, too."

Now it was Tatiana's turn to tear up. "Mama Sally came all the way here to see me?"

"Of course she did. You know we love you."

Tatiana's face scrunched up, and she began to weep. "I'm gonna fuck up my makeup," she said.

"Shhh," Charlotte whispered. She put down her poboy and went to Tatiana's bedside to gently hug her friend. She was surprised to find Tatiana crying harder under her arms.

"It's okay, Tati. I'm here."

"That's the problem, Snow. *You're* here. The bitches from the club came—I mean, look at this room! Your aunties came. Mama Sally came. You know who didn't come? My own Mama."

Charlotte stroked her friend's arm gently. "Did she even know you were here?"

"Yeah, she did. She's one of my emergency numbers. Jake talked to her."

Charlotte picked up her sandwich and sat back in her chair slowly. "Oh, wow. Okay."

"She said she'd pray for me, Snow, but it was in God's hands. And she told Jake not to call her unless I left my sinnin'. Her own child." Tatiana sobbed. "I could have died."

"I'm so sorry. She doesn't know what she's missing out on."

"I don't even know anymore. Like, I was at the park that night for a Grindr date. What if she's right? What if I got attacked because I'm a sinner?"

Makeup smeared down Tatiana's face, and Charlotte struggled to find the right words to comfort her friend. "You really believe that?"

Tatiana breathed heavily, her voice shuddering. "No."

"Good. 'Cause it's nowhere near the truth. God has a lot more on his plate than worrying about your Grindr dates."

For some reason, Charlotte's words struck both women as funny, and they started to laugh—slowly at first, and then more loudly.

"I'm gonna need you to write that down for my headstone," Tatiana laughed, wiping away her tears.

"I don't know about that," Charlotte smiled. "And looks like we got a long time to think about a headstone."

Charlotte began to grow nervous about Vasile's appearance at Jack's right around the time she left Moonchild. She'd had Sylvie roll her hair into soft waves and fussed about her makeup more than she normally would have.

"You look like a goddess," Sylvie said when she finished.

"Come on," Charlotte laughed dismissively.

"No, I'm for real. Sybil, come see. Doesn't she look like a goddess?"

Sybil came over and assessed her niece. "Woooooo, she does. You're gonna bank tonight, baby. You really do look like the moon gave birth to you herself."

"Now you know it's true if Sybil and me agree on something," Sylvie chuckled.

Cassie approached the trio, took a look at Charlotte and said, "Wow, baby. I forget how beautiful you are sometimes."

Sybil and Sylvie looked at Charlotte victoriously, both with a hand on her hip.

"Thanks, y'all. Wish me luck. Fridays are usually big biz, and I'd like to keep building on this good streak we've had going here lately."

"Now you see?" Cassie said. "Even better—you got brains to go with them looks. Sybil, come help me count the till."

Sybil kissed her niece on the cheek. "Be safe, boo. No walking home alone."

"Yeah, you make sure you get a car after work," Sylvie seconded.

"I will, don't worry. Love y'all." Charlotte kissed her aunties goodbye and stepped outside to start the short walk to Jack's.

If the crowds on the streets were an early indication, the club would have a good night, Charlotte guessed. The atmosphere was one of excitement and money, both positive elements for the city.

She reached Jack's around 11 and let Big John know to let Vasile in without a cover, then headed to find Bobbie.

"Hey, Mama," she said as she found her boss near the bar, watching the crowd pick up.

"Hey, baby," Bobbie said, hugging her side. "Looks like we're gonna have a good night."

"Good. We still got that table for my friend? He helped me out the other night, and I wanna make sure he has a good time. I got his drinks and food."

"I'll let the door and servers know," Bobbie said. "Name?"

"Vasile. He's tall. Dark, curly hair."

"That's like half of this state," Bobbie laughed. "Come on."

"He dresses nice?" Charlotte offered.

"Attractive?"

"Yeah," Charlotte said, grateful the club was dark enough to conceal her blushing. "Accent, too. He's Romanian."

"Romanian. That's quite a ways away off."

Charlotte nodded. "He's my new neighbor. I know he'll tip well."

"Don't worry," Bobbie said. "We'll take good care of him. You know if he prefers redheads, Latinas...?"

"No idea," Charlotte said. "Maybe just ask the girls to rotate? I bet he lets them know. Oh, and he mixes some Romanian bullshit with his drink. Maybe let security know he's cool? I'm gonna head back."

"Will do. You look *hot,* by the way. They're gonna love you," she said, nodding toward the crowd.

"Thanks, B," Charlotte said, squeezing Bobbie's hand.

Charlotte headed to the dressing room to put on a vintage-looking black lingerie set with a leopard-print sheer robe and heels.

"Holy shit—you look *amazing,*" Jade said as she walked past Charlotte toward the back. "You're gonna love the vibe tonight—tips are already slamming."

"Badass," Charlotte said. "Hey, my neighbor is coming, and I wanna make sure he has a good time. Can you give him a dance if he wants? I know you'll be cool."

"Of course," Jade smiled. "He got an Asian fetish or something? Because ugh."

"I'm not sure what he's into," Charlotte said. "He just helped me out the other night when some assholes were hassling me."

"Ooooh, a gentleman. You got it, babe."

"Thanks, Hoa," Charlotte said.

As she walked to the bar, Charlotte scanned the crowd to see if Vasile had shown up yet. She breathed a sigh of relief that he wasn't there and walked the floor to visit with customers and make some money. About an hour into her shift, she'd already made around three hundred dollars with requests from multiple tables for her company and found herself regretting she hadn't brought at least one vial of Sucka Punch.

Out of the corner of her eye, she saw Bobbie leading Vasile to a table near stage right, places usually reserved for generous customers. After she made sure he was seated, Bobbie pulled aside a cocktail waitress, who nodded and immediately went to Vasile's table to take his order. Charlotte breathed a sigh of relief. He was getting the VIP treatment.

As Mandy, the auburn-haired dancer, passed her, Charlotte reached out for her. "Mandy, I gotta favor to ask."

"Sure doll—oh shit, you look great!"

"Thanks, so do you. You see that guy at table four?"

"Sure do—friend of yours?"

"Kinda. Neighbor. He did me a solid, and I wanna make sure he has a good time."

"I gotcha. I'll go see him now."

"Thanks, baby. I owe you."

"Anytime," Mandy smiled. "He's cute!"

"I gotta work that table," Charlotte gestured toward a pair of men clearly enjoying the evening. "I'll head over there in a song or two."

As she danced for her table, Charlotte glanced over at Vasile's table a few times. He was grinning broadly at everything going on around him and happily accepted the drink when the cocktail waitress approached. Mandy was sitting and talking to him, and when a new song began, she began to dance for him.

Charlotte began to relax. Her father was right after all: Vasile was young enough to appreciate a strip club outing as a thank you. As she walked to the back to take to the stage, Charlotte saw Jade walk toward the table, hug Mandy, and sit down by Vasile's left side.

"Ayyyy, Snow," Johnny C said enthusiastically as she approached him. "What we dancing to tonight?"

"Rhianna. 'Pour it Up.'"

"Right on. Good choice—this crowd is throwing up the bills."

"That's what I like to hear," Charlotte said. "Let's go!"

As the first notes of the song pounded through the club speakers, Charlotte stepped out onto the stage and pumped her arms up. The crowd clapped and cheered receptively, and she gracefully landed a cartwheel into a full split. All eyes on her, she grabbed a pole and began to dance to the beat around it, stopping only during the verse, to encourage the crowd to throw money onto the stage.

The crowd roared every time she made the motion and tossed so many bills that the front of the stage was littered with cash. Enjoying the energy and the sight of the money, Charlotte smiled widely and rolled in the cash by the close of the song, and the audience roared with delight.

As she blew a kiss to the crowd, Charlotte looked to Vasile's table: he was on his feet, clapping wildly. By the time she reached the floor, Charlotte already had multiple requests for appearances at tables, but she walked to Vasile's table first.

"Hey, you made it!" she said, reaching out a hand. Vasile stood and took her hand but also pulled her in to kiss both of her cheeks.

"This is wonderful, Charlotte! You dance so well. It seems they like you, too," he said as he motioned to the crowd.

"Yeah, I gotta make a few rounds—make that cash, you know?"

"Of course, of course," he said. "I am enjoying it."

"I still owe him a dance," Jade said.

"Vasile, this is on me. Don't pay for anything, understand?"

Vasile laughed. "No, you already taught me about tipping. Don't worry. I won't embarrass you."

Charlotte smiled and relaxed. "Yeah, the girls do like tips. Jade, can you make sure the girls keep checking on him? I wanna make sure he's got booze, food, and boobies in front of him at all times."

"You're very kind," Vasile said. "I did eat."

"All right, but we got you for the rest. I better go."

Vasile gave a half-bow, smiled, and sat back down while Jade jumped into his lap.

After Charlotte's performance, the DJ continued to play up-tempo songs, and the club atmosphere was upbeat as well. It was the type of evening Bobbie called a "disco party" because the clientele was light-hearted, just the right amount of drunk, and ready to spend. All of the dancers were energetic as well; to Charlotte's recollection, this was the first *normal* evening they'd had since Pixie was murdered.

Although she was busy working the floor, Charlotte would walk by Vasile's table to make sure he was having a good time or give him a thumbs-up sign. In truth, she knew he was having a great time. The dancers at Jack's were beautiful, most of them good conversationalists.

By the time she decided to take a break, Charlotte had made nearly $800, not including the tips thrown onstage. She went to the bar to order a drink, threw her robe back on, and headed to Vasile's table, where several of the dancers were now seated with him, Mandy on his lap. Charlotte laughed to herself; he was clearly tipping well, and he was attractive.

"Snooowwwwww," the girls called out to her as she approached.

Charlotte took a seat next to Vasile, noting he had his cloudy half-vodka concoction on the table in front of him. He was at ease, in the same way the drag show hadn't flustered him one bit. He grinned broadly at Charlotte and pointed to the cash tucked into the straps on her lingerie. "You are doing well!"

"Yeah, fun night here. You look like you're having a good time, too." Charlotte winked at Mandy.

"Yes, of course we have clubs in Romania, but nothing like this—and the women are nowhere near as beautiful," Vasile said.

"Awwww," Mandy said. "Your friend is so sweet, Snow." She stood to go. "Come on, girls—let's let them talk. See you, Vasile!"

The dancers left the pair at the table, and Vasile lifted his drink. "My dear friend," he said, "A toast?"

Charlotte smiled and lifted her glass.

"Noroc," Vasile said, tipping his glass with hers. "To new friends and new experiences."

"To new friends," Charlotte said, and took a sip.

"I think I like this show even better than the one at Tatiana's club," Vasile said. He sounded tipsy.

"I'm glad you're having a good time. I really do appreciate you helping me."

Vasile smiled. "No need—you have thanked me many times, Charlotte. However..."

"However?"

"Do I not get a dance from you? You are the star here."

For some reason, Vasile's request made Charlotte warm up, and she was grateful for the drinks customers had bought for her, making the current interaction only slightly less awkward. She smiled at her neighbor, who looked at her earnestly—almost innocently.

"Really? You're not sick of beautiful women in your lap yet?"

Vasile howled with laughter. "You are very funny." He finished his drink, and a cocktail waitress came over almost immediately. "One more, please," Vasile instructed. "I can feel I am losing my senses already. Of course, that may very well be the present company."

Charlotte looked at him. His eyes were glossy with excitement, his cheeks flushed. There was no denying he was attractive, charismatic even. She could feel something pull her to him, and this time, she didn't resist. As The Weekend's "Wicked Games" sounded over the speakers, Charlotte eased into Vasile's lap and began to dance for him. He kept a small half-smile on his face, his eyes locked with hers, as she danced, and it seemed as if they were alone in the dark.

When the song ended, Vasile nuzzled into her neck and whispered, "You should invite me over."

For some reason, his voice pulled her from the lure, and she remembered who—what—he was.

"Nah," Charlotte smiled. "We ain't like that, my friend."

A brief flash of pain crossed the Romanian's face, but he concealed it quickly and took a swig of his drink.

"Well, thank you for the dance," he said, pulling a hundred from his wallet and tucking it into her waist. "I better get back to my flat. I still have work to attend to."

Charlotte stood up. "Thanks for coming, Vasile. And thanks again."

Vasile smiled. "Thank you for a wonderful night." He kissed her cheeks again and slipped out of the club into the crisp November evening.

By the time Charlotte reached Moonchild for work, the back of the shop was already a loud hive of activity: Mama Sally's longtime friend Maime had stopped in for a visit. Charlotte smiled the moment she heard the familiar voice, recalling childhood days at the feet of the pair as they happily gossiped away.

Mamie was closer to the twins' age than Mama's, but she had experienced enough history with Mama—

Hurricane Audrey, Jim Crow Laws, World War 2—to be thick as thieves.

As Charlotte approached the kitchen, Mischief was happily squawking, showing off his favorite words. "MERDE!" he screeched, to which Maime asked, "Is that damn bird ever gonna die?"

"Oh, mais, you know that's what people say about you and me, Maime." Mama laughed, and both women fell into a fit of giggles.

"Well, hey, baby," Maime said as Charlotte entered the kitchen. Charlotte gave her a hug and kiss, then kissed her grandmother's hand and cheek.

"Well, look at this," Charlotte said. "I bet the whole city's ears are burning from the gosspin' y'all doing." Maime and Sally laughed like schoolgirls.

"You know it," Maime laughed. "Come sit with us."

"All right, but only for a few minutes or else Cassie will come looking for me. You look good, Maime."

Maime laughed. "For what? My age?"

"Nah, just in general. It's good to see you, and I know Mama's happy you're here."

"I am," Sally smiled. "It's been a good minute."

"How's Ernest?" Charlotte asked. Ernest, Maime's son, was mentally disabled.

"He's good, baby. Strong as ever. Don't know what he's gonna do when I go. He's the reason I get up and work every day."

Mama fell silent, as if she saw something but didn't want to put her thoughts into words. "He's gonna be fine," she offered at last.

"I never wanted to put him in a home," Maime sighed. "Ain't got no family left. Ain't got no money."

"You got us, Maime," Charlotte said.

"Well thank you, baby," Maime said, patting the younger woman's hand. "I sure do."

"Y'all have breakfast yet?" Charlotte asked. "Want me to make some biscuits?"

"That would be wonderful," Mama said. "I think I got some breakfast sausage in the freezer. Eggs, too."

"Breakfast sandwiches it is," Charlotte said. She pulled out flour, salt, butter and began to sift the flour and mix the ingredients, and the women seemed to forget about her as she cooked.

"So like I was saying, I just can't sew as fast as I used to," Maime said, continuing a conversation Charlotte guessed had started before she arrived. "They got these Vietnamese tailors now who can work so much faster than me. Ain't the quality that's different, or better, or worse. I just struggle to get them pins set."

"Oh, I understand that," Mama sympathized. "Arthritis, the tremors. Aging just ain't for the weak."

"You right about that. Now Ernest's dad paid off our place before he died, so it ain't the rent or no mortgage worries me. But the place is falling apart. And Ernest, bless him. He can't keep a hammer steady. He can paint good, but he loses interest too quick."

"Can't blame the boy for that," Sally laughed. "What's that phrase—like watching paint dry? If it weren't for the girls, this place would be in shambles."

"Yeah, you got lucky," Maime sighed. "Y'all live long, healthy lives."

"Not *all* of us," Mama corrected. "The Baron Samedi always looks for balance. He gives with one hand, but he always takes with the other."

"I'll have to take your word on that, Mama. I don't do them vodou gods."

"C'est bon. They watch over you anyway, whether you want them to or not."

Charlotte put the biscuits into the oven and set the sausage into the microwave to defrost, but the women still seemed oblivious to her presence.

"You think about what your girls are gonna do when you go?," Maime asked.

"All the time," Sally replied. "Lately, more than ever."

"What? How come?"

"I've been alive a long time," Mama said. "And all things have their reckoning."

Over the loud humming din of the old microwave, Charlotte struggled to listen in to the conversation, concerned.

"But little pitchers," Mama smiled, nodding toward Charlotte. "Grands Oreilles."

"You right, you right."

While the biscuits finished, Charlotte fried up the sausage and eggs. Her mind whirred as she wondered if her grandmother were being sympathetic, dismissive, or serious about her own end. It was something Charlotte couldn't even picture, so after a moment, she pushed the thought from her mind and pulled the biscuits from the oven.

"Whoo, those biscuits smell good," Mama said.

"Mmm-hmmm. Sausage, too."

Charlotte served the women a plate and then divided the remainder on three additional plates to bring to her aunts. "I'm gonna head up front," she said. "Y'all holler if you need anything. Maime, don't leave without telling me 'cause I have something for you."

"Well, thank you, baby," Maime said.

Charlotte kissed both women on the cheek and carefully balanced the remaining plates on her chest and arms before heading to the front of the store, where her aunts heralded her approach with excitement.

"Ooooh, fresh biscuits!" Sylvie called.

"Looks good," Sybil said. "They wear you out already?"

Charlotte smiled. "Nah. I just figured they need time to visit alone. Here you go."

As she placed the plates on the countertop in front of her aunts, her phone buzzed—a text from Brigette.

Not sure if you heard. Chanel who used to work with us got murdered last night. Found her body at St. Roch's.

Although she vaguely remembered the name, Charlotte struggled to remember the face.

Who? She responded.

White girl, brunette. Remember Bobbie fired her for hooking?

The additional information helped. Charlotte had warned Chanel not to solicit customers at Jack's—a strict rule of Bobbie's—but the dancer hadn't listened and inevitably got fired. Last Charlotte had heard, she had moved on to another club and continued escorting for extra cash.

Shit. That's awful, Charlotte replied. *I know she was picking up random johns on Bourbon.*

Word is she put up quite a fight. Prolly left some marks on the dude.

Charlotte breathed a prayer for the dead woman under her breath. Once again, a murder hit too close to home.

"You okay, baby girl?" Sybil asked. "You look like someone walked over your grave."

"I'm good," Charlotte said. "Just reading the news. You know how it is."

"In this city?" Sylvie scoffed. "That explains your look."

"Yeah. Y'all know—not easy to be a woman here."

For once, Sylvie and Sybil didn't argue on a point, but nodded wordlessly. Charlotte found her appetite had left her, and she sipped her black coffee in silence. A nagging suspicion had her wondering where Vasile went after he left Jack's, and she made a mental note to inspect his face and hands the next time she saw him.

Chapter 20

As she approached her apartment after work, Charlotte noticed that one of Vasile's lights was on in his place.

She hesitated briefly before knocking but decided she needed some answers. Since he had moved in, Charlotte noticed too many deaths, and that was either the most unusual set of coincidences she could remember in her life, or—

"Why, Charlotte, what a lovely surprise."

Cloaked in the dim hallway light, Vasile looked even more handsome, and more dangerous, than usual.

"Hey," Charlotte said. "I—uh—wanted to check up on you after your night out."

"Would you like to come in?" Vasile gestured to his interior.

"No, I'm tired. It was a long day at both the shop and the club."

"Ah, I understand. I had a wonderful time, Charlotte. Thank you again."

"Right on," Charlotte searched his face. There were no visible signs of a scratch mark on it. "So what did you get up to after you left?"

"Well, I must confess I was more than a little disoriented from the alcohol. I apologize for being so forward."

"Not a problem," she said. "So did you come home or—?"

It was Vasile's turn to examine Charlotte's face. The silence between them lasted long enough to become tense.

"Why do you ask?" he finally said.

"Just curious." Charlotte pulled both of Vasile's hands to hers and glanced at them quickly, but the light was too dim to examine them for any signs of injury. His hands were ice cold in hers. Vasile looked at her curiously, then withdrew his hands from hers.

"I don't understand you, Charlotte," he said at last. His face strained into a gloomy look. "I need to get back to work. Good evening."

"All right," she said. "'Night."

Vasile closed his door with a harsh click, and Charlotte couldn't help but feel a wave of embarrassment. As she entered her own apartment and went about her evening routine, she tried to remind herself that she was within her rights to question his actions—after all, didn't neighbors of serial killers always express surprise when they learned of the misdeeds of people living just feet from them?

Chapter 21

Winston was in pain, and no amount of ibuprofen or aspirin was helping. A cracked tooth marred his weekend, and the entire right side of his jaw was swollen, bruised, and ugly.

He struggled through half of the workday before his usually surly demeanor turned uglier. He was working with Marcella, a coworker he loathed even on a good day. Marcella was nowhere near as efficient as he was, and she'd gotten in his way one time too many.

The last time he felt her breeze by his right side, the rush of air alone made him wince in agony.

"Hey!" he hissed. "Come here."

Marcella looked at Winston blankly, her eyes impassive. She was used to Winston's outbursts and tended to ignore them.

"What?"

"Look here," Winston snarled, angry he had to form words with his aching mouth. "I'm gonna need you to *stop coming anywhere near me.* This place is big enough for you to stay the hell out of my way for the next four hours that I have to suffer your presence."

Marcella's face rapidly shifted from impassive to heated. "It ain't like I *want* to be anywhere near you," she said. "But since you're behind on the sorting, I gotta grab it from your bin to put in the boxes."

"Just...just leave it," Winston said. "I don't need your help, and you actually slow me down with the mistakes you make."

Marcella smirked. "No, you slow yourself down with your bullshit. Don't you *dare* blame me for your nonsense. I'm here doing my job."

"You're doing *a* job. Then we have to go behind you and—"

"Oh no, no you don't," Marcella snapped, her voice raising. She stepped just inches from Winston's face. "Ain't no 'we' here. *Nobody* here likes working with you because you're such an asshole, but *we* don't say shit because you're one of them guys that shows up to work and shoots people."

Winston glared at his coworker, his eyes narrowing. "I would never shoot anyone," he protested. He gave this some thought; if, for instance, he planned to kill Marcella, shooting would be much too impersonal for the grief she caused him. He imagined a much more dramatic outcome—a guillotine, with her round moon face held in place with a wooden frame before the fatal drop of the blade. The idea was comical, and he found suddenly found himself laughing at the image.

Marcella recoiled with horror and stepped away from him. "See, you can't even say that without laughing. Like how is that funny?" She shook her head and walked away from him, looking back over her shoulder in a mix of fear and disgust.

Winston shrugged. If it only took fear to keep her away from him, he would have to up the ante when he felt better. He made a mental note, wondering how far he could push it without getting summoned by HR.

During his brief break, Winston made several phone calls to try to find a dentist who could see him as soon as possible, but because he hadn't retained a regular one, the earliest he appointment he could get was a week away.

Winston tried to gauge whether or not he could tolerate the pain he was in for a week as he sifted through mail and decided he would look through his mother's medications when he returned home. He suffered through the rest of the afternoon in a tense détente with Marcella, who was now making theatrical sound effects to indicate her disgust for him.

But she kept her distance, so Winston considered their interaction a personal victory.

Charlotte was busy with a new concoction: remoulade for fried okra to go with a steak. Tatiana was due home from the hospital any moment, and Charlotte wanted to make sure the queen had homecooked food waiting for her. And just in time, she heard Tatiana calling her thanks to a driver and unlocking her door.

After searing the steak quickly and then popping it into the oven, Charlotte packed up the remoulade and okra and a bowl of fresh strawberries and cream. She let the steak set briefly and then placed it on a covered plate with a knife and fork and headed downstairs.

"Hey, Mama!" she yelled as she knocked. "Got some hot dinner for you!"

"Well, hey!" Tatiana said. "What is all this?"

"I figured you'd be hungry. Made you a steak—"

"Ooooh, girl, yes!"

"And some fried okra."

"Keep talkin'."

"And some homemade fresh remoulade."

"This is music to my busted-up ears, Snow. Come in, come in."

The pair headed to Tatiana's living room, where the drag queen already had the TV on and several pharmacy bags on her coffee table. Charlotte looked her over, assessing her friend's healing. She could see the bandages covering Tatiana's lacerations were still in place on her back and shoulder, and a huge wound crossed her neck and down onto her chest.

Her face was still bruised, with a large gash stapled together with sutures crossing her left check, barely missing her eye.

Charlotte realized she must have been looking at her friend for too long and felt Tatiana staring back at her.

"That bad, huh?

"What? I just—"

Tatiana shrugged. "You know, it's good I been doing my own makeup for years. Ain't nobody gonna be able to tell in a few weeks when the scars come in."

Sitting down, Charlotte uncovered the plates and bowls and arranged the dinner for her friend. "No hurry, boo, but once you feel strong enough, I really wanna to know what happened."

"Oooh, and strawberries?" Tatiana gasped. "You spoil me. Mmmm." She cut the steak and took a large bite, savoring it. "You know, y'all brought me good food, but nothing—nothing beats a steak done just right."

"That mean you don't wanna talk about what happened?"

"Naw, that ain't it. I just couldn't tell you, Snow. He hit me from behind, and I don't remember a damn thing after that."

"So was it the guy you were supposed to meet? The cops follow up on him?"

"Yeah, he's actually the one who found me—about thirty minutes after I got attacked, I guess."

"Hmm," Charlotte said skeptically. "How do they know it wasn't him?"

"I mean, girl—he stayed with me all the way to the hospital. The nurses said he didn't have no blood on him and was crying. I guess it could be him, but it doesn't seem like the cops think so. He still messages me, see if I'm okay."

"And how about now? Are they following up with you?"

"Who, the cops?"

"Yeah. Any news?"

Tatiana shrugged and dipped a piece of okra into the remoulade. "Beat-up drag queens are last week's news, and ain't nobody care then, either," the queen sighed, then popped the okra in her mouth. "Oh my god, Snow. This remoulade—I could eat this alone."

"I'm glad you like it. I gotta run out in a while. Looks like you got your medicine. You need anything from the pharmacy, the grocery?"

"I could use a blunt."

Charlotte picked up a bag of pills. "If any of this interacts with weed, you ain't getting any."

Tatiana laughed a deep, throaty laugh. "Oh, now you the mom. Okay, *Mom*. You know, if you can get me some mascara, that would be good. I'm running low—it can be drugstore. I'm gonna wear lashes any-way."

"Wear them where? Where you planning on go-ing?"

Tatiana rolled her eyes. "For when I entertain peo-ple here, until I can get out again without feeling like a monster. Plus I got my standing date with Mr. D. I told him no sex, but he can take me out to dinner."

Charlotte laughed. "And of course you did."

"Hey, gotta keep that hustle goin', you know? So what's been goin' on around here? Did our friend up-stairs turn into a bat yet?"

"Funny you should ask," Charlotte said, her face clouding over. "I don't know what to make of him, Tati. He *seems* nice, but I can't help thinking something is wrong."

"Well, based on what your family does, I wouldn't push those feelings away. You try any of the hocus pocus on him?"

"Yeah, and no. It's complicated. I'm not sure it's working."

"Mmm-hmmm."

"What do you mean *mmm-hmmm?*"

"I mean y'all seemed cozy at the Honey Pot."

"No, Tati, listen, please. I'm not one for conspiracies, but ever since he moved in, seems like people close to me are getting hurt..."

"And we still don't know if it's him."

"Exactly."

"Well, he ain't come over to your balcony, right? Still got the crucifixes up?"

"I do."

"And the salt ain't seem to do anything."

"Right."

"I guess we can't stake him until we know for sure."

"You *guess?*" Charlotte's expression was so exasperated that both of them began to laugh.

"Mama know anything about this? Like what we need to do next?"

"No. She'd had her mind preoccupied with other things—losing a member of the coven, the store."

Tatiana opened the box of strawberries, dipped one into the cream, and bit into it thoughtfully. "Maybe we need to consult with an expert."

"An expert? Who do you know that's an expert in maybe-vampires?"

"I don't know anyone, but we in New Orleans, and this is the home of Anne Rice. Vampire Ball. All that shit. Somebody's gotta know something that can help us. I'll get on the internet later and see what I can find, make a few calls."

"I don't know that you should do that today, Tati. You need to get some rest and heal." Charlotte stood up. "I'll come get the dishes later and bring your mascara."

"All right, baby. Thanks for everything. For the food, for being here for me."

"You got it. If you need anything, just text me. And stay off Grindr."

"I will. At least until my face heals, and a bitch is pretty again."

Healing rapidly, Tatiana Manhunter was bored. Her week in the hospital, where she was unconscious and clinging to life, was fading with her wounds. Thanks to Charlotte's magical intervention, she was healing more rapidly than anyone expected, including the queen herself.

Without her weekly shows, however, she found herself longing for excitement and finally ventured to head out on this clear November morning, and having consulted with few members of the local goth community online, she had a mission.

Still sore, Tatiana threw on a muumuu with a matching head wrap and some oversized shades to hide the fading sores and bruises. "Okay, not bad, you still pretty, Miss Thang," she said as she looked in the mirror. She emptied a bottle of pills onto a jewelry tray in her bathroom and packed the bottle in a handbag.

The morning was crisp and clear, with feathery wisps of cirrus clouds lazily moving across the robin's eggshell-blue skies. Tatiana walked with a steady purpose to Jackson Square and around the corner of St. Peter's to the cobblestone in front of St. Louis Cathedral.

The crowds hadn't started to form in the square at the early hour, and Tatiana wondered if she should return later, when a 6'3" black drag queen walking into a church would be less conspicuous. "Jesus loves everybody," she whispered to herself, and marched confidently to the gray façade.

Once inside the narthex, Tatiana's eyes quickly rested on the object of her mission: the bénitier or holy water font. She looked around cautiously. Far down the aisle of the church, near the front, a floral arranger was talking to a priest as the former attended to his work.

Moving silently and quickly, Tatiana unclasped her handbag, walked over to the font, and pulled out the empty pill bottle. She had just dipped the bottle into the water when a voice behind her rang out.

"Well, good morning!"

Tatiana spun around and sloshed water onto her sleeves; another small portion dripped from her bottle onto the floor.

"Oh shit," she said, her eyes wide. She faced a beefy priest with a toothy smile on his face. "I mean, oh, sorry about the language, Father."

The priest chuckled. "Oh, I've heard worse. Are you here for penance before mass?"

"Oh no, no, no," Tatiana stuttered. "I mean, unless you have coffee and a few hours."

"Well, my dear, if it's that bad, I'm sure we can find the time."

Tatiana cupped the pill bottle with the holy water behind her back, struggling to put on the childproof cap without the benefit of sight.

"I'm afraid not today," Tatiana laughed nervously. "I just always been curious what the inside of this place looks like."

"Ah, you're a native."

"Yup. And you know us locals. We do love to sin."

"Hah, yes. Well, locals also know they can come here to pray and be forgiven of their sins. If you are staying for mass, that begins right after noon, but you really should be shriven if you plan to take communion."

"Oh, yes, sir. I'm a big fan of these church rules and etiquette and such."

The priest looked at her quizzically.

"All right, then. I'm Father Paul if you need anything. You are welcome to come in and pray if you'd like. It's nice and quiet right now."

"I sure do appreciate that, Father. I might just do that one day, but I need to get to my job."

"I see," the priest smiled bemusedly. "Well, our doors are open when your heart is."

"Thank you," Tatiana said. The cap behind her back clicked shut, and she slipped it into her handbag behind her back. "I'll make sure to do that." She backed up toward the front doors and turned to leave.

"God be with you," the priest said. "And if you need any more of that holy water, it's free, my dear. No need to hide it."

Tatiana cringed but walked back into the square, gripping the holy water victoriously.

As soon as Charlotte came home from work late Saturday night, Tatiana was waiting for her.

"Finally! Girl, I got something for us."

Charlotte yawned. "Is it a vacation? Because that's the only thing I need right now."

"Nah," Tatiana lowered her voice to a stage whisper and pointed overhead. "It's for our friend."

Despite her fatigue, Charlotte felt obligated to entertain her friend. "All right. One blunt unless you're still on the opioids."

"Yayyy!" Tatiana yelped. "Lemme grab my purse."

As she waited for Tatiana, Charlotte looked up to Vasile's apartment, where one light illuminated the interior.

"I wonder do revenants smoke," Tatiana mused as she walked out of her apartment and locked the door behind her.

"Shhhh," Charlotte reprimanded, stifling a laugh as the women climbed the staircase.

Once inside her apartment, Charlotte dropped her backpack and collected a box with her rolling papers and Kush. She followed Tatiana outside, and the two women took a seat on the balcony. The women shared the joint as Tatiana regaled her friend with her tale about the holy water.

"Just when I think you can't get any crazier, Mama..." Charlotte laughed.

"Okay, but we gotta figure it out one way or another. Like you said, something's been wrong since he moved in. Now I ain't sayin' for sure he's a vampire, but we gotta try these tests, and then once we know for sure, BAM!" Tatiana slammed a fist into her palm.

"Bam what?"

"I don't know. We'll have to see. Lemme get him to come out and smoke with us."

"I guess that's one way to find out if he smokes," Charlotte laughed.

Tatiana stepped back into the apartment, and Charlotte heard her footsteps on the wood between the doors, her loud, flirtatious laughter, and her short walk back. She had a glass of water with her, sat down, reached into her purse, and dumped the holy water into the glass and set it next to her before winking conspiratorially at her friend.

"Well?"

"Oh, he's coming. I told him you really wanted him to come hang."

"Come on," Charlotte groaned.

"I didn't think he'd come otherwise. We *need* to know, Snow."

Charlotte relit her blunt and inhaled deeply. "He's gonna smoke with us?"

"I don't know. I just told him to come over."

"Well, then I guess that part about vampires is still a mystery."

"What part of vampires is still a mystery?" a heavily accented voice asked bemusedly from the balcony adjacent to Charlotte's.

"Shit!" said Tatiana. "You ever gonna learn not to sneak up on a bitch?"

Vasile laughed. "It's not intentional, I assure you." He had a drink in his hand and approached the gate. "May I?" he asked, his eyes locking with Charlotte's.

"Of course," Tatiana interjected. "Come on, baby. Got you a seat right here."

Keeping his eyes on Charlotte, Vasile raised an eyebrow. Charlotte took a deep puff from her joint and shrugged.

Vasile reached through the gate and unhinged the lock on Charlotte's side. "Thank you for the invitation," he smiled. "I have been meaning to call on you, Miss Tatiana. I saw your story in the newspaper."

"Wait, *what*? I was in the paper? Oh shit. What picture did they use?"

"No photo of you, just mention of your assault. I'm very sorry this happened to you."

Tatiana motioned for Vasile to sit next to her. "I appreciate that, baby. Ms. Thing is surviving."

"Yes, you look like you are healing well." Vasile took a sip from his glass after sitting. "And I'm sure Miss Charlotte is looking after you." He looked in Charlotte's direction again, and she nodded.

"This girl is *the best*. She and her family been here for me when my own wasn't."

"Family can be difficult indeed," Vasile sighed. "Please let me know if you need anything."

Clearly flattered by the attention, Tatiana giggled and placed a hand on Vasile's arm. "You are just too sweet, Vasile. So what have you been up to? Are you getting used to the city? Lotsa ways to get into trouble here, I can tell you that."

"I did get to go see Charlotte dance," Vasile said.

"Uh, what?" Tatiana looked at Charlotte, her eyebrows raised in an expression of great surprise.

"He did a big favor for me," Charlotte interjected.

Tatiana's face broke out into a huge grin. "And this is the shit I missed when I was dyin'.'"

"It was a very nice evening out," Vasile said. "Your friend is a very talented dancer."

"You mean she's hot as fuck," Tatiana corrected.

Vasile took a large quaff from his glass. "Yes, of course. She is beautiful."

"Hey, y'all can stop talking about me like I'm not here," Charlotte said.

"Oh, right," Tatiana said. "And you can pass that blunt."

Charlotte passed the weed and scowled at her friend. Tatiana took a deep drag and tried to pass the blunt to Vasile.

"Ah, no thank you," the Romanian said. "I still have to work. This will be my only drink tonight as well."

Tatiana turned to pass the weed back to Charlotte, her eyes wide and triumphant: *vampires do not smoke Kush.*

"Can I get some of that water, Tati?" Charlotte asked pointedly.

"Oh damn, right," Tatiana winked. She grabbed the glass and sloppily splattered some of it onto Vasile. The Romanian leapt out of his seat, his face twisted in shock, as if the water were hot grease.

"Cacat!" Vasile yelled, his face twisted in shock and anger. "What is this?"

Tatiana stood up, leading Charlotte to leap out of her seat as well. "Ah-*HA!*" the drag queen yelled gleefully. "I knew it. I *knew* it! We were right, Snow!"

"Right about what? You play games too much, both of you, like schoolgirls."

"You just go ahead and confess," Tatiana said loudly. "That's holy water. We know what you are."

From the darkness, Vasile laughed a deep, ugly laugh. "So that's it? You tested with salt, now holy water? This, in the age of science?"

"And the blood," Charlotte said. "And the murders."

"Ah, so what? Now the plan is to kill me?" The Romanian cried furiously as he backed up toward his balcony. "What's next? A stake through my heart?"

"Bitch, we should ask you that!" Tatiana yelled, her voice echoing down the street. "Who else you gonna eat?"

"WOULD YOU ALL SHUT THE FUCK UP?!" A voice from across the street called. "IT'S 2 A.M., FOR GOD'S SAKE." Awoken by the din of his neighbors yelling, Winston stood on his porch, shaking with rage.

"Bitch, you shut up!" Tatiana yelled back, gripping the railing on the balcony.

"You're all garbage!" Winston seethed. "You sound like a bunch of damned crows, squawking back and forth. Just shut up. *SHUT UP!*" He cradled his cheek and grimaced in pain.

Charlotte approached the edge of the balcony and put her arm around Tatiana's waist. "Man, you live with your mom," she sneered across the street. "What are you—forty? Get your ass back in your apartment before Tati and I come over there. And you know we will."

Flustered with wrath, Winston met Charlotte's gaze, spat into the street, and spun around to return to his apartment.

"That's what I thought!" Tatiana called after him. She turned to Charlotte. "The *fuck* is wrong with these men?"

Charlotte looked over at Vasile's balcony, but the Romanian had disappeared back into his apartment. "Fuck if I know," she said. "I just want them to stay the hell away from me."

Chapter 22

"Mama wants to see you before you leave," Cassie said with her usual flat tone.

"Okay," Charlotte slung her backpack over her shoulder and headed to the back, where Mama was beading necklaces.

"Hey, Mama." Charlotte kissed her hand and forehead. "You needed me?" "ARROMBADO!" Mischief screeched.

"Well hi to you, too, you naughty bird."

"Sit down, child. I wanna talk to you before you run off again."

"I always got time for you, Mama. You know that."

"I'm more worried if you got time for *you*," Sally said, punctuating her thought by gently pressing a finger to her great-great-great granddaughter's chest.

Charlotte sighed. "Yeah, I know. Doesn't feel like it lately. There's so much going on."

"Truth be told, baby, I'm worried about you. I know you're hustlin', and you come by that honest, but when's the last time you got to slow down and enjoy life?"

"I mean, I try to. Here, at the club..."

"That's all work. I don't know how you could enjoy it up front with them girls bickering all the time," Mama laughed. "You ever look at their lives, Charlotte?"

"I guess?"

"My poor Cassie—just so absorbed with loss that she can't enjoy the girls she still has here now. And the twins—lord! They're all content to stay here all day, every day. That ain't because of me, baby. I don't want you to end up like them."

"I can't see Cassie going for that. I had to argue with her to get her to take Brigette on."

"Mmm-hmm. It's not for lack of trying." She squeezed Charlotte's hand. "I don't want you to end up the way they are."

"What do you mean?"

"I think you know what I mean. Girl your age should be out with friends, going on cruises, dating. You're so strong for everyone else, but when are you gonna take care of you?"

Charlotte's eyes welled up with tears. "I can't help it, Mama. I feel like I have to be strong for everyone. You all been so good to me, raised me, accept me. It's my turn to give back."

"I understand," Sally said. "I spent way too many lifetimes trying to protect my babies and grandbabies, to give them something of their own to be proud of. But then look here, what happens: you end up old as dirt with people fussing over *you*. And the Baron is gonna get his due anyway."

"Shhh," Charlotte whispered. "Let's don't invite him yet, huh?"

Sally fumbled with the beads in front of her thoughtfully. "I been avoiding my dance with him for a long time, my baby. I'm not scared anymore, and you all will be fine without me."

The idea of her grandmother no longer being here in the kitchen—fussing at Mischief, warmly giving readings to customers, brewing her extra strong coffee—formed a heavy weight in Charlotte's chest. She wanted to protest, but there was no denying the truth of Mama's words.

"It's okay, Charlotte." Sally pulled her granddaughter in for a hug and kissed her forehead. "I just need to know that you will start to take care of you. You gotta promise me you won't get stuck alone, mourning over things in the past you didn't do or should have done. Promise me?"

"I promise," Charlotte said. She sat quietly in her grandmother's arms, listening to Sally breathe, her heart thump-thumping along, hoping that she would get to hear that sound for many more years to come.

Chapter 23

After a long shift at Jack's, Charlotte climbed
the stairs to her apartment wearily, her great grandmother's words on her mind. As she turned the key in
her door, she heard Vasile's door open slowly behind
her. Mr. Andrei stepped out and looked at her with
disgust.

"Voi reveni mai târziu cu o anumită hrănire," he
said over his shoulder, where Vasile was nodding
grimly.

The smaller man stepped down the stairs lightly
and into the dark night.

"Charlotte," Vasile said.

"Hey," she said. "You look like shit."

Vasile smirked. "Thanks. You always know the
right thing to say."

"What's *he* gonna do—go grab another kid?"

Vasile stepped into the hallway and looked Charlotte in the eyes. "I think you know the answer to that.
What a strangely judgmental woman you are, especially for the work you do."

"What the fuck does *that* mean?"

"I mean you are a witch, so—"

"So what? We've been around since the beginning
of time. And *we* don't eat babies."

Despite his frustration, Vasile laughed. "*I* don't
eat babies, either."

The pair stood silently, Charlotte looking at the
wood flooring beneath her sneakers.

"What do you want from me, Vasile? You want me to validate who you are, what you do? You think that's what I want from you?"

Vasile took a step forward. "I would be very interested to hear what you want from me, Charlotte. And why you and your friend downstairs find it necessary to persecute me."

"Persecute? Are you serious?"

The Romanian sighed deeply. "And again, I do not understand how you think. I feel we could be friends, but then you get angry with me for things I do not understand." Vasile tried to get Charlotte to meet his gaze, but she continued to stare at the floor, scowling.

"I just want you to stay away from me. My friends. My family," she said at last. "You do what you gotta do—but don't think for a minute you can hurt the people I love."

Vasile took a step back. "You think I would hurt you? Really?"

Charlotte met his gaze and tried to read what was in his mind, but she wasn't Sybil or Mama. All she saw was pitch black emptiness and danger.

"Just stay away from me," she said.

"I see," Vasile said. He retreated further, his face masked in fury, and stepped back into his apartment. "I will trouble you no further, Charlotte. Good evening." And with that, he closed the door firmly behind himself, bolting the door.

Drained, Charlotte let herself into her apartment where Ghost greeted her with a series of gentle mewls. "Hi, baby," she said, bending down to pet him. "Let's get you some dinner and go to bed."

Chapter 24

Although the night was uncharacteristically calm for New Orleans, Winston was awake. The cracked tooth had been pulled three days ago, but now the pain surfaced when the pain medication wore off, and the medication had the unpleasant side effects of irritating his stomach to the point of dry heaves.

Winston thought of *The Odyssey* and Scylla and Charybdis, wondering if he would ever feel whole and pain-free again. He loathed the medication, how it made him feel airy and stupid, so he delayed taking it until the throbbing from the hole in his mouth was excruciating.

As if influenced by her owner's behavior, Sophie was active as well, moving back and forth in her terrarium, following Winston's movements. Winston began to wonder if, having had a taste of his blood, the python was now stalking him. He had taken to barely opening the top of the enclosure at all, just tossing her prey in on feeding days. He tried to make sense of her behavior, her impassive eyes, but there was nothing to read there.

While the medicine would bring sleep and numbness, Winston resisted the urge for the moment. He stepped onto the balcony and cautiously inhaled the cool November air. The chill momentarily numbed his cheek, so he closed his eyes and took several hesitant breaths.

When he opened his eyes, he saw the stripper across the street illuminated in her bedroom. She was undressing, and he could see her cat on the bed. He had watched a similar scene unfold many times in the past, but tonight, with the pain and irritation, he found himself wondering how she could be so openly brazen. As she peeled off her tank top, he could see her round breasts, her nipples, erect from the cold.

And unlike the men who paid to watch her undress, Winston found himself disgusted by what he considered another one of her performances. He resented that he could not even step on his balcony to gain some relief from his pain without being reminded of how filthy the city was, how abysmally amoral and repulsive everyone living in it was.

He found a strange gnawing in his stomach and threw a pain pill in his mouth. Nothing in the deteriorating apartment fridge would abate his hunger, so Winston decided to go out into the night, hoping that something in the city would satisfy his urgings.

Past experience, however, taught him that both pain and frustration were bottomless voids, like the gullet of the patient, ravenous Sophie.

It was the hour of the wolf, and the sky was pitch black as Sally rose and made herself a cup of coffee. Confused by the early rising, Mischief muttered a host of curses to himself but then settled back to sleep on his perch.

Sally thought about the many tense nights she had seen this hour, like when she ran from the Thibodaux plantation years ago. Luck and faith had seen her through dark days hiding in the swamps, her babies suffering all manner of bug bites, snakes a constant source of worry.

But they made it through mostly unscathed, and the likeness of her drawn up for the escaped slave bulletins looked nothing like her or her children, the artist depicting Cassie and Apollo as dark black instead of biracial.

She was largely forgotten and ignored once they began life in the city, and when the sugar jar ran low and the new house slave mistakenly added the sugar and oleander to the master's and mistress's tea, there was no one left to identify Sally in person. Death brought a final anonymity.

In the dim light from the hood of the stove, Sally sat down to pen a letter to her family, to remind them of their history, of how she chose the LeNoir surname because she wanted them to be ever proud of their blackness and unashamed of how they came to have whiteness.

And she told them that she owed the Baron two lives at least and was lucky to have lived this long.

This task finished, she walked slowly to the side door, opened it, and waited while humming "When It's Sleepy Time Down South" to pass the time.

Hardly had she finished the final notes when she heard the footsteps heading from the outside into her kitchen.

"You smell like rot," Sally growled.

"You know who I am?" the stranger asked.

"You're Death, and I do not fear you."

The man drew nearer, stealthy as a black cat hunting at midnight.

"You're not going to scream? Beg for your life?"

Mama laughed, a laugh full of a life spent in love and richness. "I've lived long enough. More than twice the lifetimes I should have. And I don't beg. If I can't live proudly, I'll die proudly."

A heavy stillness descended on the small kitchen as the man seemed to ponder Sally's words. Suddenly, he sprang into action, and Mama felt a sharp pain on her clavicle. She heard the sound of her own blood spray up against the wall and smelled it as it hit the air.

"Is that all you got?" she snickered, raising her hand to the wet area near her neck. "Come on, *boy*. Do better."

With a fury as black as the night outside, the stranger leapt on her and tore her apart. And while he'd hoped to hear her cry, or scream, or whimper, Sally did none of these as her body drained of its life-force, the only sound in the room issuing from Mischief, who rustled his wings and cooed, at last, "Shit. Oh shit."

It was Sam the delivery man who found Mama's body. He brought frozen seafood to a restaurant just two buildings down from Moonchild, as he had for the last ten years, twice a week.

The late hour, the open door, and blood trailing from the stoop to Mama's kitchen caught his attention, and he went over to the threshold once he'd parked his truck and put the hazards on.

Sam met the gory sight in front of him with horror and called 911, barely able to describe what lay on the floor in front of him. He knew the block, and he knew of the store, having gone into it to see what it was about several years ago.

What was left in the small kitchen was nothing he could recognize nor identify, and he was grateful that the police came to cordon off the area and check the remainder of the store so that he could go finish his delivery and then sit in his truck and cry. Sam regretted that his delivery took long enough for him to hear the wails of the family members, sounds he would carry with him for the rest of his days.

Because she did not live with her aunts or great grandmother, Charlotte was the last to find out that her grandmother was dead. An early morning phone call from Sylvie summoned her to the store, where twilight was creeping over the city.

Unlike her aunts, Charlotte couldn't find her voice to scream or cry. She slumped down into a chair and wept quietly, disbelief chilling her. Sybil struggled with the officers to get to the back to see her mother, but they held her back, and she moaned and fell into her sister's arms.

Cassie's response was one of ire. She screamed at the police, at Damballa, at all the gods she could think of. When she grew hoarse from screaming, she fell to the floor and wailed and prayed until Charlotte pulled her from the ground and held her while she wept, shaking with anger and sadness.

As news spread, the women of the coven begin to show up with food and offerings, whispering in hushed tones reverently. The detectives spent the better part of the morning taking photos and collecting evidence while Mischief watched over them and cursed. And once they left, Brigette and Jade silently headed to the kitchen to clean up Sally's blood.

No one could even think of the magic to cast or candles to light; the coven was dazed and weeping, weak and powerless. The moonless sky overhead was also draining, their powers frailer from the pain and emptiness in themselves, mirrored in the lunar cycle.

Charlotte watched the day's events pass in a fog, wondering how they were going to survive such a loss. She couldn't bring herself to call her father until the sun set, and the agony she felt she caused him with the news tore at her soul. Her stomach empty, she went to the bathroom at the store and threw up bile. Everything was black and poisonous, and no one had any clear vision on what to do next. It was as if Mama, in her blindness, was the only one who could see.

Chapter 25

The sky was gray and cold the morning of Mama's Second Line march to Holt Cemetery. The coven wore all white, their dresses whipping around in the wind like doves taking flight.

Andre pulled Charlotte in close to his side as they followed the brass band. "Be strong, baby," he whispered to her, and looking at his teary eyes, Charlotte wondered if he was talking to himself as well. No one looked particularly strong in this grave march, least of all the LeNoirs.

Because Mama was a fixture in the city, her funeral was being documented by the press, and all manner of people came out to pay their respects, from the local witches from different shops to vodou practitioners to city elites with money who gave Mama thousands for her guidance.

Maurice and Joan Patois attended in matching black and purple outfits, with black parasols they clung to in the cold wind as they moved to the music. Tatiana came in a long black dress and sunglasses, wiping away tears frequently.

A horse-drawn hearse followed the crowd, its elegant, shiny black horses pulling a coffin that looked so impossibly tiny that it made Charlotte gasp to think of her grandmother in it, unmoving, and not the larger-than-life woman she'd always thought Mama Sally was.

It seemed to Charlotte that the whole of New Orleans had poured out of their houses to watch the procession. The onlookers made the sign of the cross as the hearse passed, some of them reaching out to touch the chariot carrying the coffin.

Charlotte had never felt so utterly lost in her life. Even if Cassie or Sybil made a decision in the shop, behind it all was the calm feeling that Mama was the security there, that if anything went wrong, the coven could go to her for guidance. Mama's death left a void no one could fill.

Looking around, Charlotte sucked in her breath both at the cold and at seeing Sylvie and Sybil arm in arm, weeping together. Seeing their pain tightened the knot in Charlotte's stomach, but watching Cassie walk alone, her head down defeatedly, led to a fresh freefall of tears.

"Daddy," she said, pulling her father's arm and nodding toward Cassie. Andre understood immediately and walked her over to Cassie and put his arm over his great aunt's shoulders. He stopped her briefly to let Sybil and Sylvie catch up and grabbed Sylvie's hand. Charlotte put her hand into Sybil's and leaned her head on her aunt's shoulder, the family moving slowly toward the cemetery, where Mama would be laid to rest with her ancestors, all of whom she had outlived, under the watchful eye of the mighty oak.

Chapter 26

After a week of grieving with her family, Charlotte needed to be alone. She smoked at home and spent the day wondering whether or not Mama's murder would be like Pixie's—unresolved. The police had interviewed the family and a number of friends and customers, but Charlotte sensed the sheer randomness of the crime was a hurdle.

Vasile, too, was on her mind, and she considered talking to the police about him, but what evidence did she have? A half-hearted investigation into whether or not he was a vampire?

Nothing from the past week could console her, whether it was the coven—who cast spells of protection and even thought to collect some of Mama's blood from the kitchen for her family—nor the many friends of the shop, who brought food and donations, flowers and cards. Even her father's presence, as comforting as he tried to be, just left her feeling empty.

She couldn't even bear to go into Mama's kitchen, knowing there was a void instead of her grandmother's wise, loving, and calm presence. As day turned to night, Charlotte opted for drinking alone, ignoring phone calls and texts.

Charlotte lighted a white candle for clarity and closed her eyes. She blocked out the sound of the city and turned the vial of Sally's blood over and over in her hand. The whiskey warmed her as she listened for guidance.

Please, Mama, she whispered, her breath making the candle flame flicker. *Please tell me what to do.*

The room was still, too still, and Charlotte began to cry. "Fuck this. I'll go to you, Mama." She emptied the contents of her backpack onto the floor as Ghost watched her sleepily from his seat on the ottoman.

Desperate, Charlotte scrambled from kitchen to bedroom, tossing anything she thought might prove useful—candles, charms, mirror, rum, beads, a sacred cup—into her bag. She slipped the vial of blood into her back pocket and headed for the door. As she opened her door, one of Mama's rosaries ticked back and forth against the wall. Charlotte grabbed it as well and put it around her neck. Once outside, she called for a car and rode to the cemetery almost wordlessly, responding only her thanks to the driver's comment expressing surprise about her destination.

As the driver pulled away, Charlotte scaled the fence and crept toward the large oak tree. The waxing moon overhead was pale with sorrow, and Charlotte was grateful for its pale glowing presence.

Although she had been at Sally's gravesite every day this week, something about being there alone at night eased Charlotte's mind. She lighted candles and prayed for Mama's soul.

And then, she stretched out next to the fresh mound of dirt where Mama's body lay, listening for any advice she hoped would surface. An hour or two passed, and the moon continued its journey overhead. Charlotte watched it peep through the tree branches overhead, like an impatient child playing hide and seek. She pulled the rum from her backpack and took a swig, spitting some out toward the tree for Legba and some on the ground for Sally.

Charlotte lifted the remaining contents from her bag, her hand seeming to hum when she touched the rim of the chalice. Following her instincts, she sifted through the remaining materials she'd brought with her. Suddenly, it occurred to her that Mama was there guiding her, and all she need do was close her eyes and let her hands follow her grandmother's guidance.

The mirror was the next item her hand landed on, and it felt right to place it under the chalice. As she did so, she caught the moon's reflection and understood that this was all intentional.

"What next, Mama? I'm listening."

As she ran her hands over the other items, her hand came to rest once more on an item—this time a small ampoule of mercury. She peeled open the cap and poured it into the chalice, and under the moon's gaze, it too became luminous, reflecting the light.

Charlotte ran her hands over the remaining contents, but nothing felt right. There was no electric feeling when she touched the other items, and she began to worry she had misunderstood. Frustrated, she sat back on the heels of her boots and put her hands on her knees. Something nudged the side of her back, and she ran her hand over her back pockets, it brushed the vial of Mama's blood.

"Got it. I got it!" she said excitedly. Peeling open the vial, she poured the viscous, dark blood into the chalice, swirling the mercury with the blood.

But something was still missing. At this point, she could feel it, and she understood Mama wanted her to lure whatever was stalking the city with this potion. *What else! What else do I need?*

A cold breeze swept through the tree, rattling the branches. The leaves whispered back and forth, and Charlotte closed her eyes to listen to them, and suddenly she realized they were saying her name.

Pulling the ebony-hilted Kalfu and the ivory-hilted Legba from her boots, Charlotte realized the last ingredient belonged to her. She swiftly moved the blades across both her right and left wrists, letting the blood drip into the cup to mix with the mercury and Mama's blood.

With this, the trap was set. Charlotte set the chalice next to Mama's grave and leaned back into the large roots of the tree, using her hoodie to slow the flow of blood from her wrists. She shot rum until the bottle was nearly empty, her head nodding into her chest as both alcohol and sleep claimed her mind.

She wasn't sure how long she stayed there in the roots, sleeping, only that the crackle of footsteps on leaves woke her abruptly, and she jumped from her spot, gripping both knives in her hands. From the darkness, a voice she should have known laughed malevolently.

"You!" she gasped.

In front of her, his hands clutching a sharpened ice pick, stood Winston. "I guess you people really are witches," he snarled. "You seem to be the only people who know I'm coming."

"Yeah? Well don't mistake me for my defenseless grandmother," Charlotte threatened, lifting her knives. "Let's see how well you do preying on the strong instead of the weak."

"They'll bury you right here next to her," Winston mocked, circling her to try to gain advantage.

"I'm gonna bury *you*, motherfucker."

Like a viper impatient for its prey, Winston lashed out at Charlotte, the point of the pick landing in her right shoulder. As he withdrew the makeshift weapon, Charlotte sliced through his forearm with Legba, blood splattering into the fresh mound of dirt at their feet.

Surprised and maddened by the sight of his own blood, Winston lashed out again quickly, stabbing Charlotte repeatedly, the pick connecting with her sternum and ribs. The shock from the attack brought her to her knees, and she knocked over the chalice, the blood and mercury mingling with the earth.

Charlotte steadied herself, blood blooming across the front of her hoodie and dripping down onto her jeans and shoes.

"Won't you just give up and die already?" Winston growled. "Why cling to your shitty life? Let it go."

"You first," Charlotte said, swiping the blades in an X-formation in front of Winston's face, leading him to stumble backward over Mama's grave, where he leapt up and righted himself.

"Dirty—you fight dirty. You live dirty, and you will die here, in the dirt of your grandmother's grave," Winston said.

"You got me wrong," Charlotte winced. "I'm gonna make sure she gets to taste all of your blood, her and Legba. And then this city will forget you as it remembers her."

Winston sprang at Charlotte again, and this time, he only glanced her arm while she dug Kalfu into his chest. The blow made him grunt audibly, and he stumbled backward to catch his breath, rubbing the wound with his hand and looking at his dark blood under the moonlight. His face twisted into a sinister mask of wrath, and Charlotte felt that she was fighting with a demon because he resembled nothing human at all.

"Enough," he yelled and rushed her with all the force he had. The pair fell into the dirt, and it mingled with their blood, caking into their wounds. Winston quickly gained the upper hand, punching Charlotte's face and using a knee to pin down her right arm. Her left arm caught his hand in the fray, but he punched her again to subdue her and raised the ice pick to deliver the coup de grace.

Dazed and in pain, Charlotte looked to the moon overhead and prayed for a quick end. She tasted blood and dirt in her mouth and spat it into his face. As the ice pick descended toward her neck, a dark shadow drew over both of them, pulling Winston off Charlotte.

As she watched, stunned, Vasile had Winston pinned back against him, his fingers gripping Winston's hair to reveal the strong rope of veins in his neck.

Winston's eyes were wide with horror as Vasile tore into his vein with his canines, now prominent and glistening under the moonlight. As Charlotte began to struggle against unconsciousness, she watched as Winston's legs twitched before he became completely limp.

Blinking heavily, Charlotte watched the moon until she passed out, and all was darkness.

Chapter 27

Although the emergency room doctors wanted Charlotte to be admitted for a day or two for observation, she declined after getting sutures and medication. Exhaustion setting in, she let Vasile call a cab for both of them after two hours of interviews with detectives from her hospital bed.

When they reached the apartments, Vasile looked at Charlotte with grave concern. "You don't want me to stay with you, to make sure you are okay? What if you need something?"

"You know, I think it's time we exchange numbers," Charlotte chuckled, then winced in pain. "You can have the night shift."

"I guess you have your answer about me, then."

"Oh, in more ways than one," Charlotte said.

The Romanian bowed. "I need to get in before the sun rises, as you know. Please, please let me know how you are doing or if you need anything."

"You know I will. Vasile, thanks. I owe you. Again."

"I will expect a personal dance when you are healthy," he said and winked. "Good night."

Once she slipped under her covers, Charlotte slept like the dead and didn't wake until Sybil and Sylvie pounded on her door in the morning.

"Girl, what in Hades is wrong with you?" Sylvie started.

"Oh my god," Sybil interjected. "What happened? Who did this to you?"

"Can we get some food?" Charlotte asked. "And then I can explain. I'm starving."

The coming days were a flurry of activity. Charlotte had to change her number as the press wanted to interview the woman who caught and killed the city's most infamous murderer since the Axeman stalked his victims in the early part of the 20th century.

Charlotte longed to heal from the pain and loss of the last few months. She watched as a forensics team descended upon the apartment Winston shared with his mother, removing a corpse that was surely his mother. Tatiana rushed to her apartment that afternoon with burgers and gossip about how the creep across the street had beheaded his mother months ago, keeping her head in the freezer with dead mice.

With constant care from her aunts, coven, and Tatiana, Charlotte did physically heal quickly—imperative now that the letter Mama had been writing had been returned to them from police custody and was, in effect, a last will and testament that made Charlotte head of the coven and store in her stead.

Overwhelmed, anxious about her ability to lead the women, Charlotte stepped onto her porch to smoke and watch to moon grow to its full glory. As she sat in silence, Vasile slipped onto his porch.

"Charlotte! It's good to see you up and about— that's how you Americans say it, yes?"

"Thanks, Vasile."

The Romanian approached the gate between their balconies. "May I come over?"

Charlotte hesitated, thinking about the vampire myth preventing the creatures from entering a home without the owner's consent.

"You know what? Yes, you can."

As he crossed the threshold, Vasile smiled to himself and pulled up a chair next to Charlotte. The pair sat silently for a few moments, enjoying the cool night air and one another's company.

Vasile extended his hand and Charlotte let him cup her hand in his. After a few moments, he raised it to his lips.

"So now do you trust me?" he asked.

Charlotte looked at his earnest brown eyes shining with happiness in the dark.

"With *your* life," she said with a smile, and settled back into her chair.

Epilogue

The December moon—the Cold Moon—glided in and out of the clouds lingering over the apartments on St. Peter. Most of the building's inhabitants were asleep, save for a vampire and Tatiana Manhunter, drag queen and diva.

The latter was looking in a mirror, plucking hairs from her neck and face.

"The fuck is all this coming from?" she said, frustrated. "I'm gonna need to go get some wax."

Tatiana felt electric, reinvigorated. Her wounds had long since healed, and her libido was raging into overdrive.

"I gotta get outta this apartment," she said aloud, grabbing her purse and reapplying her lipstick.

She wandered the streets for about thirty minutes before she felt a strange sensation grip her gut. Just two blocks from Armstrong Park and thinking she needed to relieve herself, Tatiana dipped behind a row of bushes. Suddenly, her arms and legs trembled in agony, and she fell to the ground.

Hair began to sprout rapidly from her body, which itself was elongating to resemble a wolf. Emerging from the bushes, Tatiana was no longer Tatiana but the Manhunter, and she howled her hello to the sleeping, guileless city.

Acknowledgements

My deepest gratitude goes to the friends and family worldwide who encouraged me to turn my jokes about living next to a vampire into a novel. There are too many of you to name individually, but I love you and am eternally grateful. Thank you to my editor, Denise Bartlett, who made this work the best it can possibly be. I'm grateful for your guidance and knowledge. Thank you, too, to Charlotte Holley for giving *Terrene Moon* its home at Gypsy Shadow Publishing.

About the Author

Moxie T. Anderson is an avid horror fan and writer who lives with a very patient rescue mutt, a very assertive (former) street cat who beats up the very patient mutt, and one very patient partner who edits her work.

TWITTER: @MoxieT2
FACEBOOK:
https://www.facebook.com/Moxie-T-Anderson-Author-110848621215312/
TIK TOK: @moxietanderson
INSTAGRAM: @moxietanderson

CPSIA information can be obtained
at www.ICGtesting.com
Printed in the USA
BVHW071006200622
640191BV00003B/204